I0589182

POOL OF KNOWLEDGE

BOOK ONE OF THE HIDDEN WIZARD

VAUGHAN W. SMITH

FAIR FOLIO

ISBN: 978-0-9874694-6-5

For Hugo

PROLOGUE

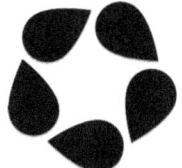

G ranthion awoke with a start. His heart was pumping, and he knew that something was very wrong. He rose from his bed, cursing the aches and pains he felt in his lower back. He could overcome many things, but not age.

After a moment, he identified the feeling. It was danger, which could only mean one thing. He retrieved the sapphire ring from his bedside table and slipped it onto his finger. He chanted a few words under his breath, concentrating on visualising his target: the matching ring.

He cleared his mind and let the spell do its work. He started to see images, and with an icy rush found himself looking into a room. He saw his son, surrounded by dark shapes. He strained to look further, to see more details but he could not. The tightness in his chest and physical reaction were now confirmed in his vision. His son had been taken and was in terrible danger.

"Fool," Granthion said, including both his son and himself in the comment. His own pride and arrogance had driven his son away. But also, it was his son's foolishness and lack of care that had landed him in this predicament. The trouble was, there was no time to save him. Granthion ran his hands through his white hair, trying to think of a solution. If he didn't act fast, his son would cease to be his son. They would transform him into something else, something similar but not the same. The essence would be there, but people were never the same after the turning. He could not allow that to happen.

There were many spells at his disposal, but his mind kept going back to one. One he was saving for his final hurrah, his final gift to the world. But it came at a cost, and there was no going back.

No matter how he approached the problem, this was the only solution. It was his life's work, but it looked like fate was forcing his hand ahead of schedule.

"Oh well, now is as good a time as ever," he said. But before he left, there were preparations to be made. Granthion shuffled over to his desk and retrieved paper and a quill. He wrote swiftly but legibly, two letters. One addressed to his new successor and one to his son. After he was done, he donned his travelling robe, packed a satchel with two crystal orbs and took one last look around the room. It was his home, and he would never see it again. Relics from his many journeys littered the room: magical artifacts, books, treasures, and keepsakes. Each one told a different story. But now he had to leave, and forge one last tale. He left the room and closed the door behind him.

The tower was still and quiet, as the other elder wizards were all asleep. But he didn't want to take any chances and quickly cast an invisibility spell with a secret inverted hook that would hide him from the other wizards. He would now be completely invisible and not even a trace of magic would be detectable by standard methods. He crossed the large chamber and headed towards the stairs. He never enjoyed them, they were entirely too small, and he always felt unsteady on the long walk down. But this time they were like friends, speeding him on his way. He had a new purpose, and it would be fulfilled soon.

Once he had descended from the tower he looked out across the courtyard. It was empty as expected, but he could still see images of many of his triumphs and those of his students played out before him in his mind's eye.

"Nostalgic old fool," he told himself and kept walking. He headed straight for the stables, to retrieve his trusty horse, Whitemane. They had been on many journeys together, and it was fitting that they would go on one last quest. As he entered the stables Whitemane was awake and waiting, quietly.

"You always seem to know something before I do," Granthion muttered to the horse. He led Whitemane out and prepared him for travel. Granthion walked out the main gates beside Whitemane and looked back at the Wizard Academy. His legacy.

"May you stand the test of time, and solve that which I could not," Granthion said, then mounted Whitemane and rode off into the forest.

Once he was out of sight of the academy, Granthion let the invisibility spell lapse, now that the immediate danger of being spotted by other wizards was over. Next, he needed to travel somewhere elevated to perform the spell. He knew of a smaller mountain nearby, more of a lofty hill if he were honest. But time was against him, so he decided that it would have to do. It was also centrally located within the country of Avaria, and he knew that his son was also somewhere in the vicinity. But he could not track him further.

Whitemane ran with incredible speed as if he understood the urgency. Granthion was glad; he didn't want to push the horse too hard. There were other means of speeding this up, but he needed to preserve his strength. He would need every ounce for the spell.

He thought over his plan as he rode. By casting the spell from a height and drawing the right kind of power he could cover the entire country of Avaria. Not knowing where to target the spell wouldn't be a problem, and he would help many other people at the same time. But the cost was so great. Doing the spell would take everything he had, and most likely his life. That was the price for him doing it this way. But it would save his son and countless others.

There would be repercussions of course, not just for him. Doing this would create an imbalance in the world. If he succeeded, then Avaria would be the only country free of the Blight: something that would cause conflict and jealousy.

Not my problem now, Granthion thought. He had spent a lifetime carrying all the problems of the world on his shoulders. Today would be the last day for that.

He looked up as they were emerging from the forest. He saw the mountain peak in the distance. It didn't look that big from where he was, but he knew it would be enough.

I must make it in time.

He felt Whitemane increase his speed in response and patted his old friend in thanks. The morning sun was starting to emerge, as Granthion arrived at the mountain path. He dismounted from Whitemane and stroked the horse on his head.

"You have done well, my friend, thank you," Granthion said. Whitemane neighed in response and waited patiently. Granthion gave him one last pat on the white mane that had earned him that name and continued on foot.

The path was rough and steep, it was not meant for a lot of traffic; especially not an old man like himself. He imagined all the ways he could cheat his way up but restrained himself. It kept his mind busy, but he couldn't waste the energy. Physical exertion was one thing, but exertion of his Spark was another. He had to save up every last scrap that he had to pull this off.

Slowly, he trudged up the mountain leaning heavily on his staff. It felt like every two steps he took, he would slide back one, but he persevered. He had an important task, one that he could not fail to do. He took a moment to examine his thoughts and feelings. It wasn't out of love that he was doing this, but regret. Regret in the way he and his son had fallen out, regret at what could have been.

I set him on this path. I must set him on a new one.

He pushed harder, winding higher. Finally, he saw signs that he was reaching the top, and made one last effort to make it. As he rounded the last wind of the path he emerged at the top of the mountain. The peak was flat and cleared. There were only a few rocks strewn about.

"This will do," Granthion said, surveying the view and what he could see. The sun had risen now, and filled the sky with amazing orange colours.

The start of a new day, and a new beginning, he thought. He slowly walked over to the middle of the mountaintop and set down his satchel and staff. He retrieved the two crystal orbs. One was snow white, the other jet black: two components of the spell, two aspects. The white one was the source of the cleansing spirit, the black one the conduit and connection to the Blight. By using the two in tandem, he could accomplish the impossible. He could cleanse the taint of the Blight. But the cost was high; his life force was the currency. It was an imperfect and incomplete spell, but it should work.

Granthion took a deep breath and pictured his son.

"I love you, and I'm sorry," he said. He held the orbs in his hands, the black one in his left and the white one in his right. He prepared his mind and started to visualise the spell.

He pictured the country of Avaria, and a white silky net covering it. All those within the net would be affected. Next, he supplied his own Spark, powering up the white orb. He funnelled more and more into it and created a link between himself and the orb. Only the smallest amount remained in his body.

He sent out his purified Spark, resulting in columns of white light streaking down from the sky, each one targeting a person in the country. The light touched each person, and if they were not tainted by the blight, it dissipated immediately. But those who were couldn't shake the strange column of light that hovered over their heads.

With this done, he started the final push. By using the black orb, he drew out the Blight from each person, through the orb and into himself. Each time another person was drained of the Blight, he saw a quick flash of their face and soul. Tirelessly he continued, hoping to see the face of his son. When he least expected, it came and went, like all the rest. A feeling of peace washed over Granthion.

It came in two parts. Firstly, he was relieved that he had found and saved his son. The other more pragmatic part was that it had worked; this whole effort was not for nothing. Hopefully, he had acted before the full transition had completed. As grand a gesture as it was, this act wasn't the proper solution he had been working towards. But he was glad that at least his final act would be a successful one.

However, he didn't stop there; it was too risky, and he had a job to finish. He continued pushing until he had touched every person tainted by the Blight. Then he switched the link between him and the orbs, trapping the entirety of the Blight within himself. He felt the taint, corruption, and filth like black sludge on his soul. A monumental amount that no single person should ever have to endure. He understood what those afflicted must have felt, and the effect it had on them. It was terrible, and left unchecked it would turn him into something else entirely.

With the spell in full effect and the taint of a nation within him, he did the only thing left to do. He used the small amount of his Spark left within to call down one more ray of light from the sky. But this one was not to heal, it was to destroy.

He felt the white-hot heat searing him, and with it peace. As he was burned away, so was the sludgy taint from his soul. His final gift was to himself, a fitting end to an incredible life.

1

A WIZARD ARRIVES

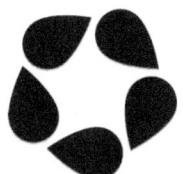

Vincent unlocked the workshop and ushered his son inside. The lanky young man hurried in, used to the routine. Vincent opened the doors all the way and let the light flood in.

He looked around, making sure everything was as it should be. The workbenches were clear, the anvil was clear, and the forge was ready. There was a clean version of the workshop smell filling his lungs.

Good, Vincent thought.

"Alrion, how does the workshop look?"

"Everything is fine. What did you expect?" Alrion didn't hide the annoyance creeping into his voice.

"It's a good habit to always assess the situation. Otherwise, you can get yourself into trouble." Vincent walked around the room, passing his eyes and hands over each of the workbenches.

"Well, a locked building is usually a safe bet." Alrion stood rooted to the spot, watching his father's routine.

"You can't always be so sure," Vincent said, with a chuckle. He had seen many strange occurrences over the years, some random accidents, some not so random. He finished his inspection after giving everything a proper look over. He was not usually so careful, but he had a strange feeling.

"It's going to be an interesting day," Vincent said.

"If you say so." Alrion looked bored already. That wasn't a good sign for the beginning of the day. Vincent decided to spice things up a little.

"Let's try and finish all the outstanding orders." Vincent watched his son's reaction closely.

"I don't think we can." Alrion looked unsure of his answer, however.

"Well, let's try." Vincent walked over to the wall and grabbed some charcoal. He wrote up all the orders for the day. There were simple knives, tools, horseshoes, and other assorted implements to be done.

"Looks doable," Vincent said, stepping back. Alrion didn't comment.

"So, do you think you can go buy me the required materials to knock these off?" Vincent watched his apprentice with interest. Alrion looked up at the board and ran his hands through his dark hair.

"Not sure."

"C'mon son, you've done this a while. Just think carefully and break it down." Vincent wanted to break through, he knew Alrion was capable. The lad just needed the right push.

"No, you've done this for a while. I just help out. You never actually let me do the work. I'm a grown man now, you know. Everyone else in the village is actually doing something with their life, not just acting as a hands-off apprentice." Alrion paused, looking a little surprised himself at the outburst. Vincent shook his head slowly.

"Well, I do admit I've been a little strict in my teaching. But there's a good reason why you haven't been doing the bulk of the work. You're just not interested in being a blacksmith. You've no focus and no desire."

"Then why keep me here? Why keep going through the motions?" Alrion looked ready to just walk out. His eyes were daring Vincent to give him a reason. But Vincent wasn't going to let his son off the hook that easily.

"I don't know exactly what the world has in store for you. I had hoped that you would follow in my footsteps. But I do know that I can teach you all you need to know through blacksmithing. It was my lifeline when I was drifting around, looking for a purpose. And also, how I met your mother." Vincent walked over to Alrion and had to crane his neck a little. He still found it difficult looking up at his taller son.

Why are kids always bigger than you?

"Seriously? I can learn all I need to know in the world from blacksmithing?" Alrion said. Vincent smiled. He had his son's curiosity aroused now.

"Sure you can. To be a successful blacksmith you need three things: the knowledge of how to work the metal, an iron will to bend it to your purpose, and a passionate heart to bring out the best in it. Those three things are the building blocks for success in any field."

"Sure, maybe." Alrion turned back to look at the list of jobs. Vincent watched carefully, curious to see how his son responded.

"Sorry, I don't know what you need," Alrion finally said. Vincent's hopes sank. Something was still missing, he hadn't quite gotten through to Alrion.

"You do, but you don't trust yourself. Fair enough, it's probably my fault. It's often easier to learn through doing. I'll write you up a list," Vincent said. He scribbled the list on a piece of leather and handed it to Alrion. He delighted in watching his son's face as he read through, the realisation coming together that whatever he had been thinking was not far off what Vincent had written down.

"Show off," Alrion muttered, then left the room. Vincent smiled as he watched his son leave.

Some things get through, as much as he doesn't like to admit it, Vincent thought.

~

Alrion walked quickly through the town. He was annoyed by the way his father handled things, especially when his father was right. He couldn't fault the man's approach too, which made it all the more irritating. But it still didn't help his frustration at being stuck in the same loop. He needed to move on to something else. But for now, he would complete his errands.

The first stop was the tanner. He knew intimately where the shop was, but his nose could have guided him blindfolded. The smell was strong, even from this distance. He expected to see Bruce, the tanner when he arrived. But instead, he saw Gavin. The blonde-haired apprentice was lounging around.

"Hey, Gavin," Alrion said. Gavin looked up and smiled.

"Hey, Alrion, you running errands?"

"Yes, we're doing a big push today. Are you minding the shop?" Alrion kept looking around, but saw no sign of Bruce.

"Actually, my old man is out today so I'm running the show."

"That's great." Alrion tried to hide his annoyance. Either he did a good job at masking it or his friend didn't notice.

"What do you need?"

"Just these," Alrion said, handing the list to Gavin. The young tanner glanced over the list.

"Yeah, that's no problem, I have everything here. Although you just made more work for me. If I fulfil this whole order, I'll have to push hard to finish it." Gavin was frowning.

"Oh well," Alrion said, not worried about Gavin having to do actual work. At least it seemed like meaningful work, rather than buying materials. He watched Gavin go and collect and trim all the hides he needed and let his eyes wander over the rest of the town. It seemed so slow and sleepy, that he couldn't imagine what would keep him here.

"Hey, are you coming out stargazing tonight?" Gavin called out as he worked.

"Maybe. What's the plan?" Alrion had forgotten all about it. Suddenly his day didn't seem so bad after all. There was nothing more freeing than seeing the clear night sky full of stars. They offered more than Hamley ever would to Alrion.

"We're going to Pyrin's Peak and we have a good group going. Looks to be pretty clear, no clouds at all."

"Sure, why not?"

"Great. Meet us at the town gates after dinner and we'll hike over."

Soon Gavin returned with a pile of hides, all perfectly cured and ready for use. He dumped the pile in Alrion's arms.

"This should do it," Gavin said, taking enjoyment in Alrion's awkward handling of the hides. He was trying to carry them all without dropping them.

"Thanks. My father will come around later and pay."

"No problem, we know where you live," Gavin said with a laugh and Alrion quickly joined him. He left a bit happier than he had arrived and rushed back to the workshop, so he could drop off the hides. Alrion peeked inside and saw his father staring into space.

There he is, off in his own world again, he thought. But he didn't disturb his father and went off to find the carpenter.

Allan the carpenter was inside his own workshop. Alrion could tell that from the consistent sawing noises he heard as he approached. He walked in and watched Allan work, knowing that he wouldn't be heard until there was a natural break. Allan had several large logs lined up on his workbench, and he was methodically cutting them down into more standard sizes that he could use.

"Hi," Alrion said when Allan had finished sawing one of the logs. The older man turned to see who had addressed him.

"Oh, Alrion, how are you doing?" Allan beamed a full smile as he always did.

"I'm fine."

"Good to hear. Say, I still need an apprentice. I know you've been helping your dad, but would you be interested in trying your hand here?" It wasn't the first time Allan had asked, but there was a real earnestness to the man that made Alrion almost consider it.

"Sorry, it's not for me."

"No problem. You know me, I have to ask. Would you believe I had to ask my wife out eight times before she said yes?"

"Yes, actually I would." He really could picture Allan going back again and again with that enormous smile until she finally relented.

"Ha-ha yes she's a tough customer. But it was well worth the effort. So, what brings you in today?"

"I need a few materials, so we can complete our current orders." Alrion showed Allan the list. The carpenter nodded his head slightly as he read each item.

"Hmm, that's fairly easy. Most of it I can give you straight away. I'll need to make a few cuts first." Allan moved with purpose through the workshop, picking up planks that seemed to be placed at random. After he had a small pile assembled on one of the workbenches he set about cutting some logs to fulfil some of the other sizes that Alrion had requested.

As Allan was working, Alrion could see what his dad meant about passion. There couldn't be anything less exciting than cutting logs to a specific size. Yet Allan was some forty years into it, and cutting away with the enthusiasm of an apprentice. Alrion hoped that one day he would find himself a similar role, something to hold his passion and excitement the same way.

"There we go, all done. You need a hand hauling this back?" Allan said. He looked eager to help.

"No, it's not far I'll be fine. Thanks again." Alrion didn't want to take advantage of the man's good nature.

"No problem, I'll sort the details out with your father. Don't forget my offer."

"I won't," Alrion said, meaning that he wouldn't forget but also wouldn't take the man up on it. He struggled with all the planks, but didn't want to go back and ask for help after he had already refused it. He kept going despite almost losing his grip multiple times, dropping them in a loud heap at the entrance of his father's workshop. Vincent ran out immediately.

"What's all this? Is there a battle out here?" he said before looking over the pile of lumber and hides.

"Job's done." Alrion gestured at the rather messy piles.

"I can see that, maybe a little more care next time. Help me bring them in, and try not to drop anything." Vincent sighed and started collecting materials. They carefully brought everything inside and stacked them up according to Vincent's instructions. Alrion let out a sigh of frustration.

"There's a method to this. I've set up a workflow to quickly churn through all the jobs to be done. You'll be impressed," Vincent said. Alrion looked over the stacked benches and just felt tired.

"I'll be the judge of that," he said.

"And now we start," Vincent said with a big smile. Alrion just looked at him.

"You having fun yet?" Vincent asked, reaching for the first piece of iron.

Falric pulled his brown cloak tighter around him as he approached the outskirts of the town. It was a very small town, more like a village.

This has to be it, he thought, although it did seem odd. He hadn't expected to arrive at such a place. But he had done several magical pulses and the location had been confirmed every time without fail.

His cloak was too warm for the conditions, but it was more to avoid any unwanted attention. Now he just looked like a normal traveller. It was very important that he pass through the town unnoticed until he had completed his task. A small sign on the side of the path announced the town of Hamley.

I'm about to put Hamley on the map, Falric thought with a chuckle. Well, his actions here would do so, but it would take a while for the world to take notice. Such was the fate of wizards.

The town looked to be well-maintained and bustling, although from the clothing of those he saw that they were not rich. The houses had well-thatched roofs that showed signs of proper care. The people he saw looked happy and content, but busy.

A nice place to grow up I think.

Perhaps the perfect environment. There weren't many places like this left in the world. He let his horse determine the pace, only gently guiding him in the right direction. He received a few looks, but nobody paid him much attention. An old man in a dusty cloak riding a horse didn't look that out of place after all.

He passed several workshops, men and women alike working hard. There was a tanner, a blacksmith, and a carpenter servicing the town. Probably more trades as well, but those were the most obvious. He thought back to his task, a strange one. He had enjoyed the trip over, a good distraction from his otherwise administrative duties. Heading up the Wizard Academy was a busy job, and not as exciting as many would think. He enjoyed it but longed for trips such as this. Precious opportunities to explore the world.

He gently pulled on the reins, bringing his horse to a stop. It was a normal looking house, white with a red door. He dismounted and hitched his horse to a wooden post out the front. He stepped up to the front door and knocked soundly twice. At first, nothing happened. He focused more and could hear movement and footsteps within the house. Finally, the door opened, and a young woman with bronze skin and long bright blonde hair opened the door.

"Hello. Can I help you?" the woman said. She was dressed as the other villagers, in simple clothes, but Falric noticed something else about her. She seemed much more refined and was looking at him critically, trying to size him up.

"I very much hope so. My name is Falric, may I come inside?"

"You're not from around here. Care to explain why you are here?" The woman was polite but firm.

"Well, I had hoped to broach the topic inside, but why not. I am the head of the Wizard Academy, and I am here to locate the grandson of the great wizard Granthion. I know that he lives here," Falric said. He took amusement from the stunned look on the woman's face and hoped that she wouldn't leave him outside.

2

FAMILY HISTORY

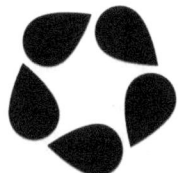

Alrion moved the last knife into its proper place on the workbench and took a step back. They had completed all the work and placed each of the items together with the name of the requester.

"This was a good day's work. I think we're ahead," Vincent said.

"Yes, you did well."

"We did well. You played your part, son." Vincent clapped Alrion on the back.

"Thanks." Alrion had to admit that it was satisfying seeing all the raw materials converted into useful items for their customers. From experience in his home, he knew that the items lasted well. His father built things properly and they could be used for years with only minimal maintenance. While he didn't make particularly exciting things, they were definitely built to last.

"Well, let's head home then. I've worked up a fair appetite, how about you?" Vincent said.

"I'm starving." Alrion thought that perhaps his stomach was trying to gnaw its way out and find someone else to properly feed it.

"That's the reward for a good day's work. And your mother's

cooking is also its own reward. Step outside and I'll lock up the shop," Vincent said. Alrion left and turned back to watch his father. Vincent was initially just staring at Alrion, and then nodded to himself and resumed closing the workshop.

I wonder what he's thinking.

The two of them set off to walk home. The town wasn't particularly large, so after a few minutes they had already arrived. No conversation was required. After a long day working together they usually had nothing else to say. Vincent stopped suddenly and pointed to the horse tied up outside the house.

"You expecting visitors?" he said to Alrion.

"No." Alrion was surprised. Their friends and neighbours all lived close and didn't need to ride over.

"Maybe your mother is," Vincent said. But his tone of voice suggested he wasn't confident. The two of them walked up to the door, Vincent entering first and Alrion rushed in just behind him.

Alrion saw his mother sitting in the lounge, an old man in robes sitting across from her. On the wooden table between them was a pot of tea and two cups.

"Welcome home, dear," Celes said to Vincent. Her voice sounded strange. Alrion darted his eyes between his two parents, trying to figure out what was going on.

Something is wrong, I've never heard her call my father dear.

"Thank you, my dear wife. Who may I ask is our guest today?"

"I thought you might be able to answer that," Celes said. The old man rose quickly and approached them.

"Hello, sorry to impose. My name is Falric," he said looking at Vincent and Alrion. A look of recognition passed over his face.

"Ah, now the mystery is solved. Good to see you again, Andar," Falric said. Alrion was shocked and could see the surprise in his mother's face as well.

"I'm afraid you are mistaken. The name is Vincent."

"Really? My facts are correct, but perhaps more has happened that I am not aware of." Falric had a cautious look on his face, but still seemed quite confident.

"Who is Andar?" Celes asked, her voice rising in pitch. Alrion didn't know where to look, but settled his gaze on Falric.

"Andar ... sorry Vincent here, is the son of Granthion. That means you must be his grandson," Falric said, nodding at Alrion.

"Who is Granthion?" Alrion asked finally. There was something going on here, and he seemed to know the least about it.

"Why Granthion was the saviour of Avaria, and the great wizard who founded the Wizard Academy," Falric said.

"Let's all just sit down," Vincent said. He gave Alrion a look that made him swallow what he was about to say next and sit down on the couches provided. Celes was similarly quiet.

"I see I have caused a bit of a commotion. I'm very sorry about that. I should start again from the beginning. I am the head of the Wizard Academy, and I came here to find the grandson of our founding wizard, Granthion. I recognise Vincent here from when he was younger. And you, young man, have your grandfather's look about you. There's no mistaking it."

"My name is Alrion. I've never heard about my grandfather." Alrion looked at his father, who avoided eye contact.

"Oh, well I'm surprised your father never mentioned him. He's the most famous wizard that ever lived. He died over twenty years ago, sacrificing himself to cleanse our country of Avaria from the Blight."

"Wow, I had no idea. This is all so strange. Why are you looking for me?" Alrion felt like something was off. His stomach churned away.

"It will become much stranger soon, I'm sure. But I came here to find you because you must be tested and trained to be a wizard."

"I see," Vincent said. Alrion felt something shift. That nervous energy became a mix of curiosity and fear.

"Because my grandfather was a wizard?" he said.

"Of course. Magic is accessible by all, in various strengths and means. But the talent of a true wizard is passed through the family," Falric said.

"Shouldn't that make my father a wizard too?" Alrion looked over but again, his father avoided eye contact.

"It should," Falric said, looking at Vincent.

"Sometimes it skips a generation," Vincent said, offering no additional details. Celes gave him a questioning look.

"Well regardless, Granthion left specific instructions to search for his successor when the time was right. And here I am."

"How did you find me?" Alrion said.

"Magic. With the right spell and the right focus, you can find just about anything."

"I still don't understand, though. My grandfather was a famous wizard but until now nobody has ever talked about it. It doesn't make sense." Alrion just wanted some sort of explanation.

"It doesn't make sense, does it?" Celes said, giving Vincent a pointed look. Alrion felt better that his mother also seemed to be in the dark. It wasn't just something kept from him.

"Well, that's a fair question. To put it simply, having such a famous father is the kind of thing that follows you around and gives people the wrong impression. So, I changed my name and left it behind me. There was nothing good to come of it for me."

"But you don't deny your son the opportunity?" Falric said.

"If he's got the gift and he has the desire he can be a wizard. If it is his true calling I won't stop him." Vincent had a resigned reluctance to his voice. Alrion had never heard him sound so defeated.

"I can't believe you are the son of Granthion," Celes said, looking at Vincent with new eyes.

"I am, but that doesn't change anything," Vincent said.

"Yes, it does, a wizard has come for my son." Celes was raising her voice again.

"Are you saying that he cannot go?" Vincent said. Celes looked at him, exasperated.

"No, I just need time to adjust to this. If he does go, you must join him and make sure he is safe."

"Sure, I can accompany him. It might even be fun," Vincent said. Celes did not look impressed.

"Falric, can you tell me more about wizards and my grandfather?" Alrion said. He needed to know more about what they were talking about. Nobody in the village discussed wizards at all. Only in stories were they referenced, and rarely.

"Certainly. Wizards have been around for a while. They are the masters of magic and can do wondrous things. But for the longest time, it was a master to apprentice relationship. The skill of a wizard was very much dependent on the quality of his master. It developed a strong bond between the two wizards, but kept out other wizards and bred secrecy and competition. There were some other drawbacks too, but they were the key ones," Falric said.

"What was the answer?"

"Your grandfather realised that there was a better way to do things. A way to share the knowledge evenly to make every wizard better, and at the same time have stronger bonds with his fellow wizards. He conceived of an academy where all wizards could go to train, and absorb the knowledge from other skilled wizards."

"That sounds pretty good." Alrion liked the idea of such a place. It just seemed more open and exciting than the constraints of Hamley.

"Yes, it's a fantastic thing. Knowledge is such a key component of being a wizard; it's largely what sets us apart from others. Building a place to gather and distribute knowledge to all wizards was a fantastic idea. And now the academy is thriving and becoming bigger and bigger." Falric's excitement was obvious. He gestured with his hands to show the growth of the academy. Alrion saw in him the same passion that his father had invested in blacksmithing. Maybe this would be the answer he was looking for. But there was more to it than that. This was a whole side of his family that had never existed until now.

"What was my grandfather like?" he said.

"He was a kind soul, but a little abrasive at times. He was very abrupt and to the point. He didn't tolerate silliness at all. But he was fascinated with the world, and even without his final gift he contributed more to wizards than any other."

"You mean when he sacrificed himself?"

"Yes. He devised a means of cleansing the Blight from people. And he used it to great effect to save Avaria. Our peace and prosperity are largely due to him. But I believe he was working on something bigger, a way to cleanse the Blight for good," Falric said.

"So, are we in agreement then, that Alrion will undergo wizard training at the academy and see if it is the life for him?" Vincent said, standing quickly.

"Yes, provided you accompany him," Celes said.

"Yes, I want to try it out. This could be what I've been looking for," Alrion said. It was an unbelievable opportunity. And he could always return here and help his father if it didn't work out. That wasn't going anywhere.

"I'm not particularly comfortable with going to the academy. But I won't deny him the opportunity," Vincent said.

"There is still a matter to discuss before we proceed. The test," Falric said.

"The test?" Alrion said. The nervousness came back.

"Yes, it's a simple matter that won't take long. As I discussed, many people can use magic to some degree, but wizards have a special talent. We have a test that proves whether you have the gift, even if it is untrained. Given your lineage I don't foresee any problems, however, you must pass to undergo the training," Falric said.

"What does this test consist of?" Alrion was fine with the idea of being a wizard, as a new concept. But this whole idea of a test made it more of a reality, one he wasn't quite ready for.

"That I will explain in due course. Is there somewhere safe to perform the test?" Falric looked at Vincent.

"Let's use the workshop," Vincent said after a short pause.

"Very good. If you don't mind, I'd like to administer the test straight away." Falric rose and stretched his legs.

"Fine by me, let's head over now," Vincent said.

"I have to see this so I'm coming as well," Celes said. Alrion looked at them both. He was trying to hide his concern, but he wasn't sure he was doing it well. He wasn't ready for a test. Not when they just announced he was a wizard.

"Don't worry, lad, you'll do fine," Falric said. Vincent strode towards the door, opened it, and waited for the rest to leave. Alrion was last.

3

THE TEST

They walked in silence to Vincent's workshop. Alrion's steps were heavy and slow. He wanted more time.

He looked over at his mother and she also seemed nervous. She kept stealing looks at Vincent, trying to find an opportunity to talk. However, his father just walked on, his posture stiff and unnatural. Falric looked like he was somewhere else, his mind processing something.

This is really happening.

"We're here, let me open up," Vincent said. He unlocked the front door and swung it open, disappearing inside soon after. Again, Alrion waited and was the last to enter the workshop. He could see everyone congregated around a few lit lamps in the middle of the room.

"This should be fine," Falric said, looking around.

"Good. How is this going to work?" Vincent said.

"There's nothing to it. I'll explain as we go." Falric walked over to the nearest workbench. He reached into his bag and removed an ornate gilded lamp with a gold base and glass sides.

"This here is a magical artifact. It operates like a lamp; however, instead of being lit by oil, it is lit by the Spark of a wizard. If you have the gift, it will light without any additional spells required." Falric placed a hand on the lamp and it instantly ignited, a controlled flame dancing inside.

"Wow!" Alrion was amazed. Seeing that flame suddenly appear was magical.

"Pretty nice, isn't it?" Falric looked to be enjoying himself.

"Dad you should try it too," Alrion said.

"No thanks, this is for you," Vincent crossed his arms and took a step back. Falric extinguished the flame and looked over at Alrion.

"Care to give it a try?"

Alrion looked around the room. He shuffled his feet on the floor, hesitating. Finally, he crept closer to the lamp.

"What do I need to do?"

"Just place both hands on the lamp, close your eyes and think about it lighting up," Falric said.

"And that will work? Is that a spell?"

"No, it's just a useful way of focusing yourself to make the test work better. This is a spell," Falric said, and he made a flame appear above his open hand flickering in the slight breeze. Alrion rushed over and looked at it, curiosity overtaking him.

"Does it burn?" Alrion was tempted to wave his hand through it.

"It sure does. But let's not get too distracted. You will learn this as part of your training." Falric let the flame wink out and he pointed to the lamp.

Alrion nodded and headed back to it. He inspected it closely, procrastinating. He didn't feel magical, surely that was something you could tell. He was going to look quite foolish when he failed this test.

"It's just as simple as holding it?" he said.

"Absolutely," Falric said.

"OK, I'll try." Alrion placed his hands on the lamp gingerly, like he was afraid to hold onto it.

"A firmer grip will work better," Falric said, seeing the hesitation. Alrion held on a little tighter but was still tentative. He looked over at his parents. His mother was holding his father's hand, and squeezing it hard. He gave her a reassuring look, then returned his gaze to Alrion.

There's no other way, I just have to try.

Alrion closed his eyes, trying to think about a spark or flame lighting up the lamp. He felt so awkward with this wizard and his parents staring at him while he held a magic lamp. What if this was all some kind of prank?

Here goes, he thought, focusing his attention more. But his mind wandered. He wondered what might happen, and if this thing really was magical. He got angry about how he had been put on the spot since he knew nothing about magic or wizards. He felt a sudden intense heat within him, then realised it was real. He opened his eyes and saw a giant flame leaping out of the lamp. He removed his hands immediately, panic rising within him. The extent of the flame, and the wild manner in which it had risen scared him. He had done almost nothing, and yet the flame was colossal.

"I need some air," Alrion said, and ran for the door. It was like the flame he had created had sucked all the air out of the room, and he just needed to breathe again.

~

"There's no debate about that result." Vincent peered at the black scorch mark on the ceiling.

"That was a success," Falric said.

"Go after him," Celes said. Vincent nodded and left the room.

He stepped into the cool night air and looked around for Alrion. He saw his son striding down the street, towards the town exit. Vincent upped his pace and followed close behind. He needed to catch up with his son and calm him down.

Alrion was slowing, and Vincent slowed too. Soon they were walking together.

"Hey, slow down a minute," Vincent said. He put a hand on his son's shoulder.

"Sorry, I just had to get out of there. I couldn't breathe." Alrion finally stopped and turned to face Vincent.

"That's fine, tell me what happened."

"Well, I just felt awkward and on the spot. And I got angry and annoyed at you all. And I felt the heat of my anger and saw the flame. I don't know how else to say this, but it scared me." Alrion looked down at the ground. He seemed ashamed of himself.

"Because it was so strange?" Vincent needed to understand what was behind this sudden panic.

"Yes, and because it came from me. I know that. It was uncontrolled and unexpected. Even if that lamp was magic, it came from me."

"Well, there's nothing wrong with that. It means you have a powerful gift, and you need to learn to control it."

"What if I can't?" Alrion had a desperate look about him. Vincent sighed. This wasn't what he had wanted, but this wizard business was really happening. He had to support his son in it.

"Well, think about it. Clearly, this is something you were born with. Have you ever mysteriously burned any houses down?"

"No." Alrion looked more hopeful. Vincent could see him coming around.

"Well, there you have it. You were doing just fine up until now, and from now on, you will be safe. Falric is an old hand; he will teach you how to control your gift."

"You're right. But what about you? Why didn't you go through this?" Alrion looked at him for an answer, but Vincent just turned away.

"Let's walk back to the house," he said. He started walking and Alrion followed. After a minute or two, Vincent spoke up again.

"Like I said before, I didn't have what it takes to be a wizard. My father was one and it consumed his life, so there was a bit of friction there. He wanted me by his side regardless. I left to live my own life."

"Why me then?" Alrion stopped and looked into Vincent's eyes.

"Who knows? The world works in mysterious ways. But you clearly have his gift, so it's up to you to nurture it."

"What do wizards do anyway?" Alrion started walking again and Vincent breathed a sigh of relief.

"Well, Falric will be the best person to tell you. But, I can imagine that you will travel the world and help people. When you're not working on becoming a better wizard, that is. I don't think it's the type of thing you master overnight."

"I think you're right," Alrion said. They were back in front of their house.

"Come with me, I have something for you." Vincent entered the house and walked straight to his bedroom. He rummaged through his wardrobe and removed a dusty wooden box. Instead of a normal lock it had a strange mechanism. Vincent pressed special parts of the box and it opened. He withdrew a soft blue pouch, closed the box, and put it back where he found it.

"Here, this was given to me by my father. Now I'm giving it to you." Vincent handed Alrion the pouch. Alrion opened it and removed a silver ring with a blue stone set in the middle. The ring was on a silver chain.

"What is this?" His eyes were bright with curiosity. Vincent chuckled.

"It's a magical ring. He told me it would keep me from harm. I'm not sure how it works, but here I am. So maybe it will be of use to you."

"Thanks, I'll keep it with me." Alrion returned the ring to the pouch and put it in his pocket.

"You know it's funny, after all this time I never lost it. It always showed up when I felt like I needed it. Anyway, take good care of it and keep it with you always."

"Why didn't you ever mention all this before?"

"I wanted you to have a normal upbringing. This magic stuff is about as far from normal as you can get. I didn't even know if you would have the gift. So, I did the best job I could raising you, without all that hanging over your head. You always felt that you were meant for more than blacksmithing, and I guess this is it."

"I guess so."

"Think about me for a moment, I'm about to lose my best apprentice!" Vincent hoped he could lighten the mood.

"I'm your only apprentice," Alrion said, but he did crack half a smile.

"I think I hear your mother, let's go take a look." Vincent walked back to the living room. Falric and Celes had just arrived.

"So, you'll set off tomorrow?" Celes said. Vincent looked over at Falric.

"Yes, tomorrow is best. You will need to make a few preparations before you leave," Falric said.

"True, and the workshop will have to remain closed while I'm away." Vincent started thinking through what he needed to do.

"Well, in that case, we should celebrate. A farewell feast for my wizard son," Celes said smiling at Alrion. He returned a cautious smile.

"Don't worry, you'll become accustomed to the title soon. You will feel it in your very being," Falric said.

"If you say so." Alrion shrugged his shoulders.

Vincent disappeared to help Celes in the kitchen with the final preparations for their meal. Alrion began to realise that it would be his last meal at home for a long time.

Saul drank deeply, like he was dying of thirst. He didn't even taste the ale. He slammed the tankard down, drops of ale flying out and spilling onto the tiny, grimy table.

Never again! he thought. Images of the hideous creatures came unbidden to his mind, their screams and ferocity. He needed to distract himself. Thrusting his trembling hand into his satchel, he found and removed the sack of coins. He only dared peek inside. The glint of gold was enough of a reminder, and he hastily stashed the sack. The inn wasn't particularly safe, and even worse if you invited trouble.

Dingiest place in Altarbright, just how I like it. But he pushed the thought away. It was time to start a new chapter. He had enough gold now to start afresh. Live out his life somewhere else in peace. No more smuggling. And as far away from the Blight as possible. The memories started flooding back again.

I never should have taken that job, he thought. But maybe the gold was enough. He heard footsteps and looked up. A hooded man sat down gracefully, occupying the chair opposite. He rested his arms on the table, like he had been invited.

"Saul, I knew I could find you here. How are you?" the man said. Saul didn't recognise the voice. In the low light he couldn't see the man's face under the hood.

"I don't think we've met. Who are you?" Saul tried to hide his fear, but his voice was thin and weedy. He gulped down more ale.

"You can call me Dale. I was your most recent employer." Dale pointed to the satchel, and Saul reflexively covered it with his hand.

"I see. What can I do for you, Dale?"

"I'm in need of your services again."

"Why?" Saul swallowed hard, his throat sticking.

"The last job was just a test. I needed to make sure that everything went according to plan. This time, it will be a lot bigger. It's the real deal."

"I'm not sure," Saul stammered.

Why is this man so intimidating? Just stand up to him. The job was done, now you are done.

"I'm done with that. Sorry." Saul managed to sound more confident. Dale shook his head.

"Saul, Saul. Why would you say that?"

"I never signed up for that." Saul forced the images away.

"Oh, but I took care of everything. Everyone played their part, correct? Nobody challenged you on the way through?" Dale had a dangerous tinge to his voice. Saul swigged more ale.

"No, of course not. But, those creatures ..."

"You mean the Blighters?" Dale said. Saul shrunk away, and looked around.

"Don't worry, nobody will overhear us. You had a problem with the Blighters?" Dale talked even louder.

"Sshh. Yes, alright the Blighters. Horrible creatures. And I saw what they did to a man. I want no part of it." Saul looked around, nobody seemed to have noticed their conversation.

"I thought you were the best." Dale sounded disappointed.

"I am. Or I was. That wasn't part of the deal."

"We were upfront about the cargo. You saw it yourself before you left."

"Well it was too late then, wasn't it? Look, I won't say nothing. I'm done. Find someone else." Saul tried to lift his satchel, but Dale's hand came down quickly and held his arm.

"I'm afraid that's the wrong answer. Such a pity, you would have been more useful had you the stomach for it." Dale reached out with his other hand. As it passed through the light Saul saw a long black nail, dripping with a thick black substance.

"Welcome to the fold," Dale said and jabbed Saul's chest.

4

FINAL PREPARATIONS

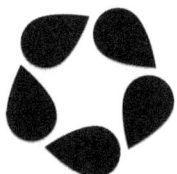

"How far will we be travelling?" Alrion said to Falric.

"Not too far, only a couple of days' ride. The majority of it is on established roads, so it's fairly quick with horses and quite safe. Have you travelled much?"

"Not really, no." Alrion couldn't believe how little he had travelled now that he thought about it. Life had so easily revolved around their little town.

"Well, I think you'll enjoy the trip. Being a wizard will eventually require a lot of travel, once you have trained. Wizards are an important part of society."

"I didn't even know about them!"

"No offence intended, but a small place like this has little use for a wizard. We are generally more involved in cities and countries. There is a lot we can do, and a lot that people require us to do."

"I suppose I'll understand that later."

"Of course, don't worry. You will learn these things gradually. There are many mysteries to being a wizard, but I'll try and keep your training as straightforward as possible. There are enough things we don't understand without adding to that list." Falric started to speak again but suddenly stopped.

"Now, what do we have here?" he said, eyeing the food that Vincent was carrying.

"This is lemon potatoes with assorted vegetables. My wife is about to bring in her famous roast chicken," Vincent said with pride while laying down some dishes.

"We don't get that at the Wizard Academy. Looks great," Falric said.

"It's not that famous," Alrion said.

"Trust me, lad, you'll be missing this." Falric looked to be mentally devouring the food. Alrion couldn't understand the extreme reaction. Celes walked in with the roast chicken platter, placing it at the centre of the table. She put generous servings on everyone's plate.

"I feel like I should say a few words," Vincent said. He paused before continuing.

"It's been a pleasure bringing you up, Alrion, and now you are about to take your first big steps into the world beyond. There are many things that you have not learned by being here, in this village with us. However, I think that what you have learned, are the tools to becoming a great man. The path of a wizard will be a challenging one, but know that we will always support you. Always remember that you have a home here."

"Thanks, Dad," Alrion said. He had never heard his father talk like that before. He had always been kind and supportive, but this seemed different.

"He spoke for both of us, but let me add one thing. You be careful out there, Alrion. Not just of the dangers of the world but watch out for women. They'll see how good you are and will be on the attack. Remember that if you get serious with a woman you need to bring her back here to meet us," Celes said. She had a serious look on her face.

"Mum, that's just embarrassing." Alrion turned away.

"It had to be said," Celes said with a devious smile.

"Let's dig in." Vincent started to eat, and everyone else joined in.

After they ate, they returned to the living room and the couches there. Alrion continued through the room, leaving the house. Vincent followed him out. He found his son staring off towards the town gates.

"Is something up? Do you have somewhere to be?" Vincent said. Alrion was lost in thought. He wondered where his friends were right now.

"No, it's nothing. Let's go back inside," Alrion said. Vincent nodded and gave Alrion an affectionate squeeze on the shoulder. They headed back in together.

"Amazing meal Celes, I'll be dreaming about those potatoes," Falric said.

"Thanks, you are too kind." Celes beamed with the praise.

"I need to come up with a spell for that."

"I don't think there's enough magic in the world to recreate that," Vincent said.

"Do you want to stay here tonight?" Celes said to Falric.

"No, I'll go sleep in the workshop actually, if you don't mind. I have a few preparations to make myself."

"Are you sure? It'll probably be uncomfortable and cold," Celes said.

"Cold? Did you forget who you were talking to?" Falric said.

"Just don't burn the place down," Vincent said.

"I'll do my best. Would you mind accompanying me, Vincent?" Falric said, rising from his chair.

"Sure, let's go," Vincent said, and the two left the house together.

* * *

"What kind of preparations are we talking here?" Vincent asked once they were alone.

"Nothing too special, just a few things I need to go over myself. I want to see if the road ahead is clear and try to communicate with the Wizard Academy. They need to know we are on our way," Falric said.

"Sure."

"You do remember me, don't you?" Falric looked at Vincent.

"Yes, you were my father's star pupil. You've aged somewhat, though."

"Good. At least you've kept some of your faculties, if not your name."

"It was important to get a new start. You can't imagine how hard things were after that happened."

"You should have come to us. We could have helped you."

"No, you couldn't have. Here we are," Vincent said, unlocking the workshop once more.

"Thank you. I will come around in the morning, then we can set off."

"Good night. See you tomorrow," Vincent said, leaving Falric to enter the workshop.

* * *

The next morning Alrion woke up early. He hadn't slept well, his mind churning about becoming a wizard. He had so many questions, but he couldn't even articulate half of them. There were just too many unknowns. Nevertheless, he was excited to be leaving the village. It was like a huge weight had fallen from his shoulders, and the possibilities seemed endless.

He felt a little bad for how ungrateful he had seemed for his upbringing and his dad's insistence on being a blacksmith apprentice. But now he was truly discovering what he should be doing.

Alrion packed some clothes, then went to check on his father. Vincent was sipping coffee in the living room, a bulging pack sitting next to his chair. Propped up next to the pack was a sword with an ornate scabbard.

"I see you've packed already. What's that sword?" Alrion said.

"It's a relic from another life," Vincent said.

"Do you even know how to use it? I know you refuse to make weapons, so it's strange to see you with one." Alrion couldn't reconcile his father with having a sword. It seemed so foreign.

"I have made swords before, a long time ago. I may be a bit rusty using one again, but I can certainly handle myself. It's just a simple precaution. Are you packed?"

"Almost. I just need to check a few things."

"Don't worry; you won't even know half of what you really need until you need it. Just make sure you have clothes." Vincent grinned at Alrion.

"I don't remember the last time I saw you this excited," Alrion said.

"It's an adventure, even if it's a small one. We should celebrate things like this. It's a break from routine, and we're going out into the unknown."

"Well, when you put it like that, it's pretty exciting even for you."

"It's not every day you accompany your son to begin his wizard training."

"True. It's not every day you set out to train as a wizard either."

"See, something to be celebrated," Vincent said.

"How long will you be away?" Celes said as she entered the room.

"Probably a week," Vincent said.

"That doesn't sound too bad. How long until Alrion comes back?"

"No idea, that's one for Falric." Vincent shrugged his shoulders.

"I heard my name," Falric said from the front door.

"Come in!" Vincent called out. Falric opened the door and walked in. He was dressed the same as the night before.

"Celes was just asking how long Alrion will be at the academy before he can come home."

"To visit? Or for good?" Falric said.

"Both," Celes said.

"He really shouldn't visit for at least six months. That gives us time to get some traction and build in some good safeguards once he starts learning more."

"And then?" Celes said.

"Well, truthfully if his training goes well he should never return here to live. Once he becomes a wizard, he belongs to the world, and not one place. Of course, he can and should visit you when he can, but his duty will be elsewhere: either at the Wizard Academy, in a royal court, or on an expedition. I'm afraid your son's days in Hamley are numbered," Falric said. Celes nodded. She looked over at Alrion.

"This really is goodbye then. Should he go say goodbye to his friends?"

"I would advise against it," Falric said.

"Why?" Alrion said. He didn't have that many, but they deserved to know he was leaving.

"How will you explain it? They either won't understand or won't believe you. Of course, I won't stop you, but I think it's easier to just leave, and explain when you return."

"I'll think about it," Alrion said. But he suspected Falric was right about this.

"Whatever you decide, we will tell people you left to study," Vincent said.

"That is an excellent idea," Falric said.

"Are you ready?" Vincent said to Falric.

"A wizard is always ready. Occasionally they need more preparation, though."

"Are you fully prepared then?" Celes said with a laugh.

"Just about, but I do seem to be lacking some quality food, though." Falric licked his lips and looked at Celes.

"Don't worry, I'm sending some with the boys. Come over to the kitchen and take a look," Celes said. Falric rubbed his hands with glee and followed her.

"I'll bring horses and meet you outside," Vincent said. Alrion nodded and watched his father leave. A few minutes later he saw Falric return from the kitchen. But his face was white, and he looked unsettled.

"What happened in there? Did you get the food?" Alrion said.

"Oh yes, of course. Nothing important. Your mother just ... err ... shared her concerns about our trip." Falric chuckled, but it didn't have the same energy to it. Alrion wondered what could have spooked the wizard so badly.

"Excited?" he said to Alrion.

"Yes, but I'm also a bit unsure what to think," Alrion said.

"I know the feeling. It'll be a true adventure, though, you can count on that."

"I don't doubt that. Compared to Hamley, anything is an adventure. We are almost ready, I'm just waiting for my father to return with some horses," Alrion said. Celes distributed the last of the food she had prepared. Alrion watched her closely, and she stole a pointed look at Falric. The wizard pretended not to see and Celes looked satisfied. Then they all left the room to wait outside. It didn't take long to see Vincent leading two black horses over.

"Saddle up," Vincent said, handing the reins of one of the horses to Alrion.

"You can't leave without saying goodbye to your mother," Celes said. Alrion hugged her and gave her a kiss goodbye. Then he threw his bag over the back of the horse and climbed up into the saddle. Vincent and Falric followed suit.

"This is it. Are you ready?" Falric said.

"I'm ready," Alrion said with more conviction than he felt.

"I expect a full report when you get there, write me a letter," Celes said.

"Can't you just ask Dad?"

"No, it's not the same."

"Alright, I'll do it."

"You two keep him out of trouble," Celes said looking at Vincent and Falric.

"Sure thing boss," Vincent said grinning at her. Falric turned his horse around and they started to ride off. Alrion looked back at his mother one last time. But that was it. He didn't look around as they left the village, instead he just stared ahead. Once they were clear of the village, he finally turned back and had one last look.

I don't know when I'll be back, or who I'll be when I do return. Goodbye Hamley.

He watched the village go about its business and realised that apart from his mother he probably wouldn't be missed. His destiny lay elsewhere. Turning his horse, he raced to catch up with his father and Falric.

5

WIZARD PRINCIPLES

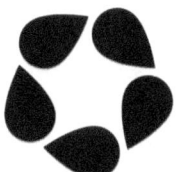

There was little conversation at the beginning. Alrion did not know why, but he was preoccupied with checking out the landscape. It was ground he was familiar with, and he could identify every farmhouse and building that they passed. He didn't know what he was looking for at all. After riding for over an hour they passed a point at which he finally understood. He had been waiting to pass from the area he knew into unknown terrain.

The transition was so subtle and fast that he did not notice it at first. However, once he did, he sat up straighter in the saddle, looking more intently at the surroundings.

"You're in unfamiliar territory now," Vincent said, confirming Alrion's reaction.

"The adventure is finally starting. It's exciting."

"It should be, there's a whole wide world out there for you," Falric said. He gently pulled on the reins, nudging his horse closer to Alrion.

"Now that we have some riding ahead of us, is there anything you want to ask me about?" Falric said.

"Too many things. But, I was wondering if you could explain magic a bit more. I don't understand it at all." Alrion shuffled his position so he could more easily ride and pay attention to Falric as well.

"Of course. The first thing that people usually don't understand is that magic is not just for wizards. Wizards are just the most well-known and complete practitioners. I'll explain that point in a minute. But it should be made clear to you that your mother could use magic with a little instruction."

"Really?"

"Absolutely. There are forces in this world which anyone who has the knowledge of how to do so can summon and use. Of course, the effect is generally quite tame because you are leaning heavily on the natural order of things and not supplying any force of your own. But there you go, that's a common misconception."

"You just need a recipe then?" Alrion tried not to sound sceptical, but it just seemed too simple.

"We do like to call them spells, but yes. With the proper instructions available, if you follow them to the letter you can achieve many things. However, this kind of knowledge is not widely available and usually guarded quite stringently because anybody can use it. It is something that Granthion started to combat with the Wizard Academy."

"And that was so wizards could collect and share these spells?"

"Exactly. This leads me to describe the first pillar of magic: Knowledge. With the right knowledge, you can cast spells with nothing else. Or, you can enhance or unlock capabilities unavailable to other people. Knowledge is something very important for wizards, as we need to be able to access and use all types of magic."

"I understand that. Is that what I'll be focusing on at the Wizard Academy?"

"Mostly, yes. There will be many types of training, but one key thing that sets wizards apart is knowledge. We will be transferring as much as possible to you. That is something you can learn most effectively at the academy."

"What about other ways of using magic? Are there ways that do not require knowledge?"

"Well, yes and no. Let's just say that knowledge is a pervasive element that usually helps. However, to answer your question, yes, the other two pillars of magic do not necessarily need knowledge. The next one is Will. By force of Will, you can perform feats thought impossible. There are monks who train exclusively in the development of the Will. They can command their bodies and the world around them to behave in different ways. You could argue that there is an element of knowledge and training to this, but there have been examples of those who discovered these abilities with no prior knowledge or instruction."

"That sounds interesting, but I can't picture it. What are some examples?" Alrion nudged his horse closer to Falric's.

"They can move objects with thought alone, and break things with their body that should be too strong. They hone the strength of their will to challenge the laws of nature."

"Wow, that's pretty cool," Alrion said.

"It is indeed and has earned them fame as a result. Nevertheless, they must undergo very strict training and mental conditioning to get to that point. It is not an easy undertaking."

"Is it easier for a wizard?" Alrion had to admit he liked the idea of moving things with his mind, or breaking the unbreakable.

"It is if they have progressed enough in the other two pillars of magic to support the Will. But, fundamentally, there are no shortcuts. The wizard should have the capacity to do more, but not skip over the development required."

"Could I just go lock myself in a cave and eventually emerge with the ability to move things with my mind?"

"Not exactly, but theoretically yes. The potential is there if you can develop yourself in the right manner. Which would be incredibly difficult without proper instruction."

"Wouldn't it be easier to use spells?"

"It's all about having the right tool for the right occasion. The most potent magic combines all three pillars."

"What's the third one?"

"Spark. This is the one that we already tested." Falric pointed at

Alrion's chest. "Spark is the only thing that a wizard cannot learn or train in from nothing. You either have it when you are born, or you do not."

"Could you have tested me years ago?"

"Yes, and you would have most likely passed. However, it is better to train wizards later when they are stronger physically and mentally. It is a hard path, but very rewarding."

"What does the Spark do?"

"The Spark is like the fuel that lights the fire. Which is part of the reason the test has been designed that way. It's an easy way to explain the importance of Spark, and why it is key to being a wizard. Spark is innate magic, but you need Knowledge and Will to use it effectively. You could recite a spell to create a tiny flame, but your Spark will fuel that flame into something else entirely."

"That's why I scorched the ceiling." Alrion had not forgotten the wild nature of that flame. It still made him nervous, the fact that he could do so much from nothing.

"Exactly. Your Spark can amplify many different spells; some require your Spark as a key ingredient. Therefore, only those with the Spark can truly call themselves wizards. Since you cannot have mastery over magic without having all three." Falric finished his explanation and waited for questions. Alrion nodded along and focused more on the ride. He needed to think through everything that he had just learned.

"Let's break for lunch over there, it looks like a nice shady spot," Vincent said, pointing ahead.

"Good idea," Falric said. The three of them pushed forward and tied their horses to a giant tree to one side of the road. Vincent directed them to a nice grassy area under the shade of the tree, and they sat down to eat some of the food provided by Celes.

After Alrion ate, he spoke up.

"Falric, how did you become a wizard?"

"Your grandfather found me. He was searching for new initiates to build the Wizard Academy. He travelled the entire world, seeking out any who were willing and able to be trained." Falric had a faraway look and a smile on his face.

"What were you doing before that?"

"I was studying to be a scholar. Destined for a life with my head in books, researching and writing papers. The funny thing is, that's how it ended up anyway. Only the books were mostly spellbooks and my writing was reports and letters."

"That sounds different to the wizard's life you explained."

"It is unusual. Before Granthion, it would have been unheard of. It was one of the sacrifices required to make his vision of the Wizard Academy a reality. The life of adventure was not for me, as it turned out." Falric sighed.

"We're happy to have provided you the opportunity for a mini adventure, right, Alrion?" Vincent said, winking at Alrion.

"And you can thank us by providing a quick magic demonstration." Alrion made a flourish with his hands and laughed.

"Of what? I'm not a performer you know," Falric said, chuckling.

"Just show me the three pillars of magic in action." Alrion leaned forward, eager to watch.

"Alright. Let me think for a moment," Falric said, closing his eyes.

"I have just the thing. Let us walk slightly further from the road, just in case." Falric jumped up and set off. Alrion followed quickly behind, while Vincent was in no rush at all. Falric stopped within a minute and looked around.

"This will do just fine," he said. Alrion watched with burning curiosity.

"First, I'm going to start with a very useful spell. This one draws out water from the atmosphere." Falric held out his hand and a small pool of water formed in his palm.

"Wow!" Alrion couldn't say anything else. He was transfixed by the sudden appearance of the water.

"Next, I will use my will to work with the water," Falric said. The water started to move, drawing up, twirling into the shape of a sphere, and hovering gently above Falric's hand.

"Hang on, what you just did there isn't magic?"

"Technically no, I imposed my Will onto the water. The right shaped container would cause it to have this shape, why can't I compel it to do so as well?" Falric said. Alrion didn't have a reply.

"Next, we can spice it up a little bit," Falric said. The sphere of water grew in size and started to crystallise. With a snap, the process was completed, and a ball of ice fell back into his hand. He threw it over to Alrion.

"It's cold." Alrion laughed as he caught it.

"Exactly. I used my Spark to draw more water and cooled it past its freezing point. And now you are holding it."

"Wow. I see what you mean. Wouldn't it be a good idea to teach people that water spell? So that they can find water when they need it?" Alrion said.

"Unfortunately, the volume is far too small with the base version of the spell. There are much better ways of gathering water, so it's not really worth it. But, for a wizard, it is incredibly useful. You just need the right training and experience."

"You'll have to teach me how to do this." Alrion kept staring at the ball of ice, turning it over in his hands.

"All in good time, that, and much more."

"Nice trick," Vincent said as they were walking back to the horses. Alrion threw the ball of ice at his back and Vincent quickly turned and caught it. He removed a flask of water from his saddlebag and crushed some of the ice into it.

"Thanks," Vincent said, enjoying a swig of the colder water. Alrion laughed.

"That was a lot of magic just to cool your drink," Falric said with a chuckle. With the demonstration over, they packed up and resumed their ride.

For a time, Alrion saw nothing much to look at on the ride. The scenery was empty woodland to either side of the path, with the occasional track peeling off.

"Those tracks probably lead to homes," Vincent commented when Alrion was staring at one of them. Farms started appearing once more and signs of civilisation were apparent. Other paths forked off the main road, wooden signposts naming them. Alrion recognised none of the names.

"Not far now," Vincent said.

"To where?" Alrion said.

"Carford. The biggest town around here, and a bit of a trading hub. I think you'll like it," Vincent said. Alrion reserved judgement but was curious to see it. Finally, he started to see buildings looming in the distance. In front of them were large stone walls. They didn't go around the whole town, but blocked off each side of the road a good distance and converged in a peak over the main entry. He couldn't see much past them but noticed a large flow of people, horses, and wagons going in and out of the entry.

"What do you think, Son?" Vincent said.

"Big," Alrion said. He'd never seen anything like it. His eyes widened as he tried to take it all in.

"Bigger, but this is still small. Just you wait until you see somewhere like Brangtur, now that's big."

"I guess this is big enough for now," Alrion said with a laugh. He looked at the people flooding the road and noticed that they seemed less carefree and happy than those from his village. A bit more stressed, and more purposeful.

There were large guards, clad in chain mail and shiny metal helmets standing at each end of the entry scowling at the people coming in. They had swords at their hips but otherwise didn't seem too threatening. Alrion wondered how active they actually were.

As their horses stepped through the gates Alrion felt a wave of wonder pass over him as he took in the sights of Carford. It was a fitting beginning to his adventure.

6

A CHANCE ENCOUNTER

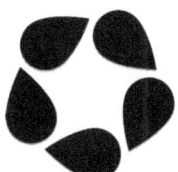

After the entry, the road opened out into a giant square. There were stalls around the edge of the square, and streets going off in four different directions. There were even a few brass statues littered about.

"Who are they?" Alrion said, pointing at the statues.

"Famous warriors from the past. Ones that either governed the town or rescued them from sieges or raids. They are immortalised in brass to commemorate their contribution," Falric said. Vincent nodded along at the information.

"Are there any statues of wizards?" Alrion didn't see any.

"Unfortunately, not, wizards don't inspire the same kind of following and support. I think it has to do with what we do. People can understand a man who fights for his people. They find it hard to understand the intricacies of what a wizard does. It isn't always clear what we actually achieve." Falric shook his head slowly. "I think many wizards would not achieve any recognition at all in their life-time, only future generations would be able to look back and join the dots."

"So, it's a fairly thankless pursuit then?"

"On a grand scale, yes, but don't worry there will be plenty of opportunities for you to make a difference for people and they will know it. Think of your grandfather, he certainly made a big difference on the world stage," Falric said, looking at Vincent.

"I can confirm that people knew about him," Vincent said, without adding anything else. As they rode through the square, Alrion looked around at the buildings. They were all bigger than those at Hamley, and many had multiple stories. They were all made out of stone and looked solid and imposing.

"How did they build all this?" Alrion said, half talking to himself.

"Over a very long time," Falric said.

"I can imagine." Alrion pushed on straight ahead, passing through the square. Many smaller buildings started to line the streets, most of them looking like houses. They approached a corner and noticed a huge and striking building sitting there. It had a grand entrance, stables off to the side and a giant shield-shaped sign hanging from the roof.

"We are here," Falric said. Alrion read the sign.

"*The Sundered Shield*?"

"Yes, that's it, there's a great story to this place. I'll tell you once we are inside. Vincent, can you take care of the horses?" Falric said.

"Sure." Vincent dismounted and retrieved his bag. Once Alrion was ready Vincent threw his own bag at his son's feet and started gathering up the horses. Falric dismounted with grace and shouldered his bag, walking into the establishment.

Alrion bent down and grabbed both the bags, quickly straightening as he balanced the weight. As he rose he bumped into something, and stepped back in surprise. There was an olive-skinned woman walking past. Her short blonde hair and plain clothing surprised him.

"Sorry," she said, and kept walking. Alrion watched her go, fascinated. There was something different about her. It wasn't just the way she had dressed, but something about her mannerisms. She soon disappeared into the crowd and he turned back to enter the inn.

The interior of *The Sundered Shield* was dark, even though a few lamps were strung from the ceiling. There were so many long wooden tables Alrion had trouble seeing the floor and where he could walk. He saw that Falric was up at the bar talking to one of the women working there. Alrion joined him.

"If not three rooms, surely we could get two?"

"We're almost full, we could do two rooms if one of you is willing to pay for a prestige room." The woman spoke the words like that was a goodbye.

"I'll get that. What's the difference?" Falric said without hesitation. The woman looked confused.

"Nicer furnishings, private water jug and so forth."

"Sold," Falric said, dropping a small pile of gold coins into her hands. The woman counted them carefully and deposited them behind the bar.

"Excellent. Your assistant can come with me and drop off your bags," she said. Alrion wanted to say something but Falric waved him off and handed Alrion his bag as well.

With a sigh, Alrion followed the woman up the stairs. She was dressed in a blue and white dress, and it swished left and right as she ascended. She moved swiftly, her curly brown hair bouncing along as she walked. At the end of the hallway, they stopped and she unlocked the door.

"This is the prestige suite," she said. Alrion stepped inside and placed Falric's bag on the bed. It looked nice but didn't seem that special. Once he left the room, she locked the door and gave him the key.

"Next stop is your room," she said. They returned to the other end of the hallway and she stopped outside a dingy looking door, covered with scuffmarks.

"This is your room," she said as she unlocked the door. Alrion could see how cramped it was, with two tiny beds taking up most of the room. He placed the bags inside and stepped out again.

"Here's your key," the woman said, and handed it to Alrion. He locked the door and headed downstairs. He saw his father sitting with Falric in the corner of the room and walked straight over.

"We all settled in?" Falric said.

"Yes, and here's your key." Alrion threw it over. Falric almost dropped it, but kept a hold of it and tucked it into his robes somewhere. Vincent looked at Alrion with disapproval.

"You just keep our key, take a seat," he said, shuffling over. Alrion sat down next to him.

"So how far are we?" Alrion said.

"From the academy? Not far we will get there tomorrow," Falric said.

"That's not too bad." Alrion thought he could get used to this adventuring business. It seemed pretty good so far.

"Not at all. Although I think your father will be disappointed by how short his trip will be," Falric said. Vincent shrugged.

"I'd like to know more about being a wizard. And you were also going to tell me about this place," Alrion said.

"Ah yes, *The Sundered Shield*. As it so happens I can do both at the same time. I was involved in the story that gave this inn its name."

"I didn't know that," Vincent said.

"There's a lot you don't know about me," Falric said, a crafty smile on his face.

"This particular town was originally a smaller village, like your home. One day a group of mercenaries and bandits camped nearby. They were passing through and needed supplies so they performed a few raids on the local villages. Nobody put up much resistance, so the hardened warriors decided to settle in for a longer stay, which was the start of it all." Falric paused to take a swig of the ale in front of him.

"Right, so after a few of these raids, there was a man called Ryder who took issue with the bandits. He was just a local farmer but was sick of dealing with them. But, what could he do? He was just one man. So, he decided to do what one man could do: steal from them. He snuck out to their camp at night, after they had all passed out from drink. While they were asleep he took as much food as he could lay his hands on, and rose away with the food and the leader's horse."

"I bet they weren't impressed," Alrion said.

"Not at all. The townsfolk were divided. Some praised his action, some criticised him for making trouble. They decided to eat all the food and set the horse loose so there was no evidence. The bandits came back the next day, demanding answers. But the town denied everything, and they left."

"He got away with it?" Alrion said. It sounded too easy.

"Well, not quite. You see Ryder felt bolder after his success, and went back again. He crept back to their camp, made sure they were asleep, and started to steal more food. This time the bandit leader was lying in wait and caught Ryder red-handed. Ryder fled, but it was no use. The bandit leader had recognised him. Fearing reprisals, the farmer came to the Wizard Academy and begged for help."

"So, you met him there? Ryder?"

"Yes, I did. He made a convincing case, but we didn't want to get involved. That would just direct the ire of the bandits to the academy, and we didn't want that. Besides, I believe the role of a wizard should be less direct. There can be a truly incredible power imbalance, and the more we stay out of things the better," Falric said.

"He just left then?"

"Not before he stole a shield from our inventory. It was a curious piece that looked completely generic. But, it had a special power. I let him take it of course, curious as to what he would do. I followed him back to see what would happen next."

"You let him steal from you?" Vincent said, surprised.

"It was all very controlled; I could have stopped him at any time. He returned to the village with the shield, and told them all, that he had found a magic shield and they would now be safe. I still, to this day, wonder if he really believed that without even seeing it in action. However, the bandits were waiting in ambush; his town had sold him out. When they attacked, Ryder held up the shield, and it deflected every attack. He managed to push them back, the bandits mystified as to why all their attacks were powerless."

"It actually worked? He got away with it again?" Alrion said. This Ryder seemed to have incredible luck.

"Not quite. After they retreated, the town had a big celebration. Ryder as the hero drank a little too much, and fell into a deep sleep.

While he slept, the leader of the bandit group snuck into the town and swapped the shield with an identical one that was not in any way magical. A significant downside to that particular shield."

"Because it could be so easily misplaced or changed. Were you aware of the swap?" Alrion said.

"Of course, I could tell. However, I didn't act, I just observed. The next day the bandit leader returned and said that if Ryder defeated him in single combat, they would leave the town alone forever. Ryder immediately accepted, thinking that his shield would keep him from harm. So, with the townsfolk and the bandits watching on, the bandit leader and Ryder faced off in a sword fight." Falric paused for dramatic effect. Alrion made a gesture to Falric to keep going, he needed to hear what was next.

"The leader wielded two swords, and Ryder used a sword and shield. They traded blows, and the shield held up, but something was amiss. The perfect deflection abilities of the old shield were not there, and the shield started to show damage. Ryder, to his credit continued fighting, even though it was obvious to everyone that his shield was weakening."

"And what happened?"

"Well, seeing his victory was nigh, the leader surged with a final assault, both his blades whirring at great speed as he attacked Ryder. The plucky farmer parried what he could, but kept using his shield to protect himself. His battle prowess could not match the bandit leader. Finally, the shield split in two and dropped to the ground. The bandit leader had his sword at Ryder's throat and demanded that he surrender."

"So, that's where you stepped in?" Alrion was trying to figure out what role Falric had played in this.

"Not quite. Ryder refused to surrender and rolled away. He grabbed one half of the shield and kept fighting, with a ferocity and energy that was unmatched. The leader was suddenly on the back foot. But he counter-attacked and went for broke, trying to finish Ryder once and for all." Falric again paused for drama. Alrion let go a sigh of frustration and then Falric continued again.

"It all came down to one final swing. The bandit leader had attacked high and was following up with a piercing thrust. Ryder had parried the first attack with his blade, but the shield was too small to protect him. Therefore, instead of trying to block the attack, he used the sharp jagged edge of the broken shield to attack the bandit leader. Both men took critical wounds, and neither could continue the fight."

"What did that mean for the town?"

"The bandit leader retreated and left the town alone. Ryder recovered, but could not return to a life of farming. He took to hanging around this very inn, and soon people would come from all over the area to hear his story. To capitalise on this, the owner renamed it *The Sundered Shield*, to commemorate Ryder's actions and to profit on his popularity. With the town safe from bandit attacks, and now on the map for the heroic actions of Ryder, it quickly grew in popularity and prosperity." Falric finished with a flourish and sat back in his chair.

"Hang on, there's no mention of wizards in that story at all. Apart from what you have mentioned to us," Alrion said.

"Exactly. So, you see, I knew that direct involvement would change the struggle, and maybe even escalate it. But by letting Ryder take responsibility, and a relatively risk-free item from our stores, I let the story play out to a complete and proper resolution," Falric said.

"But he profited by stealing from you? What kind of message is that?" Alrion liked the story, but didn't see the point of it. Not from a wizard's perspective anyway.

"It shows that he was prepared to do what was necessary. It also shows that his actions cost him dearly, but he still managed to win a victory for his town."

"Whatever happened to the magic shield?"

"Well, I visited the bandit camp and retrieved it without them noticing," Falric said with a grin.

"Sounds like wizards do a lot of nothing," Alrion said. Vincent grunted in agreement.

"Sometimes, yes. However, one thing you will learn is that every action has consequences, even inaction. And acting only when required will have a greater impact." Falric let his gaze linger on Alrion, and then turned his attention to Vincent.

"That's enough stories for the evening, let's get some food, then turn in," Vincent said. Alrion's stomach rumbled in agreement, and he looked forward to what was on offer.

After the meal, they all walked upstairs to retire for the evening. Alrion showed Falric to his room, and the wizard was satisfied with it. Vincent was less than impressed with their room, but at the same time, he seemed to be expecting it. Alrion lay down to sleep and dreamed about being a wizard and hurling fireballs everywhere.

When he awoke, he was alone. His father had packed up and left the room.

I don't know how he's always up so early, Alrion thought, as he started to prepare himself. He reached into his pocket to look at his ring again, only the pouch wasn't there. After a few seconds of panic, he tried his other pocket, then went through the rest of his clothes looking for it. There was no ring.

He thought back to all the things he had done since they left Hamley. The whole time it had only been the three of them, and neither his father nor Falric would have taken it. Then he had a flash of insight. When he was outside the inn, he had bumped into that young woman. She must have taken it, there was no other explanation.

But how is that possible?

He realised that perhaps he had a great deal to learn about the world, and chalked it up to experience. However, he couldn't admit to his father that he had lost such a precious heirloom so soon, so decided to keep the incident to himself. He justified it to himself by thinking back to the words his father had spoken about the ring: 'After all this time I never lost it. It always showed up when I felt like I needed it.'

7

THE WOODED PATH

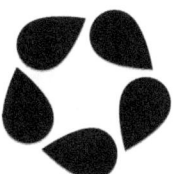

Alrion descended the stairs and couldn't see his father or Falric. He handed the room key back to the woman behind the bar, then left the inn. He could see Falric standing outside, waiting.

"Good morning," Falric said.

"Good morning. We're leaving immediately?" Alrion said.

"Yes, the sooner the better. We can stop a little later and have something to eat. Your father is readying the horses." Falric pointed to the stables.

"That's fine," Alrion said. He looked around to see if he could see the girl who had stolen his ring but didn't recognise any of the people nearby. It was foolish to think she would still be here; she was probably long gone. When his father emerged, Alrion slung his bag onto the back of the horse, then mounted it.

"How are you feeling? Have you ridden this much before?" Vincent said.

"Not too bad. I don't think I have ridden this much, but I doubt it will get much worse." Alrion was a bit stiff and sore, but it didn't bother him.

"I think that's fair. We should arrive by evening, right, Falric?"

Vincent said.

"Correct."

"Then let's head out." Vincent took the lead, guiding his horse back towards the main gate. Alrion followed but continued to peer into the crowd. He knew it was fruitless, but he had to look for the thief. If there was a chance he could recover the ring, he had to take it.

As they passed through the main gate, Alrion finally accepted that the ring was gone. He would keep that information to himself for a while, and tell his father later. After they left Carford, they back-tracked a little, before taking another direction back at an earlier fork in the road.

"Any other towns on our route?" Alrion said.

"No, that was it. We will stay on this path initially, then cut through the forest. That will be a good place to stop and eat," Falric said. Alrion nodded and watched the countryside pass by.

The land still looked familiar, even if he hadn't travelled this far before. The grass was a lush green, and there were many trees around. The occasional dirt roads branched off the main one, with signposts directing people to homesteads or smaller tracks.

After an hour or two Falric slowed his horse and Alrion and Vincent followed suit.

"This path here to the left, leads to the Wizard Academy," Falric said, pointing it out. Alrion noticed a wooden sign next to the path.

"Needle Forest," Alrion said, reading the sign.

"That's the one. We need to pass through there to get to the academy."

"Why not have a sign for the academy?" Alrion said.

"It's better this way. The people who need to find us can do so anyway." Falric immediately set off once more. Alrion followed, and Vincent lingered, taking up the rear position.

They had to ride down the new path in single file, as it was quite narrow. The trees were incredibly tall and had long fine bristles on them. There was a fresh woody smell that filled Alrion's lungs and instilled a sense of calm.

"I can see why it is called Needle Forest." Alrion grabbed the bristles on a nearby tree and broke some off into his hand so he could take a better look at them.

"Not very imaginative, but quite apt." Falric had his eyes focused on the road ahead. Alrion continued to look around. The trees in their size and numbers were imposing and menacing. Like they didn't want him to be there. He shuddered instinctively.

"Let's stop over here." Falric turned off the path abruptly. He pushed between two trees and Alrion followed closely behind. It seemed like a poor decision at first, but they quickly emerged into a small clearing.

"I love this spot, I always stop here," Falric said. Alrion could see why. It was covered and secluded. You would never know to look for it. Yet the grass was short and looked soft. They tied up the horses and sat down to eat.

"What do you know of the Blight?" Falric asked Alrion.

"Not much really. People talk about it in hushed tones, but nobody seems to be able to talk from experience," Alrion said.

"That's a good thing. It is best to avoid experience of the Blight if possible. Although as a wizard you will have to confront it at some time or another."

"Why is that?"

"From a practical perspective, the Blight is everywhere. You have been lucky enough to grow up in the country of Avaria. Due to the sacrifice of your grandfather, this country is free from the Blight. Strong border controls at key locations do help keep it in check as well."

"It's a problem elsewhere?"

"Yes, a big problem. Every person deals with the Blight in different ways."

"But what is it?" Alrion had trouble imagining what it was.

"That's a good question. The Blight is an infection, a disease as the name implies. But, it's more than that. It has a life of its own, and it connects all those infected. The Blight cannot create creatures, but it twists creatures to its purpose."

"Can it be destroyed?"

"Wizards can cleanse the blight, as your grandfather demonstrated. But so far only he has been able to do so. Our current options are either to destroy the infected, contain them, or keep them away."

"That doesn't sound good. Weren't the infected originally people?"

"Yes, they were, so as you can imagine it's a huge problem. One that you must learn to deal with as a wizard. You will initially be sheltered as you start to learn at the academy. But eventually, you will join the world. And the Blight is a part of the world."

"How long has it been around?"

"The stories vary. Some say it has always been around. But regardless of the origins, it is well catalogued when it became a problem. Over fifty years ago, the Blight became a major problem and swept across the world incredibly quickly. We were not equipped to deal with it. It took many hard lessons to get to the point we are at today." Falric sighed and his facial expression was bleak. Alrion didn't have any follow-up questions, he just pondered what had been said. It was an explanation, but he didn't feel like he truly understood.

"That look on your face, I have seen it before from others when hearing about the Blight. Trust me, once you encounter it, you will understand." Falric turned his gaze toward Vincent.

"I would normally say I hope you don't encounter it, but it seems like you will have no choice," Vincent said.

"So, you've dealt with it?" Alrion was curious. His father never spoke of his life before Hamley. And if he had experience about the Blight, it had to have been earlier.

"Yes, quite a bit. I travelled a lot before I met your mother and we settled here. Avaria is a precious gift. Unfortunately, when you venture forth to other countries, you will see something a lot grimmer. It is the state of the world right now, and hopefully one day we can end the Blight for good," Vincent said.

"It was your grandfather's wish to end the Blight. I don't believe that his cleansing of Avaria was the final piece in his plan, just the beginning. However, the fact that he already achieved so much means that it is possible for us. We just need to find the right way." Falric had a hopeful look again.

"That makes sense. If it's so bad, and it's a more recent thing, then maybe it's not as hard as you think?" Alrion said. Falric and Vincent laughed.

"Maybe not, we'll see," Falric said.

Alrion however, had another question.

"What happens when we get to the academy?" he said.

"You and your father will be welcomed, then there are some formalities to go through before you can start your training," Falric said.

"What kind of formalities?" Alrion had already had the surprise test. He wondered what else was in store for him.

"There is an induction ceremony. You will be introduced as a new student to the rest of your peers at the academy. Then you will take part in the ceremony and receive a gift given to all the wizards."

"But what does that actually mean?"

"It means that there are a few secrets that are yet to be revealed," Falric said, a crafty smile on his face.

"Get used to this." Vincent pointed at Falric.

"Mystery and secrecy are important tools in a wizard's kit," Falric said.

"Can't you at least give him a little more detail?" Vincent said.

"Honestly, there is some value in it being a surprise. I have sat through countless induction ceremonies, and still find them interesting and moving. So, I'm very hesitant to say more."

"Has there always been an induction?" Alrion said.

"Yes, there has. When your grandfather established the academy, he was adamant that all initiates must take part in the ceremony. He designed it himself. It's a unifying moment that gives all wizards a shared history, and a greater connection to each other."

"Sorry son, but I think that's all you are going to get," Vincent said.

"It just sounds like that is the way it is."

"Well put. Should we get going then?" Falric said.

"Sure, let's pack up." Vincent stood and started packing their bags. They each carefully guided the horses out of the clearing and onto the main path once more.

Alrion looked around the forest as they progressed, and noticed there didn't seem to be a lot of wildlife.

"Is there something wrong with this forest?" he said.

"Why do you ask?" Falric said.

"I don't see any animals."

"That's a good observation. Mostly smaller animals live here, and they are nocturnal. It is very quiet during the day."

"Is there a reason for that?"

"I'm not entirely sure; I've never looked into it. The academy has always been nearby, but I didn't think that this forest had any significance," Falric said.

"I guess it's just different to what I'm used to." Alrion kept looking around in vain. The lack of animals was really obvious once he had spotted it.

"You have good instincts, Son, there's definitely something different about this forest. There must be a history," Vincent said.

"Tell you what; I'll have someone look into it later. Even if for educational purposes, it would be worthwhile understanding more of the history surrounding this place," Falric said. They continued in silence, as if in keeping with the wishes of the forest. Falric looked like he was about to announce something but stopped. Alrion soon found out why.

The trees began to thin, and the path snaked around a bend. As they followed it, Falric slowed down and let Alrion and Vincent ride ahead.

"Wow," Alrion said as he caught the first few glimpses of their destination. At the edge of the forest stood a massive structure, a cross between a manor house and a castle. Its walls were made of stone, with large windows wrapping around the building. Rising behind the main building was a tall tower also made of stone.

"Welcome to your new home," Falric said, gesturing at the academy with a sweeping arm movement.

8

A WIZARD'S WELCOME

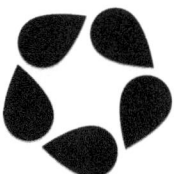

Alrion took it all in as they rode closer. The sun was setting behind the academy, an orange and pink glow illuminating it. He was impressed; he had never seen anything like it.

"How many wizards live here?"

"It varies; we have had up to one hundred. Around fifty are here at the moment," Falric said.

"Why so few?"

"Various reasons. Some move away for long periods, some leave the academy never to return. Some are lost." Falric's voice dropped a little and he looked away.

"I see."

"But they are a good group. You will meet them all tomorrow." Falric's tone changed back to normal.

"What's the plan?" Vincent said.

"We shall get you settled inside tonight, and tomorrow the ceremony will be performed. You can stay as long as you like, and return home when you are ready."

"Sure. I think I'll stay for a few days to make sure Alrion is comfortable."

"Of course. We always have room for Granthion's family," Falric said. As they neared the front gate, a robed man was waiting for them. He seemed a bit shorter with a stocky frame. The hood of the robe was pushed back so you could easily see his thick black hair.

"Hello, Falric, welcome home," the man said. He opened his hands in a welcoming gesture.

"Hello, Branthor, thank you. It is good to be home." Falric dismounted and Alrion and Vincent followed his lead.

"Were you successful? I see you have guests." Branthor studied them closely, and Alrion felt uncomfortable.

"Yes, I was. This is Vincent, and his son Alrion. Alrion will be inducted tomorrow morning."

"Alrion. A good name. Nice to meet you, I am Branthor, and I am Falric's right-hand wizard. I knew your grandfather, and I am honoured to make your acquaintance." Branthor bowed then offered his hand.

"Thank you, nice to meet you too." Alrion shook Branthor's hand and was surprised at how firm the grip was.

"I didn't know Granthion had any surviving family until recently. Vincent, was it?"

"Yes. I kept out of my father's business and also out of his shadow."

"Yes, quite a big shadow, and a big legacy. We have high hopes for Alrion." Branthor gave Vincent a hard stare.

"So do I." Vincent returned the stare.

"Let's all get inside before it turns dark," Falric said. Branthor walked ahead, and the rest followed, leading their horses on foot. As they neared the main building, two young men ran out to attend to them.

"Please take your bags, and leave the horses. We will bring them through to the stables," the shorter of the two men said.

"Are you wizards too?" Alrion said.

"No, we are apprentices." The man sounded proud. Alrion was surprised.

"And they have you doing errands?"

"Everyone must pitch in here. It's a part of the training," the taller of the two apprentices said. They offered no further explanation and quickly took off with the horses.

Looks like becoming a wizard won't get me out of errands, Alrion thought. He was a bit disappointed, but realised that was silly. He had to change his expectations. Of course there would be hard work becoming a wizard too.

"This way." Branthor pointed ahead and led them inside. They found themselves in a reception area. An open door to their right revealed a giant hall. Along each wall were wooden benches with a lectern at the end of the hall.

"That is where the wizards meet to discuss the matters of the world," Branthor explained. Alrion peered into the room but said nothing. Branthor continued walking and they all followed. They ended up in a hallway, with doors on either side.

"These doors lead to the rooms, we will take you to yours." Branthor opened one of the doors on the left and stepped inside. Another corridor was within, with many doors visible. Branthor opened the first door and stood to the side. Falric stood next to Branthor and waved Alrion in. Vincent and Alrion walked over and looked inside. The room was incredibly plain, with two single beds, a chest of drawers, and bedside tables.

"Is this for us?" Vincent said.

"Yes, we live simply here. Branthor will arrange for some dinner for you both. Have a restful night and we will see you tomorrow," Falric said.

"Goodnight, and thanks," Alrion said. Falric left and after he had disappeared into the main hallway, Branthor spoke.

"As Falric mentioned I'll arrange for dinner to be brought here. Unfortunately, you cannot dine with the other wizards until you have been inducted."

"No problem." Alrion liked the idea of not meeting everyone just yet.

"If you need anything, go down to the room at the end of this corridor. There will be someone there who can help. Goodnight," Branthor said.

"Goodnight." Alrion watched the wizard leave. Vincent stepped inside the room and looked around. Alrion took one look at the hallway and stepped in also.

"At least we're not eating on our laps." Vincent pointed to a tiny table with two chairs in the corner behind the door.

"Yes, I guess so. This is it then?" Alrion said.

"This is it. How do you feel?"

"I'm not sure. Nervous."

"It'll go well, and don't forget I'm here too." Vincent threw his bag down on the far bed. Alrion moved to close the door but stopped. He saw a face just outside the half-closed door.

"Hello, could you open the door for me?" a voice said. Alrion opened the door and saw a bald young man outside balancing a tray of food in each hand. Alrion stepped out of the way and the man put the trays down on the little table, visibly relaxing after he was done.

"Are you an apprentice?" Alrion said, looking at the young man. He had a simple robe, but no adornments on it.

"Yes."

"How long have you been here?"

"A few years. My name is Eric."

"Nice to meet you, Eric. I'm Alrion, and that's my dad Vincent."

"Nice to meet you both. Are you here to study?" Eric looked at Alrion.

"Yes, my induction ceremony is tomorrow." Alrion noticed that Eric's eyes widened at the news.

"That's exciting. Well, I'll see you tomorrow then."

"Can you tell me about it?"

"No, we're not allowed to say anything. It's not bad, though, so don't worry. Goodnight." Eric left immediately.

"Isn't he a bit young to have no hair?" Alrion said.

"Maybe he cut it himself," Vincent said.

"Maybe he had a magical accident."

"Ha-ha you could be right," Vincent said, sitting down in front of one of the trays, eyeing off the food. It was a thin chicken soup and a piece of brown bread.

"It's simple but it's food," he said. He waited for Alrion to sit down, then started eating.

"Do you really think I should be doing this?" Alrion was looking at his food but not eating.

"It's your choice. You haven't really taken to blacksmithing, so maybe this is why." Vincent took a big bite out of a piece of bread.

"But you don't seem to like wizards at all. I can see that." Alrion watched his father put his food down and look him in the eye.

"I'm a little cautious with them, I agree. Hopefully, your experience will be more positive."

"What do you mean? Wasn't your dad a wizard?"

"Yes, he was, and he pulled off a lot of amazing feats, but we didn't see eye to eye on many things. And he put his duties as a wizard ahead of everything else. He wanted that life for me too, but it didn't fit. So, that caused some friction between us." A look of sadness passed over Vincent's face, but it was gone in a flash.

"But he's just one person."

"Yes, but this whole system was set up by him. I admit that I'm a bit sceptical, but I am working on having an open mind." Vincent helped himself to another spoonful of food. Alrion wasn't finished with the conversation though.

"It's our legacy, we should take it seriously. I still can't believe you never told me."

"It was for your own good."

"Would you have brought me here?" Alrion blurted out. But as soon as he said it he wanted to know the answer. His father sighed and put down his spoon.

"Maybe, maybe not. Although I was curious to see if you would show any signs of magic. Falric came and put that mystery to rest."

"I see," Alrion said. He wasn't convinced that his father would have brought him unless there was some sort of incident that required it. His father seemed to be wrestling with something, and spoke up again.

"You know, I should be clearer. I absolutely would have brought you here had you shown any signs. In fact, I think eventually I would have brought you anyway just to make sure you weren't supposed to be a wizard. Because I owe it to my father. He sacrificed so much, for me and for the rest of the people of Avaria. As much as I spent my life avoiding wizards, I can't ignore what he did." Vincent paused, watching Alrion's reaction. Alrion tried to speak but his father started again.

"I just want you to think of it this way. There's magic in our family. But, you always have a choice. You can decide that you don't want this, and we can leave and that is the end of it. There's no danger for you if you choose not to pursue being a wizard. As much as you may not believe it, I'm not advocating a choice either way. It is important to me that you understand that it's not a requirement thrust upon you. The choice is, and always will be, yours."

"Thanks for being open about this. But, I know that I need to continue. I can't make any other choice until I know more. It does feel right, though," Alrion said.

"I'm glad you feel that way. Always trust your instincts. I never felt like I was allowed a choice. It was a large part of our falling out." Vincent paused. It looked like he was going to talk again, but he just stared into his meal. Alrion started eating finally and Vincent dove back in. They finished their food and pushed the plates to the far corner of the table.

"I think it's time to turn in," Vincent said.

"Sure."

"Goodnight, Son." Vincent walked over and gave Alrion a big hug. He couldn't remember the last time his father had just done that out of the blue. Vincent then dropped unceremoniously into his bed.

"Goodnight, Dad," Alrion said. He kicked off his boots and settled into the small wooden bed. The mattress wasn't as uncomfortable as it looked, but he had trouble sleeping.

He kept playing the events of the last few days over in his mind and imagining what would happen at the ceremony. He drifted in and out of a light sleep, but didn't feel like he was even sleeping. He just couldn't switch his mind off. He tried to reason with himself, explaining that he needed the rest and it was a big day coming up, but it was hopeless.

Eventually, he did feel sleep taking effect, and felt relaxed that finally he would enjoy a proper rest. He started to dream, and in his dream, the door was knocked three times. He ignored it. The door was knocked three more times, then finally it opened. A shape appeared in the doorway and spoke.

"It is time," the voice said. Something about the voice seemed real, so Alrion struggled to open his eyes. The door to their room was open, and there was a person standing there. As his eyes opened more, he peered closer and recognised the person. It was Eric.

"Eric? What time is it?"

"It is time," Eric said, in the same monotone manner. Alrion sat up in the bed and turned to look over at his father. Vincent was sitting quietly in the bed, watching but not speaking. He nodded at Alrion. Trying to shake the cobwebs from his mind, Alrion stood and stepped towards Eric.

"In that case, let's not keep them waiting," Alrion said, sounding much more confident than he felt. Eric turned and started to walk away and Alrion followed close behind. He heard his father close the door behind them but didn't look back.

9

THE WHITE FLAME

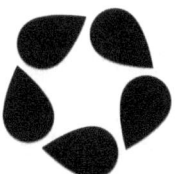

They didn't walk far, and at the end of the corridor, they stepped through a door that led to another, narrower corridor.

This place is like a maze.

He emerged into a simple room, with a table, two meals, and two chairs. Eric pointed at the table.

"The ceremony draws on your strength. Savour your last meal as a normal man." Eric left the room and closed the door behind him.

"That sounded very formal," Alrion said.

"It must be part of the ceremony," Vincent said.

"Well I am hungry, and I don't know what to expect. We should eat." Alrion sat down and started eating. The food was simple and consisted of bread, cheese, and milk.

"It looks like it is a formal ritual. That's a good thing. Just follow their instructions and you will do fine," Vincent said.

"That sounds almost positive. Not trying to talk me out of it?"

"I never was, just because I have some history doesn't mean you should be held back. Try to enjoy it," Vincent said. He even cracked a smile.

"You must have slept much better than I did." Alrion returned the smile. He appreciated his father's support, even though he still didn't fully understand why his father was so touchy about wizards.

"I did, it's a skill you learn as you age," Vincent said. Before he could say more, there was a knock at the door. Alrion opened the door and saw Eric standing there once more.

"You must be clad in the garments of your calling. Take this and wear it proudly." Eric said, handing over a bundle of white cloth. Alrion accepted it and opened it up with care. He was holding a snow-white hooded robe, trimmed in navy blue around the hood. Alrion put the robe on over his clothes and drew the hood down. He looked at Eric for confirmation.

"Come now, your brothers await," Eric said. Alrion nodded and stepped out of the room. Vincent followed closely behind. They retraced their steps through the narrow corridors until they reached the main connecting room. This time they continued, finally reaching a pair of double doors. Alrion could see light coming from behind them. Eric pushed open the doors and stepped through. Alrion and Vincent followed.

They stood outside, the sun rising in the distance. Surrounding them was a paved square courtyard, with robed figures spread around the perimeter. In the middle of the square, two figures stood in front of a tall tower.

"The applicant must step towards his destiny." Eric pointed to the middle of the courtyard. Alrion stepped forward and Vincent began to follow. Eric and another wizard stepped in front of Vincent. Alrion stopped suddenly and turned to see what had happened.

"Only the applicant can enter, observers must stay back," Eric said. Vincent nodded and retreated, watching with interest. Alrion watched his father step back, and then looked around at the wizards; they all had their head and hoods down.

Alrion continued to the middle of the courtyard. He saw Falric and Branthor standing there. They were both wearing white robes but had different coloured bands around the hood. Alrion pressed on, hoping that a slow and steady walk would calm his nerves. Even though it seemed like the wizards were not watching, he felt countless eyes following his progress. As he arrived, he saw Falric raise his head and address him.

"State your name, wizard-to-be."

"Alrion."

"Do you swear to combat the forces of darkness and bring light and illumination to the world?"

"I swear."

"We symbolise this struggle, between light and darkness by bestowing each wizard a crystal of their own. A pure white crystal that contains a vein of darkness. Select yours." Falric held up a spherical translucent bowl, full of crystal shards.

Each was about the size of his thumb. Alrion picked one up to get a better look at it. It was roughly a diamond shape and had a black streak through the middle. He turned the crystal around, trying to see how it had gotten there. He looked over to see if he should select another, but the bowl was gone.

"You have selected your crystal. Keep it with you always."

"I will."

"Now, you must activate your crystal. Show your peers the spark of magic within you," Falric said. Alrion didn't know what to do. He looked at Falric, then at Branthor. Neither gave him any direction, they just waited. Alrion looked again at the crystal. It had to be similar to how they had tested him with the lamp. If he could activate that, surely he could do this. If only he could remember how he did it.

Alrion turned the crystal over in his hands, studying it. However, he knew that looking at it would do nothing, he would need to exert some sort of force upon it. He closed his hands around it, feeling the texture of the crystal; holding the crystal within his hands. It seemed so small that way. He closed his eyes and concentrated. He felt the heartbeat within his hands. Only it was not. It was different.

Alrion isolated the feeling. It was as if the crystal itself was beating, to a different rhythm than his heartbeat. He visualised the crystal, trying to understand how it could beat. It was a hard surface, it didn't make sense. Then he had a sudden realisation. It was the black streak within the crystal, not the crystal. That streak was beating, as much as it seemed impossible. He could sense the life force within the crystal, the other alien thing inside. It could only be one thing, the Blight.

An irrational fear took over Alrion. How could he be holding something with the Blight within it? He had to protect himself, but he couldn't let go of the crystal. Something else was happening. It was reacting to him. He had to get away; he had to stop it somehow. Then he felt a surge within him, a cool heat that burned hotter and hotter until he could feel the fire on his face. He could sense a bright light, even with his eyes closed.

Confused, he opened his eyes to see what was going on. A white flame engulfed his hands, burning, yet not burning. He opened his hands to see the crystal. It was burning white, the black streak within dancing in time with the licking flames.

Burn away.

The flames contracted within the crystal, then shot out from the top, a thin pillar of white light that arced up to the sky, then vanished.

Alrion looked back at the crystal in disbelief. It looked the same as before, the black streak within it appeared undisturbed.

Was that a dream? What happened, he thought. He looked to Falric for reassurance. Falric had a strange look on his face, and so did Branthor.

"The crystal." Falric extended his hand. Alrion gave it to him. Falric removed an amulet and silver chain from his robes and enclosed the crystal within. He handed the amulet back to Alrion.

"Wear it with pride."

"I will."

"The ceremony is concluded. You are welcomed here, Wizard Alrion," Falric said, his voice projected so it echoed around the court-yard. The pronouncement shook everyone out of their stunned silence, and cheers rose out around the courtyard.

"Come with us," Falric said, and headed towards the tower. Alrion followed closely behind. He needed to find out what had just happened.

My father.

Alrion turned to see what had happened to his father. At first, he could not spot him, but then as the crowds started to disperse, Vincent pushed his way through, running towards Alrion.

I bet he didn't expect that, Alrion thought.

10

DESTINY

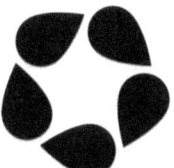

F alric and Branthor walked ahead, and Alrion rushed forward until he was right on their heels. They entered the tower together and started to ascend the stairs.

Something doesn't feel right. That can't have been normal, Alrion thought. However, he had no point of reference. As they walked, he heard hurried steps behind. He looked back and saw his father rushing up the stairs.

"Quite a spectacle, I'd like to be part of this next discussion," Vincent said.

"That is quite alright, and expected," Falric said from ahead. Alrion waited for his father to join him, then resumed walking.

"You did great, let's find out what that was all about," Vincent whispered. Alrion nodded and kept walking. Within a few minutes, they emerged into a large circular room.

The centre of the room held only a desk and a few chairs; however, the perimeter was full of artifacts of different kinds. Falric said down behind the desk and Branthor retrieved a few chairs from around the room and placed them around the desk.

"Please sit." Falric gestured at the chairs.

"What just happened?" Vincent said.

"The ceremony. However, it was a variation not seen before." Falric let his gaze rest on Alrion.

"What do you mean?" Alrion said.

"The ceremony is a rite of passage for our wizards. It is a way of binding them together and reminding them of their shared purpose to combat evil and in particular the Blight. However, as it was designed by your grandfather, it also serves a second purpose."

"A second purpose?" Alrion looked at his father. Vincent shrugged.

"Yes. It is also a test. A test to see whether the wizard can overcome the Blight, transform it if you will. To date, only Granthion has been able to do so. In fact, when he established the wizard school, he didn't tell anyone about the secondary purpose of the ceremony. Since nobody activated it, he didn't have to. But he wrote me a letter explaining what needed to be done and how to recognise the person who passed the test."

"Did he hand you the letter himself?" Vincent said.

"The note was waiting for me after he had left to perform the cleansing spell, so I didn't know about this aspect of the ceremony until afterward. In it, he explained his actions. But it was only one of two notes. Did you read the one addressed to you?" Falric said, looking at Vincent. Alrion looked over in surprise.

"Yes, I did." Vincent was intently focused on Falric.

"I wasn't able to read it, so I don't know what it said. Was any of this explained?"

"No."

"Perhaps yours was of a more personal nature. In my letter, he explained his actions and his plan for the future. The plan to end the Blight."

"What has that got to do with the ceremony? How was it a test?" Alrion said.

"The crystals used in the ceremony were all created by Granthion. They were by-products of his research into containing the Blight. That black streak within is the Blight." Falric pointed to the amulet that Alrion was now wearing. Alrion glanced down at it again.

"How is the test supposed to work?" he said.

"The normal result is a black flame. It is a reaction between the Blight, the crystal, and the spark of the wizard. It is a symbol to remember that wizards must ever be vigilant for the Blight, and the darkness within. The black flame is something that is remembered vividly by every wizard," Falric said.

"What does the white flame mean?"

"It means that your spark can convert and cleanse the Blight. We have not yet seen a person achieve that feat since Granthion," Falric said. Alrion pulled out the amulet and studied the crystal.

"The black streak is still there." Alrion was surprised at the obvious disappointment in his voice.

"Correct, but that is because you didn't cleanse the crystal of the Blight. You created a reaction where your spark altered the flame from black to white. This is very significant."

"So, I'm special?"

"Yes, you are special and you, therefore, have a special mission. To end the Blight for good," Falric said. Alrion didn't respond immediately, letting the thought sink in.

"It's up to me to end the Blight?"

"Yes, and only you can do so."

"You're sure that nobody else can do it?" Alrion couldn't understand. He was untrained, he was not who they were looking for.

"Nobody that we've identified. Perhaps there is another, but in all the years I have been head of the academy, we have not seen one. You are our best, and so far, only hope."

"How do you even know that? Are there instructions?" Alrion said. Falric laughed.

"That's a good question. Actually, the instructions and information we have are minimal. Granthion explained briefly the spell that he was about to undertake, and that it wasn't the ideal solution. And that the answers to fixing it would be available elsewhere."

"What was wrong with his solution? If it wasn't perfect, why did he do it?" Alrion's mind was racing away. This was all too much.

"I can answer part of that. The rest would come from your father."

Falric pointed at Vincent. Vincent recoiled like Falric had fired something at him.

"Dad, what's your part in this?" Alrion knew something was going on. Maybe he would finally find out what had happened between his father and grandfather.

"The day that your grandfather performed the ritual, I was captured. Held by a group of people infected by the Blight, who wanted to infect me too. I'm not sure exactly what their plan was, but I guess I was targeted because I was Granthion's son. They could get to him through me." Vincent looked away, shame on his face.

"The ritual performed by Granthion, whilst imperfect, was an incredible feat. He connected to every single Blight infected soul within the country of Avaria, drew the Blight into himself, then destroyed the Blight within him. It saved the lives of many, and prevented harm for many more," Falric said.

"And he did it to save you?" Alrion said to Vincent. He was struggling to believe what he had just heard.

"Yes. He succeeded, and I escaped unharmed."

"No. That can't be." Alrion started to understand. His father felt responsible for Granthion's death. For robbing the world of their greatest wizard.

"It's a fact not known by the general population," Falric said.

"I had no idea that Granthion was capable of that, and had plans for a better spell," Branthor said, speaking up for the first time.

"I was also in the dark until Granthion's disappearance. He did like to keep his secrets," Falric said.

"But keeping this knowledge hidden for all this time?" Branthor said. Alrion was surprised by the harshness in Branthor's tone.

"It was Granthion's wishes. He wanted his vision to be kept a secret until the right person was unveiled."

"If that spell was so effective, why can't it be used again? What's wrong with it?" Alrion said.

"I don't have an exact answer for that. My guess is that the amount of power required to target the entire world with such a spell is impossible. There would have to be another way. But for whatever reason, Granthion didn't know the way, or could not document what he had discovered," Falric said.

"What am I supposed to do, then?" Alrion couldn't see the way forward. It was all just a mess. It was one thing to throw this responsibility onto him. It was another to do so without any form of guidance or support. He shook his head.

"He did leave us with something to follow up. The Pool of Knowledge."

"The Pool of Knowledge?" Alrion's curiosity was roused.

"It is a sacred place hidden within Avaria. It is said that all knowledge is preserved there. The answers you need to complete your quest must be there."

"I'm the only one who can cleanse the Blight, but we don't know how. If I go to this Pool of Knowledge, then I'll know what to do next?"

"That's right. It may seem like an odd request, but I believe it to be the best course of action. Armed with the knowledge of what the spell requires, we can better plan our next steps."

"What warrants all this secrecy?"

"We have to trust in Granthion's approach. He must have had a good reason for having this requirement." Falric kept a calm and confident tone. It helped reassure Alrion a little.

"Have you been there?"

"No. It is a sacred place that few know of, and even fewer are allowed access. However, I do know its location."

"I'm a bit overwhelmed, to be honest. So much has just happened. First, I'm a wizard, and now I'm some special wizard who can end the Blight? It's a lot to take in." Alrion could have said much more, but held his tongue.

"Don't worry Son, we'll do this together," Vincent said. Alrion looked over at his father with surprise.

"You'll go with me?"

"Of course. You have lived a sheltered life, because of me. But I have travelled the world. I can help guide you through the dangers out there, and keep you safe."

"I will go also," Falric said. This time Branthor looked over at Falric with surprise.

"But Falric, you are needed here," he said.

"You are perfectly capable of looking after the academy. What Alrion needs is teaching in the ways of being a wizard if he is to succeed."

"Which is why he should stay here. Train with his peers then set out when he is more capable," Branthor said.

"This is an incredible opportunity; we can't just sit on it. We don't even know what is required. What if we wait around for years before setting off, and discover that we could have been preparing all along? No, this is too important. We must set out at once," Falric said.

"If that is so, I can accompany them. Your place is here at the academy!" Branthor raised his voice. But the look on Falric's face caused him to lose some of his boldness.

"My place has been here my entire life, to serve the cause of my teacher. Now there is an opportunity to continue his work, and you want me to stay here idle? No. I have earned this right and I will exercise it." Falric looked like he was daring Branthor to challenge him.

"By your command." Branthor turned to look away.

"It will be one of my last. I will arrange a proclamation today that you are the new leader of the academy."

"Won't that just be a temporary arrangement? Why go to all the trouble?"

"Let's just see. Maybe you'll do such a great job, I'll come back as a trusted advisor."

"Of course, I would be honoured," Branthor said. Alrion thought Branthor would be more pleased with such an honour.

"I knew you would be." Falric turned to address Vincent and Alrion once more.

"Take some time to wander around and think everything through. I'll send someone to find you and we can finalise our preparations."

"Sure." Alrion felt like he was in a daze.

"Thanks. Let's go." Vincent led Alrion over to the stairs. They slowly descended, not uttering a single word. As they emerged outside there were still some wizards in the courtyard. They stared at Alrion as he emerged.

"Awkward," Alrion said as he walked.

"They don't understand, this has never happened before. But don't worry about them; it looks like we won't be staying here."

"Why me?" Alrion looked to his father.

"That's the eternal question," Vincent said with a laugh. Alrion wasn't amused.

"You can't be flippant about this. Seriously, why?"

"It's fate, or destiny, or just bad luck. Alternatively, good luck. Depends on how you look at it." Vincent looked like he was enjoying himself.

"How come you're so happy all of a sudden?"

"I'm not. But this is so much more than what I expected to happen. I wanted nothing more to do with wizards, and now you're their last hope to fulfil my father's work. At some point you just need to give up, and laugh about it. Either that or cry."

"I shouldn't have complained about being bored at home." Alrion sighed.

"That's the problem with wishes; sometimes you get what you wished for."

"I still don't get it. How can you be so cheery and upbeat? This is crazy!"

"This is an opportunity. One that nobody else has. You owe it to yourself to go after it. We don't know what is involved. Maybe you'll get to the Pool of Knowledge and find out you just need to read books for a few years. We just don't know. But I bet if you look inside, and really think about it, you'll realise that, underneath this annoyance and complaining, you're excited by the possibilities." Vincent gave Alrion a knowing look. Alrion thought about what his father said and let out a deep sigh.

"You're right. Of course, you're right. But I need time," he said.

"There will be plenty of that. But you need to take that first step."

"It feels like the first step is taking me," Alrion said. He snuck a tiny smile onto his face, which Vincent picked up on.

"That's the spirit. Own the unknown. Maybe when you return here you'll get a different look from these guys."

"I hope so. I just feel like even more of an outsider."

"Your grandfather started this place. You couldn't be any less of an outsider."

"Tell that to them. The whole feeling is noticeably different since the initiation."

"Don't worry about them. Let's just go for a walk," Vincent said. Alrion nodded and they set off.

They walked around the perimeter of the courtyard and watched the remaining wizards filter back indoors.

"You've already seen the tower, let's check out indoors," Vincent said.

"Have you been here before?" Alrion said.

"No, this place was established later. Your grandfather and I and the first founding wizards lived somewhere else. When we parted ways, he came here to found the academy, and I travelled."

"Will you ever talk about him? I mean properly."

"One day. However, all you need to know is that he was a great wizard, and did a lot for many people. You have a lot to live up to in that regard."

"Sure beats being a blacksmith." Alrion pushed ahead.

After wandering through the main building, they found themselves back at the entry.

"Let's take a seat," Vincent said and settled down on a leather couch. Alrion sat down next to him.

"So, what now?" he said.

"I think they'll come and find us before long," Vincent said. As if on cue, a wizard walked in and addressed them both.

"Please come with me, your equipment needs to be provisioned," the wizard said.

"Now this should be fun." Vincent winked at Alrion.

11

ADVENTURE

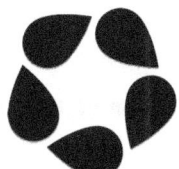

Vincent and Alrion followed the young wizard out of the main building, across the courtyard and into a smaller building that they had not spotted before. It was made of stone with a heavy steel door.

"This is our store." The wizard placed his hand on the door and unlocked it. He pulled the door open and walked inside. After he stepped in, he held his hand up and lit a lamp. As the light danced around the room, Alrion started to see what it contained.

There were shelves all around the walls, containing objects of different types and sizes. There were racks of equipment in the middle of the room. Alrion spotted robes, bags, staves, shoes, and other clothing.

"You are well stocked here," Vincent said.

"Of course, a wizard must be prepared," their guide said. He walked down the aisles, collecting things in a bundle before returning to present them to Alrion.

"Here are your things. Treat them well, and they will serve you for a long time," he said.

"Do I get anything?" Vincent said.

"You will both be given ample provisions from the kitchen store," the wizard said.

"That's a no, Dad," Alrion said.

"There is one more thing, follow me, young wizard." The guide beckoned to Alrion. Alrion handed his bundle to his father and followed the wizard. They walked to the end of the room, where there was a small doorway otherwise not visible.

"Go through and select one item. Do not show anyone," he said. Alrion turned to ask a question, but the man had left. He shrugged and decided to walk through the door.

The room was pitch black, and he couldn't see a thing. He felt around with his hand, wondering what was there. It seemed to be a collection of objects on shelves, but he couldn't tell what they were. They all had a cold, metallic feeling to them. As he brushed his hand across them, he felt a sudden surge of warmth and jumped.

He returned his hand to confirm it. One of the objects was warm to the touch, so he decided to grab it and stash it in his pocket. Then he left the room. He saw his father standing near the entrance, and no sign of the wizard except the light he had left anchored to the wall.

"All done?" Vincent said.

"I think so," Alrion said. Vincent handed back the bundle of clothing.

"Good, let's head back to the main building and get some food." Vincent stepped outside.

"Aren't you going to ask me what I found back there?"

"Not my business."

"Fair enough." Alrion was a bit surprised, but they did say not to show anyone.

"Looks like you have a full outfit there." Vincent gestured at the bundle of clothes Alrion was holding as they crossed the courtyard.

"I hope they fit," Alrion said. Vincent laughed.

"You have a lot to learn about magic, my boy."

"Now that you put it that way, it seems like they really should fit."

"You would hope so. After you." Vincent held the door open for Alrion. They walked through the hallway of the main building and returned to the room they had stayed in overnight. Alrion had a better look at the things he had been given.

"This looks like a robe." He put it on and was surprised at how comfortable it was.

"Definitely. And feel the material too. It's quite hardy, for travelling."

"Shoes, a walking stick. Why a walking stick?"

"They can be quite useful especially on uneven terrain, but I bet there's another reason for having it. Ask Falric about it," Vincent said.

"This bag looks useful; I can hang it over my shoulder. These things are all geared for walking I think."

"There are many places a horse cannot go, so that seems like a good idea. Let me know when you're ready and we can finalise our preparations." Vincent lay back on his bed and closed his eyes.

"I think I'm done," Alrion said, as he finished buckling his new shoes on. They were surprisingly comfortable, given how sturdy they looked. He looked at himself in the mirror. Despite the plain nature of everything he was wearing, he felt like a wizard.

"You look the part." Vincent stood and nodded with approval.

"They don't seem particularly fashionable, but are comfortable," Alrion said.

"Comfort is the much better of the two possibilities. Wear them in good health."

"Thanks. I guess we go see about provisions then," Alrion said. Vincent opened the door and they walked through the hallway in an attempt to locate the kitchen. They followed the sound and smells of food, and found themselves in front of a petite young woman with a rolling pin across her folded arms.

"Hello, we were just looking for the kitchen," Vincent said.

"You the travellers? This way," the woman said in a gruff voice. Vincent and Alrion looked at each other in surprise at the tone of her voice, then followed her through a door into a storeroom.

"You looked like you were guarding something," Vincent said.

"I was. You have no idea how many wizards get it in their heads to go steal some food from the kitchen. It's like some sort of ritual or initiation or something, and they don't even eat the food. It ends up being buried or exploded or something else," the woman said.

"Boys will be boys," Vincent said.

"Some of these boys are old enough to be grandparents," the woman said.

"Not surprised at all. I'm Vincent, and this is Alrion. Nice to meet you."

"Pamela. Nice to meet you too." Pamela kept on rummaging around. She started collecting food, her long red hair swishing around as she moved.

"Since you are going on a trip, I'll give you some of this flatbread. It lasts a while and is sufficient by itself at a pinch. Here, try some." Pamela handed them both a sample.

"Wow, that's delicious," Vincent said.

"I could eat that for days," Alrion said.

"Be careful what you wish for." Pamela laughed, the movement rippling through her chest.

"Sounds like you have a story about that," Vincent said.

"Yeah, it's a good one. I'll tell you when you come back. Maybe you'll have a story of your own." Pamela continued collecting other food and handed them each a sack full to the brim.

"There's a week's worth there. All I was instructed to provide. Either it's a short trip or you will have opportunities to restock yourself. But make it last," she said.

"We'll be careful," Vincent said.

"Travel safe, I'm going back to my guard post."

"Aren't you a cook?" Alrion said.

"First and foremost, but you need ingredients to cook with, so back I go," Pamela said.

"Good luck." Vincent waved goodbye. Pamela waved her rolling pin at them and marched off like she was on a mission.

"I like her," Alrion said.

"Yeah, she seems like a good sort. But regardless, always be nice to the help. The cooks, the stable boy, the assistants. Not only is it the right thing to do, you'll find yourself having allies in useful places."

"That sounds like good advice. I'll do it." Alrion guessed there were some interesting stories behind the advice, but didn't ask. Vincent looked around a bit more.

"I think you'll like it here," he said.

"If I ever make it back." Alrion hadn't even had time to unpack, and he was off again.

"Don't worry about that, you'll be back. It's just a matter of when."

"You're probably right. What do we do now?" Alrion said.

"We have equipment and food, and our horses are in the stables. I just need to do one more thing before we go." Vincent left Alrion in the hallway and walked off with purpose. He returned a few minutes later with a piece of paper and a pen.

"I need to let your mother know that I won't be back so soon. But I won't include all the details, she may worry," Vincent said while writing.

"She would definitely worry. Any reasonable person would," Alrion said.

"Then let's not cause your mother any undue distress. There, that should do it." Vincent folded the letter in half.

"I think you're saving yourself distress." Alrion was half-joking. His father laughed.

"You know her too well. Let's go see what Falric is up to."

They walked back to the central hallway of the main building, and seeing nobody around continued to the back door. They emerged into the courtyard, surprised by what they saw.

Just as in the morning, the courtyard was full of wizards. Like earlier, they had arranged themselves around the perimeter of the courtyard. In the centre, they saw Falric and Branthor with their heads bowed. Vincent and Alrion found a spot amongst the wizards and waited to see what would happen.

"Today is an auspicious day. Our newest member, Alrion, has passed his initiation and revealed his true identity. He is a bringer of light, one that can turn back the darkness of the Blight," Falric said, his voice somehow amplified so that it rang through the courtyard.

He paused. There was a quiet murmur throughout the wizards, which quickly died down.

"I have been waiting for this day, since I took over from our founding father, Granthion. Now I have an opportunity to take on his legacy and complete the work that he began. I will be leaving you, and travelling with Alrion to train him and assist with his journey," Falric said. There was louder murmuring and discussion amongst the wizards, but within a minute, it quieted down once more.

"I don't know when I will return, but I know that I cannot provide the same support for this beloved academy as I have before. Therefore, I am passing on leadership to my dear and trusted friend, Branthor." Falric gestured to Branthor, who bowed.

"This must be a big moment. There's only been one other handover of leadership, and that was when your grandfather died," Vincent said to Alrion.

"As a symbol of the transition, I am handing over the Crystal Staff to Branthor. May you lead the academy to an era of even greater prosperity," Falric said. He knelt in front of Branthor and held up the staff. It was a dark brown wood, with a cloudy crystal ball set in the top. Branthor accepted the staff and held it aloft. A pulse of light radiated out from the staff, covering the entire courtyard for a second, before disappearing completely. A cheer rose up amongst the wizards.

"They're gone," Alrion said.

"Theatrics! Let's go up to the tower," Vincent said. Alrion nodded and they walked across the courtyard as the wizards dispersed.

"This is really happening then," Alrion said.

"It certainly is," Vincent said. As they reached the bottom of the tower, they saw Falric step out of the stairwell.

"How was that?" Falric said.

"Impressive," Alrion said. He looked over at his father who said nothing.

"You have to give these occasions the proper ceremony. Otherwise, their significance can be lost. Branthor is only the third person to lead the academy, which is a major event. If we can establish something now, then future generations can carry on and keep the cere-mony alive."

"I understand that this is a big ask of you, to walk away from your life's work. I appreciate your help," Alrion said.

"Thank you. But it's also a good excuse to let go. It's time for some new blood, and Branthor has shadowed me long enough. Let's get a move on before we get noticed." Falric started walking away and Vincent and Alrion followed closely behind.

They headed straight to the stables. A young wizard was waiting there with the horses. Vincent approached the young wizard first.

"Excuse me; I need to send this letter to my wife. I've addressed it appropriately. Can you see that it gets delivered?" Vincent offered the letter. The wizard looked over at Falric.

"It's fine, send a rider to hand deliver it," he said.

"As you wish, we will take care of it," the wizard said. Vincent mounted up, and Alrion and Falric followed. They secured their bags and rode out to the main gate.

"I shall return, with more stories and more knowledge," Falric said, looking back at the academy.

"Do you always say that?" Vincent said.

"Always. It has become a mantra of mine. Always bring some-thing back, to share with the wizards. Not that I leave the academy as much these days." Falric shook his head slightly.

"That's nice. I shall return, with more stories and knowledge," Alrion said.

"I'll see to it," Falric said. Vincent grunted and started to ride. Alrion looked back and thought about how he was leaving before he had even settled in.

"When will I have a new place to call home?" he wondered as he turned his horse and began to ride.

12

PASSAGE TO THE MOUNTAIN

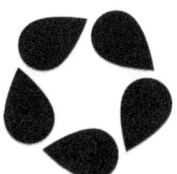

T hey started slowly, leaving the academy at a stately pace, but gradually increased their speed as they traversed the woods and reached bigger and bigger roads. Once they were back on the main road, Vincent nudged his horse closer to Falric.

"Where are we heading?" he said.

"To the Pool of Knowledge, of course," Falric said.

"I got that bit. But where is it?"

"I have been charged with keeping the location secret." Falric tilted his head down and looked at Vincent with a serious gaze.

"Can you at least tell me what area we are heading to?"

"A place near Mirror Lake."

"I see." Vincent paused and looked thoughtful, "So then, we will want to be heading to Altarbright?"

"Yes. But that's all you will get out of me."

"That's fine. In fact, I even know a shortcut."

"I'm all ears, although in my experience you never save time with a shortcut." Falric grinned at Alrion.

"It's certainly a concern. But this one is on the way, so it's low risk."

"What are you proposing?"

"We use the tunnel underneath the Thundering Mountain." Vincent carefully watched Falric's reaction.

Falric doesn't seem happy with that suggestion, Alrion thought.

"Hmm. I have heard of it, but a long time ago. Is it still in use?" Falric's voice had a doubtful tilt to it.

"I'm not sure, it's been a while. But it cuts days off the journey if it works."

"I will defer to your judgement in this case. As you said, it is on the way, so we can investigate and make a call." Falric still didn't look confident.

"Excellent," Vincent said. Alrion waited for a moment to ensure the conversation was concluded.

"Falric, I have something I wanted to ask. Why is it that all wizards are male?"

"Excellent question. One that I often wonder myself. The truth is we don't know exactly. But I can explain the main reason. Do you remember the pillars of magic that I mentioned before?"

"Yes. Knowledge, Will, and Spark." Alrion recounted them without hesitation.

"Excellent. Well, you no doubt remember, that which sets the wizard apart in the true mastery of magic is the Spark. However, women do not have it."

"Women don't have the Spark?"

"No. I don't understand the reasoning or detail behind it. But without the Spark, they cannot be wizards." Falric shrugged.

"But they can still use magic?"

"Of course, like any other, if they lean on the other pillars of Knowledge and Will they can do many things. But they cannot be a wizard."

"Seems odd."

"Certainly. There is still a lot we don't understand. I hope that answers your question."

"It does, well at face value." Alrion was beginning to realise that there were a lot of unanswered questions.

"Good. With a healthy curiosity, I expect you will do quite well as a wizard. It is only in more recent times with the establishment of the academy that we have built up a good body of knowledge about magic." Falric was lost in thought and shook his head. "In the past, the knowledge and practices were quite dispersed. There were fine wizards, but they kept many secrets to themselves, and only had one or two apprentices, who didn't even learn everything their masters knew. So much was lost." Falric sighed.

"Your grandfather had the foresight and desire to do better than that."

Alrion took in the information with interest. There was certainly a lot more that he needed to learn about magic. As they rode further along the road, they approached another wooded area.

"If I remember correctly, this forest is the best place to stop for the night, even though it is a little early," Vincent said.

"Correct. I believe the vegetation becomes quite sparse if we push on much further, and the area is very open and exposed. Stopping early suits me actually. I'd like to work on something with Alrion," Falric said.

"I'll keep my eyes out for a spot then." Vincent brought his horse to a slow clip, then stopped. To the side of the path nestled a small clearing, sheltered by a nearby hill.

Vincent busied himself getting the horses settled and comfortable, and setting up camp. Falric and Alrion walked deeper into the forest. Falric spotted a chunky log and sat down, asking Alrion to join him.

"This is as good a spot as any. Normally you would be learning a few books worth of theory and demonstration, but I think we need to start with something useful. Today we are going to work on your first spell," Falric said.

"Sounds great." Alrion ignored the uneasiness in his stomach and focused on the excitement.

"I like your enthusiasm. What we are starting with is by no means the simplest, but it has so many applications and is a good representation of the basics of magic."

"What is it? A fireball?"

"Not quite. I may be accelerating things somewhat, but I'm not looking to invite disaster! No, Alrion, we will be starting with a push spell."

"Push? Like pushing things around?" Alrion made a pushing motion with his hand.

"Exactly. This spell draws on all three pillars of magic. However, interestingly enough, it can be performed with only one given the right amount of training. Care to guess which?"

"Hmm, I'll say Spark."

"Interesting answer, but incorrect. It is actually Will."

"Will?"

"Yes, there are people who with the force of their Will alone can push objects around."

"Wouldn't they also need Knowledge?"

"No, although it is a useful component. There are accounts of people who moved things purely with the power of their Will and no knowledge that it was even possible." Falric smiled.

"That's crazy." Alrion shook his head slowly. There really was another world out there that he had no idea about.

"It sounds a bit crazy, doesn't it? However, the reality is that many things in our world are there to be manipulated in interesting ways, even if you don't realise it. Do you see why we harp on about knowledge so much?"

"Yes. The more you know about what's possible, the more you can do."

"Exactly. Part of the lesson here has already begun. I have told you that it is possible, and that you can do it without being a wizard, and without even knowing that it can be done. That is the most basic level of knowledge."

"Alright." Alrion nodded along. However, he was doubtful that he would be able to do this.

"There is a lot more that I can tell you, and we'll get to that, but let's move on. The main component to this is your Will. You need to focus the strength of your mind and resolve to overcome the laws of nature. You can compel an object to move. We won't get into the nitty-gritty details of how it actually moves."

"What are we using? What am I moving?"

"Let's start simple." Falric hunted around and placed a small stone on the edge of a nearby tree branch. It was a low hanging branch, around Alrion's head height while seated.

"You are going to push that stone off that branch. I've placed it within an easy gaze, so you can easily focus on it."

"Sure." Alrion started sizing up the task.

"What you will need to do in your mind is to will that stone to move just enough that it topples off the branch."

"I'm not sure that I know how to will things to move," Alrion said. Falric laughed.

"It takes practice. To start with, you need to think about it moving. But not the passive, intellectual type of thinking. A more direct thought. Like you are imposing your Will upon the rock."

"Should I try?"

"A little bit, just practice thinking about it," Falric said. Alrion turned back to face the stone and stared at it. He thought about the stone moving, and how he could push it. He visualised it falling. He continued the effort for a good thirty seconds.

"OK, that's a good start. Take a break," Falric said. Alrion sat back and visibly relaxed.

"Now that's just the mental part, which is absolutely necessary. The next component to help us out is to draw on your Spark."

"How do I do that?"

"This is a little more abstract. Your Spark is what you drew on when you lit the lamp and caused the light show at the academy. It is your source of power. To be philosophical, the Spark ignites your Will. If your Will is a wind of change, then your Spark ignites it into a rolling flame. It feeds on, and amplifies, whatever you apply it to." Falric waved his hands in a dramatic flourish.

"I see, so it's in a way a source of fuel."

"That's a good way of looking at it. Maybe your Will isn't targeted well or imposing enough to move that rock. But if you draw upon your Spark, you can compensate and send that rock away." Falric mimicked the stone flying off the tree branch. Alrion nodded.

"I get it. However, I just don't understand how you draw upon it. I didn't do anything those other two times."

"Each person is unique, and the exact trigger to draw upon their Spark is also different, but the mechanism is always the same. You must see the internal power that is within you, and draw it out. Open it up, or even let it loose, but you must be careful because without the right safeguards unforeseen things can occur." Falric gave Alrion a knowing look, and he picked up on it.

"Like burning the roof of my dad's workshop?"

"Exactly. So, let's give it a try again. Start as before with your thoughts, and once you feel like you are ready, see if you can draw upon your Spark to amplify the effect," Falric said. Alrion looked back at the stone and started up again.

He thought about the stone, and the force required to move it. He thought about how the stone was just teetering on the branch, and that it just needed a nudge to get it moving. He intensified his concentration and focused on the thought. He pushed everything else away. It was as if he was floating above the stone, leaning against it with all his might. It started to move, and rock back and forth in its position. As if it was under a force but resisting. Alrion kept up his focus but he needed something more, it wasn't moving.

He looked inside himself, and his focus dropped a little. He got annoyed that such a tiny stone on such a thin branch could be so solid. He felt the frustration that it wouldn't move. That his Will wasn't strong enough, and he felt a heat within him, a fire burning hotter and hotter. He opened the door to that place, and the fire leaped out and consumed him. The stone stopped rocking and flew at great speed into a nearby tree with a gigantic 'thunk' and the resulting disturbance echoed through the forest like a shockwave.

Alrion stood up swiftly, a stunned look on his face. He walked over and inspected the stone. It was embedded in the tree trunk; scorch marks around it showed the size of the impact.

"Take it," Falric said. Alrion removed the stone and held it in his hand. It was a little warm to the touch.

"I did that?" Alrion looked at the stone and then back at the branch.

"You sure did. You used your Spark, didn't you?" Falric had a knowing smile.

"Yes, I could feel it coming through, but it was wild and uncontrolled. I think my anger and frustration fuelled it."

"That's very honest of you, and perceptive. Yes, it is quite common for those kinds of feelings to draw upon your Spark. But as you grow, you will get better at harnessing it at will."

"That sounds better. It was so strange, though, like the stone was waiting for that extra push."

"I have a small confession to make." Falric had a guilty smile, and he beamed it at Alrion.

"What?"

"I was holding the stone there, so it didn't fall off by itself."

"What!"

"And I wanted to give you a reason to dig deeper."

"Unbelievable!" Alrion swore under his breath, "Why didn't you pick a bigger rock then?"

"Because I needed you to believe that it was an achievable task. The stone sure looked precarious the way it was balancing on that branch didn't it?" Falric chuckled with warmth and looked directly at Alrion. The young wizard went quiet, thinking it over.

"I see why you did that. Pretty clever." Alrion sighed. He had been played with, but Falric had come through.

"Well, I've done this a few times you know," Falric said with a confident smile. Alrion heard footsteps and turned to face them.

"What's all this racket?" Vincent said.

"Alrion used a spell to send a stone flying into that tree." Falric pointed and Vincent walked over immediately. He stopped and assessed the mark.

"This looks pretty nasty. Alrion, you did this?"

"Surprisingly, yes."

"Well, maybe you'll be protecting me pretty soon."

"That's the plan," Falric said. Alrion had a smile creep onto his face.

"It's a fantastic first effort, but there's much more to be learned," Falric said.

"I know. I don't think I could do that on the spot if I had to," Alrion said.

"That's quite alright, it will come with time." Falric walked over and slapped Alrion on the back.

"Food is ready if you've worked up an appetite," Vincent said.

"Definitely." Alrion rubbed his back and stretched his legs.

"That's enough for now, let's go eat," Falric said. They walked back to their camp and ate a simple meal of bread and cheese.

"So how was your first lesson?" Falric said once the food was finished.

"Unexpected, but I'm excited to learn more. The possibilities seem endless." Alrion felt energised, once he was over the initial shock of it all.

"That's the right attitude but remember that you must use caution and care. From now on, you have incredible potential and power, but that also means that you must act with responsibility. The consequences are significant."

"I understand," Alrion said. After more general conversation, they turned in for the night. Alrion had trouble sleeping. The world of magic had taken his mind by storm, and his mind was racing with ideas.

The next morning, they had a quick snack and packed up. The horses were keen to get moving, so Vincent suggested they make a start sooner rather than later. Within an hour of riding, they passed through the end of the forest and re-joined the main road.

"So where to next?" Alrion said.

"Wait just a moment," Vincent said. Alrion was curious but

played along. The road was still flanked by tall trees, but they were riding into a flatter, clearer area. Once they emerged from the trees, a completely different landscape awaited them.

"They call that the Thundering Mountain," Vincent said. Far in the distance, they could see a large mountain rising above the landscape. It was tall and imposing, and clouds surrounded its peak.

"Is the weather always that bad? It's like the clouds are anchored to that spot." Alrion said.

"Yes, that's how it was named. There are rumours and legends as to what is on the peak that is attracting all those clouds and storms. But nobody knows," Falric said.

"Could just be a freak weather formation," Vincent said.

"Either way, that's pretty impressive." Alrion couldn't take his eyes off it.

"It's where we will be heading today. Hopefully, it won't take too long, I'd like to investigate the tunnel below it before it gets too late." Vincent kicked his horse back into a faster gallop, and the others followed suit.

I've never seen anything that big. It's massive, Alrion thought as they rode. It felt like for the first time, the adventure was starting to feel real. He had goosebumps on his arms at the thought of exploring the mountain. He cautiously looked at both his father and Falric. Neither seemed to have noticed his excitement. They were focused on other things.

13

A DISTURBANCE

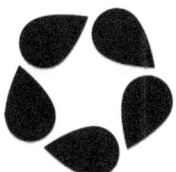

The lushness of the forest they had recently left faded gradually. At first, Alrion didn't really notice any change, but after a time he realised that something had changed. After a more focused look at the countryside, he concluded that the vegetation was dead or dying.

"This area looks different, less alive."

"You have good instincts. I've noticed as well. Not as many signs of wildlife either," Vincent said.

"I haven't been through here for a long time, how about you?" Falric asked.

"No. There should be a town up ahead before the mountain, though. A good community there of hardworking people. I'm a good friend with the blacksmith there. A man called Malcolm."

"I'll be interested in talking with him, to see if he has any information about what's been happening in this area. It's probably nothing, but it just seems so different." Falric had a worried look on his face. Vincent grunted his agreement. Alrion was pleased that he had picked up on something of note.

Every time he looked up at the mountain, it seemed to be the same distance away. But when he took the time to really look at it, and compare to other landmarks, he could tell that they were getting closer. With the comments made by Falric and his father, the mystery surrounding the mountain was even deeper now.

As noon approached, they started to see signs of the town ahead. There were a few abandoned carts on the side of the road and weathered signposts.

"These seem to have been here for a while," Vincent said.

"Agreed," Falric said. They rode on. Houses and other buildings were visible in the distance.

"Usually there would be a bit of traffic on the road at this time," Vincent said, mostly to himself. They continued. Alrion could feel the difference, between this place and his hometown. The feeling of life was not present, but he told himself that he was getting ahead of things, that he knew his own home so well that it skewed his expectations. Once they were closer to entering the town, Falric finally spoke.

"I think it's deserted."

"Are you sure?" Vincent seemed anxious.

"I can't sense any people within. It's also uncommonly quiet." Falric closed his eyes and concentrated

"Too quiet." Vincent swept his gaze back and forth. Alrion didn't say a word but just listened carefully. It was true that the normal sounds you expect; of work being done, of people and animals were missing. It just sounded empty.

They slowed the horses, making the final approach at a gentle clip. Their reduced speed increased the tension for Alrion. He didn't know what was going to happen next. As they passed through the town gates they got a better look at the buildings and the main street. Alrion read the sign.

"Welcome to Hopetarn," he said. There were no signs of life or recent habitation whatsoever.

"Certainly looks empty," Vincent said.

"There's an inn." Alrion pointed it out. A sign for *The Titanic Tankard* gently swung in the wind, squeaking as it went.

"If there's life, it'll be with the booze," Falric said with a chuckle.

"Truer words were never spoken." Vincent spurred his horse forward, heading directly for the inn.

"Let's just tie the horses out front." He stopped and dismounted, leading by example. Once the horses were secured Vincent stepped up to the entrance.

"Let's see what's in store for us." He pushed the main door open and entered the building. Falric and Alrion kept close behind. It was dark inside, the stench of rotting food hitting Alrion's nose before he could become accustomed to the low light.

"Something's off," Vincent said.

"Here." Falric raised his hand. An orb of light materialised above it and slowly floated up until it reached the ceiling.

"More warning next time," Vincent said as he shielded himself from the bright light. Alrion shied back too, surprised by the sudden brightness. Once his eyes had adjusted, he got a good look at the room. There were rows of wooden tables and benches and a bar up one end. Food was left on most tables, which was probably the source of the smell. Vincent walked over to the bar to inspect it. He turned one of the taps behind the bar and beer flowed out.

"Interesting," he said.

"Looks like they left in a hurry. Or had no form of transportation," Falric said.

"Why do you say that?" Alrion was curious how he had come to such a precise conclusion.

"The food mess. That shows that they didn't intend on coming back. Or couldn't think about that. Leaving kegs full of beer, now that's an unusual situation. I would expect either the people leaving or any people attacking the place to take it with them." Falric looked to Vincent.

"I agree, nothing raises morale like a drink or two. It was obviously considered unnecessary in the rush," he said. Alrion maintained a blank stare.

"You never liked the taste, so you wouldn't understand." Vincent laughed.

"Alrion and I will look around here if you want to take upstairs."
Falric gestured to the staircase.

"Sure." Vincent strode forward with confidence, but kept his hand
on the hilt of his sword.

"What are we looking for?" Alrion said.

"Anything of note. We want to work out why the people left."

"Why is it important? Maybe they just wanted to move on."

"This used to be a prosperous town with a long history. People
wouldn't leave without a good reason, and nobody has come back.
That's what it looks like. Let's see what we can find."

"You think there's some potential danger around here and it
forced them to leave."

"Exactly. This kind of evacuation shouldn't be happening around
here. Avaria is a very safe place. See what you can turn up." Falric
started by looking behind the bar. Alrion wandered the room. He
turned over some chairs that had been knocked over and inspected
the food that was left. But he didn't find any personal belongings.

"I don't really see anything," Alrion said after a few minutes.

"Nothing special behind the bar either. We'll see what your father
says."

"Not much to report." Vincent descended the staircase.

"Abandoned at seemingly short notice?" Falric said.

"That's my assessment. Did you find anything here?"

"Just something for the road." Falric held up a metal flask and
wiggled it.

"At least we can leave with something. I'd like to get out of here
immediately, the stench is terrible." Vincent headed directly for the
door and Alrion followed without argument.

"Any ideas on what happened?" Falric said once he was outside.

"Not really, but I want to check out the blacksmith."

"Sure, lead the way," Falric said. Vincent started untying the
horses.

"Did you know him well?" Alrion said as they walked with the
horses.

"The blacksmith? I used to, but we lost touch a while ago."

"What was he like?"

"An orderly man. Had everything in the right place, and a good system for running his shop. I definitely learned some things from his approach." A smile crept to Vincent's face as he looked in the distance, like he was remembering something.

"What do you think we will find at his shop?"

"Well, I don't know yet. But I understood him well, so whatever condition the shop is in should be very telling," Vincent said. No more was said until they arrived at the blacksmith workshop. It had no name, just a sign with an anvil on it. Vincent tied up the horses and was the first to enter the shop.

It looked like a scene frozen in time. A piece of iron sat idly on the table, with a hammer next to it. Other items were out, but most were tucked neatly away.

"He was making a sword." Vincent walked through, letting his hand linger on some surfaces or tools as he went, "Look at this. I told you he was organised. Only the parts he needed were out, everything else is packed away."

"Well, there's definitely a pattern. People left suddenly. How long ago do you think?" Falric said.

"Judging by the rust, and the decay we spotted at the tavern I'd say recently. Days or a week at most," Vincent said.

"That seems plausible. However, there's no evidence of what made them leave. I didn't notice any signs of attack," Falric said.

"Attack by what?" Alrion said. His heart started to race, and he looked at Falric.

"Could be any number of things. Perhaps even Blighters," the master wizard said.

"Let's not get ahead of ourselves. Why don't we rest here and eat, then we can move on and leave this ghost town behind us," Vincent said.

"Sure," Falric said.

"C'mon, Alrion." Vincent walked outside, holding the door open. Alrion helped him bring in some food, and move some stools so they could all sit around one of the workbenches.

"I can't believe I'm already back in a blacksmith workshop," Alrion said, trying to lighten the mood.

"You can't escape your destiny." Vincent chuckled.

"So it would seem. What do we do next?" Alrion said.

"Before we move on, I want you to practice your push spell again," Falric said.

"Sure. What do I push?" Alrion looked around the room for another object of similar size to the stone he had moved.

"Let's be careful, after what you did to that tree," Vincent said. Falric laughed.

"How about we use that." Falric walked over and opened the heavy wooden door. He left it at just the right spot that it caught on the floor and held itself open.

"This should be simple. Just close the door."

"It looks a lot heavier than the stone," Alrion said.

"Doesn't matter, you'll be fine. Just remember the process. Feel the thought in your mind, apply it to the door, and amplify it if required," Falric said. Alrion nodded and closed his eyes.

"Eyes open. You need to see your target," Falric said. Alrion opened them and stared at the door. It seemed harder to focus his mind with all the distraction of what he could see. But he managed to push his thoughts aside and focus on the door. He imagined the force building up, ready to slam the door shut. He imagined the door slamming in his mind; saw the splinters of wood flying out with the force. Then he applied that thought to the door. He could feel its resistance.

He wondered if Falric was playing games with him again, keeping the door in place. He got annoyed at the possibility that Falric was interfering.

He can't just leave things alone.

Alrion drew upon his annoyance and fanned the flame. He drew out a heat from within and forced it against the door, propping up his will and mental image. The door wobbled slightly then slammed shut, splinters of wood spraying out from the impact. Just as he had imagined.

"How strange," Alrion said.

"In what way?" Falric said.

"I imagined what it would look like when the door slammed, and it looked exactly the same when it happened."

"Of course, you imposed your Will on the door."

"Really?"

"Yes. Well, it's a bit of give and take. You understood the possible reaction from slamming the door, then you made it happen."

"But that literally?"

"They don't call it magic for no reason," Falric said.

"Nice job." Vincent walked over to the door and yanked it open, "That was shut pretty tight."

"Of course," Alrion said, delighted.

"Very good progress. You have the basics there, now we need to work on your control and speed. Eventually, a push will be as effortless as the thought required to dream it up."

"That sounds crazy, the potential. How do you just not push everything constantly?" Alrion said.

"The novelty does wear off, but there is also a price for everything and a balance. Every action has a reaction and consequences. This you will learn," Falric said.

"Alright." Alrion started looking around at the room for other things that he could push.

"Don't even think about it," Vincent said, catching Alrion's intention. Alrion shrugged and stood up.

"Let's head off then. I'm still keen to investigate the mountain," Vincent said.

"Even after what we observed here?" Falric said.

"More so. I'm concerned about what has happened, and also quite motivated to avoid the forest if at all possible." Vincent's face was grim.

He seems quite concerned. About a forest?

"Well it isn't far, and we can be safe about it. Let's head to the mountain and see if your shortcut is available," Falric said.

"Fingers crossed." Vincent stepped outside and started moving quickly.

They rode through the town with speed. Now that they were used to it, the eerie quiet was less disconcerting, but still as unexplainable. Alrion found the experience quite strange. A town full of all the things he expected, except any signs of life. Soon they had reached the town limits and joined another main road. Alrion looked up and the mountain loomed larger still.

They rode on in silence, like they were infected with the empty quiet of the town. It felt strange to speak, so Alrion didn't try and break the peace. They passed a less populated area, with evidence of the occasional farm, but it was a lot of nothing. Just a road. Every time he looked up the mountain looked different. It confused him at first, then he had a realisation.

I'm too close, I can't even take in the whole size of it.

"We're almost there." Vincent finally broke the silence.

"What should we expect?" Alrion said.

"The gate to the passage should be open, and there should be two guards posted outside," Vincent said.

"And if there isn't?"

"Then something has changed." Vincent had a grim look on his face.

Maybe the emptiness of Hopetarn has changed his expectations.

"And that's when we become awfully suspicious," Falric said.

"It's hard to see from here, but those are the gates." Vincent pointed to something in the distance. Alrion couldn't really make it out. As they travelled, he looked repeatedly and started to see the distinction.

"They look closed," Alrion said.

"Not a good start," Falric said.

"We'll see." Vincent's voice was tight, and he nudged his horse to pick up speed. The light was starting to fade and soon he was riding hard to reach the gate. As soon as he arrived he tied his horse to a nearby post and started investigating. Alrion and Falric caught up and waited on horseback. The gates were massive, the frames built from giant steel bars. They were easily big enough for five men to enter at once.

"What's your assessment?" Falric said.

"The gate is closed, but not locked." Vincent demonstrated by pushing on the door. It started to open, but all that was inside was darkness.

"Doesn't look good." Alrion surprised himself with those words. They had leapt unbidden to his mouth.

"Agreed. Are we sure about this?" Falric looked at Vincent with uncertainty.

"We have to try. The alternative is much longer and more dangerous," Vincent said.

"As you wish. Keep your wits about you." Falric dismounted and directed Alrion to do the same.

What are we getting ourselves into? Alrion thought with a sigh.

14

INSIDE THE MOUNTAIN

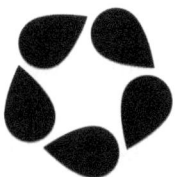

Vincent leaned heavily on the doors and they slowly swung completely open. The light from outside did little to penetrate the darkness.

"The horses will be spooked," he said.

"I'll provide light." Falric conjured up a ball of light and held it in front of him, "Follow me."

Alrion looked around at the passage. It was carved into the stone, with strong square lines.

"I think there are torches along the wall." He pointed them out.

"Well spotted, let's try this." Falric walked over to one of the torches, and his ball of light morphed into a dancing flame. He lit the torch and it illuminated the area.

"Not bad," Vincent said.

"Just the one?" Alrion said. Falric looked at Vincent, then Alrion, then waved his arm dramatically. The flame from the lit torch leapt to the nearest torch, lighting it as well. With another wave of his arm, it set off again, the flame rippling along all the torches lighting them as far as they could see.

"Much more convenient. So dramatic, though." Vincent sighed.

"I think he meant to say that was amazing," Alrion said. Falric smiled at him.

"Thank you. Let's just say it was a combination of showing you what's possible, making our lives a bit easier, and squeezing in a bit of fun too. That's allowed, right?"

"Fine by me," Alrion said.

"Now that we can see, I'll take the lead. Alrion you take care of the horses." Vincent rushed forward without waiting for a response. Alrion took all the reins for the horses and started slowly from the rear. Falric kept up pace with Vincent, staying only a few steps behind.

With the improved lighting, Alrion could see the detail on the walls. They were actually quite sparse, the same strong but basic construction as used on the door.

"What did they use this path for?"

"Mostly trade, but also normal travellers. It was the preferred route to get to Altarbright, but it doesn't appear to be in use right now. And I'm not sure how long it has been left," Vincent said.

"Does that make it safer?" Alrion said.

"Potentially." Vincent sounded unconvinced, but didn't offer any other details.

There's something he's not saying but I won't push the issue, Alrion thought and decided to keep his eyes open. The path was sloping down gently, the walls the same stark blandness.

"It was so different before. You didn't notice how plain the whole thing was, because of all the life that was flowing through," Vincent said.

"I was just thinking that there's no decoration at all."

"Exactly. Probably more due to the utility of the path than anything else. I think it was used as soon as it was completed."

"Are there any kinds of animals that live underground that we may find?"

"Generally, yes, but I'd be surprised if we did," Vincent said. Falric stopped walking and within seconds Vincent stopped too.

"What is it?" he said to the wizard.

"I feel like something is off. Just a feeling, though, it's not based on anything," Falric said.

"Firm enough to turn back?" Vincent glanced back at the way they had come.

"Not sure, we have come a fair way already. We should continue. Turning back is always an option if things change," Falric said.

"Sure, let's just take care." Vincent resumed his position out front and looked even more alert. As they progressed, he pointed out odd pieces of furniture, sometimes a table, or a wooden chair, strewn about.

"They had vendors with sales tables here to tempt the passing traffic," Vincent said.

"Again, deserted," Alrion said.

"Certainly a theme, my guess is that we will discover something here," Falric said. Vincent pushed on, staying a few lengths in front of them. Falric seemed intent on figuring out whatever in the distance had made him unsettled. Alrion himself couldn't pay much attention, he was lagging behind, struggling to handle the three horses.

"Now we're getting somewhere." Vincent stopped next to a structure built into the tunnel, with a large gate and a small building to the side. Alrion looked up to properly take it in. It looked like a checkpoint or outpost of some kind.

"Is this empty too?" he said.

"I'd say so, but there should be some books here or logs or something. This was a checkpoint with more security. I think at one stage they even charged a toll here." Vincent entered the structure and began looking around. Falric paused and started peering into the darkness ahead of them, focused on something.

"What is it?" Alrion asked. He could sense that Falric was concerned. Alrion also felt a sense of unease that he couldn't place. Falric didn't respond, but closed his eyes and put his head down. He seemed to be concentrating intensely.

"Vincent, come back and protect the horses," Falric shouted. Vincent immediately ran out of the building, confusion on his face, but after a brief pause, he continued over to stand by Alrion.

"What's the problem?" he said.

"Blighters." Falric stepped forward.

Vincent drew his sword and moved behind the horses, protecting them from the rear.

"Stay in the middle and try and keep them from bolting," he said to Alrion.

"Sure." Alrion wanted to ask more but sensed the urgency of the situation.

"Time for some fireworks." Falric conjured a ball of fire in his hands. The dancing flames lit the path ahead even more, and Alrion at last understood what was coming. He saw a horde of ashen-skinned people, hunched over, and running on all their limbs. He couldn't make out their faces but heard their grunts and cries. Once they closed in, Falric let loose.

A wave of fire cascaded out from his hands, sweeping over the first row of Blighters. They screamed in pain and fell down. Alrion had to fight the urge to block his ears. He turned back to look behind him and saw his father swinging his sword.

Vincent cut with finesse and efficiency, each strike moving into the next. He was dispatching the Blighters in one or two attacks, making a concerted effort to keep them from advancing.

"Tell Falric we need a plan. We don't know how many there are, and I can't see an end to them. We can't keep fighting them on both sides," Vincent said.

"Got it." Alrion carefully walked the horses over a bit further and called out to Falric.

"What do we do? We need a way to fight them smarter, their numbers are too great!"

"Use your head," Falric said, focusing on his fire waves. Alrion looked at the environment trying to come up with a plan. He noticed a support beam for the checkpoint building that looked unsteady. Maybe if he could dislodge it, that would cause a diversion or at least reduce the space the Blighters had to attack.

It's my only option, I have to try.

He kept his eye on the beam and started to focus. All he had to do

was push it enough to move or break it, and the weight of the structure would do the rest. He focused his will, as before, but trying to
ignore the chaos around him. He got annoyed at how slow he was,
right when the situation was urgent. And found a way to draw upon
his inner power. As he was about to release it, something jumped into
his peripheral vision.

"Incoming!" Falric shouted. A burned but not beaten Blighter was
heading right for Alrion. He froze. *What am I supposed to do?*

"PUSH!" Falric yelled out. Alrion didn't even think, he just acted.
He pushed the Blighter with all the force he had been accumulating.
Unlike before, it happened immediately. The Blighter flew back with
incredible speed, a stunned look on its face. But there was a problem.
It was heading right for Falric.

"Look out!" Alrion yelled. Falric turned in time to see what was
happening and managed to push the Blighter enough to alter its
trajectory. It slammed into the building next to the checkpoint.

*Great, I saved myself but ruined the opportunity and put Falric in
danger.*

Falric had exposed himself by pushing away the Blighter thrown
at him. Another blighter took advantage and tried to bite him. The
master wizard frantically threw a fireball at close range, charring the
Blighter instantly and sending the body flying. But the power with
which he unleashed the fireball did not stop at one Blighter.

It blossomed out, killing the rest within range and consuming the
checkpoint and nearby building. It could not withstand the resultant
force and heat and started to collapse.

"Get back!" Falric cried out and he turned to run. Alrion could say
nothing, but turned and tried to get the horses moving once more.
They were frozen still with fear, and took a lot of encouragement.
Vincent increased the intensity of his attacks in an effort to push the
Blighters back. The checkpoint building slammed to the ground with
a great crash, blocking the path and any Blighters behind.

"That's one problem solved," Falric said. As he finished speaking
a rumbling sound echoed above them.

"That could be another one," Alrion said. Falric stepped past the young wizard and stood next to Vincent, shooting streaks of fiery death at the Blighters in the rows behind. With the two of them working tirelessly, they pushed their way forward, the Blighters unable to stand up to the combined onslaught.

We might just survive this, if the tunnel doesn't collapse on us first.

Alrion followed as close as he could. He watched on in awe, seeing a side of his father that he never expected. Vincent had always been a peaceful man, working hard at the forge and supporting his family. Alrion had no idea that he was so proficient with a sword and so fearless.

Falric, too, was impressive. The Blighters pushed on and on, but the two men slashed and blasted them down as soon as they emerged.

"Where are they all coming from?" Vincent said. Alrion had no idea. On their way in they had passed no other tunnels or structures that could hold anything. He concentrated on keeping the horses under control and looked forward and back to gauge the potential dangers from the Blighters and the stability of the tunnel.

Suddenly, the stream of Blighters ended. Vincent and Falric stopped and waited. There was quiet. No more snarling or yelling. But they couldn't escape the mess of bodies and the smell of burned flesh.

"I think the path is clear, let's leave," Vincent said. Alrion nodded.

I need to get out of here as soon as possible.

He followed along as best he could, assisting the horses through.

They trudged back, away from the battle scene and back to the entrance. Alrion could smell the fresher air and knew they were close. With each step, he relaxed a bit more and could feel the horses relax too. He pushed harder and harder for the exit, feeling so enclosed by the tunnel and the battle they had just experienced.

"And here we are," Vincent said. The giant doors were wide open.

"Wait," Vincent said before anyone could move. Alrion stopped, holding the horses still. Vincent knelt to the ground and looked carefully.

"I think there are tracks. Can you do something with those Falric?"

"With magic? Not really. I'm afraid old-fashioned tracking is the way to go here."

"Hold up and let me see if I can follow them," Vincent said. Alrion kept the horses inside the tunnel and Falric stood by his side. They watched Vincent work. He stalked along, keeping a close eye on the ground and kneeling down on occasion to have a closer look. Soon he had disappeared around a corner.

"Sorry about back there," Alrion said.

"For what?" Falric gave the young wizard a questioning look.

"I almost hit you." Alrion felt so embarrassed, but Falric's face relaxed.

"Never mind that, the important thing is that we are all safe."

"But still ..."

"Listen carefully. You are still new at this, but you reacted well and protected yourself. That is the most important thing. You must never let yourself be infected by the Blight," Falric said. Alrion was about to respond but saw his father returning.

"Do you want the good news or the bad news?" Vincent said.

"Let's have some good news," Falric said.

"I was able to follow the tracks well enough to see where they came from. The sheer volume of Blighters made it relatively easy, even for a novice such as me."

"Great, so what's the bad news?"

"The tracks lead into the forest."

"Oh, I see," Falric said.

"What's the significance of that?" Alrion said.

"Now that the tunnel is closed, the forest is our only option. Even without the threat of Blighters, your father wanted to avoid it. And if the Blighters came from there, we could be in for far more trouble." Falric cradled his chin with his thumb and index finger and looked off into the distance.

"Which forest? You've mentioned it a few times," Alrion said

"The Whispering Forest." Falric's concern was clearly evident.

They left the tunnel and Alrion looked back.

Why did you have to screw up and cause all these problems?

He looked at both his father and Falric and could feel the tension. They also looked a bit shaken by the attack, and Alrion could tell that something was very wrong about the forest they were about to enter. There had to be a reason that his father was so adamant that they try the tunnel first.

"You'll have to tell me about this forest." Alrion mounted up and prepared to ride.

15

A NEW PATH

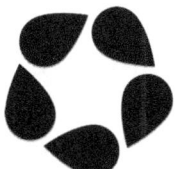

"The Whispering Forest is called that, because of what you hear within," Falric said as they rode.

"Whispering?" Alrion said.

"Exactly. It's probably something to do with the trees and the wind patterns, but the whispering sound is unmistakable. Of course, many believe that the forest is haunted and steer clear. The fact that there are many recorded cases of people disappearing within the forest keeps these beliefs going."

"Haunted? By ghosts?" Alrion wasn't sure he believed in that. The Blighters were one thing, but ghosts were something else.

"That's what the stories say. Visibility is also very poor, there seems to be a mist that hangs over the place. It would be a place ripe for theft or kidnapping, but most people avoid it."

"Maybe not as many avoid it now since the tunnel under the mountain was abandoned," Alrion said.

"You're probably right about that. I guess we shall see who we encounter," Vincent said, joining the conversation.

"Speaking of that, maybe you can tell me more about those creatures we fought. Blighters?" Alrion said. Falric nodded and prepared to explain.

"A Blighter is a person, or was a person, that has been tainted by the Blight. But more than tainted, transformed. Your grandfather studied them closely, and could not ascertain if the person still existed within. Their skin is darker, a greyish hue, and they stoop and often travel on hands and feet. As you saw."

"Why do they act like that?" Alrion said.

"It's a good question. The best theory is that the Blight changes them somehow, to a more animalistic state. They don't appear to have any leaders among them but do travel in packs. We believe there's some sort of shared consciousness or communication going on."

"What do they do? What's their goal?"

"I'm not sure they have one. If they do, it's to attack people. They can infect you with the Blight, which as I mentioned is something you absolutely must avoid as a wizard."

"Is it worse for wizards?" Alrion couldn't imagine what would be worse than transforming into a Blighter.

"The Blight reacts differently to a wizard. It corrupts their Spark. As you know, the Spark is the inner power of a wizard that makes them unique. Imagine instead of that fire you have within you, it was a lump of tar, which pulsed with a power that sickened you," Falric said.

"That's horrible."

"Yes. It would affect you in many different ways, the most obvious being that you would be unable to use your Spark in the normal way. The wizards that tried, well each spell they cast became corrupted. Usually, in ways they did not anticipate. And it hastened their transformation." Falric grew very quiet.

"You sold me on not getting infected." Alrion felt a cold shiver run down his spine.

"Good. You must avoid that at all costs. The fact that we were attacked by such a large contingent of them is concerning. Was it pure chance that they were here, or are we being targeted?" Falric said.

"A good question. We need to know," Vincent said.

"I'll think about it. However, I fear there's too little information right now to know for sure. The evacuation of Hopetarn and that mass of Blighters are likely related." Falric seemed lost in his thoughts. Alrion looked up and could see the edge of the forest.

A milky haze hung over and permeated the entire place. The trees were impossibly tall and quite narrow but extremely numerous. Their only way in was a dirt path through the middle, wide enough for single file.

"How did they even make a path through there?" Alrion asked.

"Not sure. Maybe nobody ever did?" Falric said.

"The forest is not enchanted, it didn't make the path itself," Vincent said.

"You never know." Falric shrugged.

"You of all people should know," Vincent said to Falric.

"I think you'll find, that the more you learn about the world we live in, the more you realise that there's so much we don't know or understand," Falric said.

"That is a typical wizard answer." Vincent pointed at Falric with his thumb.

"He's right about that. But for the wrong reason," Falric said. Alrion left it at that.

"We'll be in the forest soon, you can draw your own conclusions as to if it is haunted or otherwise," Vincent said.

The entrance to the forest snuck up on them, the mist making the distances harder to judge. Before they knew it, they were surrounded by giant trees. Vincent brought his horse to a halt and the other two followed. They sat in silence for a minute.

This must be for my benefit, Alrion thought. He listened out and concentrated on the sounds of the forest. He could hear the wind swirling through the trees and the sounds of wood moving. He couldn't hear much in the way of animals, though, it was quiet.

"Allllllllllllllrionnnnnnnnnnn," the faintest of whispers said. Alrion jumped with surprise, almost falling out of the saddle.

"Did you hear that?" he said.

"Hear what? The trees?" Vincent said.

"They whispered my name."

"Don't be silly, you're imagining that," Vincent said. Falric gave Alrion a curious look.

"I think the jury is out. Let's get a move on and see if you continue to hear it," he said.

"Sure." Alrion didn't trust his voice enough to say more. He was spooked. It was one thing to hear the strange whispers; it was another to hear his name.

Is it just my mind playing tricks on me?

They set off once more, slowly progressing through the forest. The heavy mist reduced visibility, so they took their time navigating the slim path. Vincent was in front, Alrion in the middle and Falric to the rear.

"I feel like I shouldn't be talking here. It's like we are interrupting something," Alrion said.

"Everyone reports feeling uneasy in here. Like they are trespassing. There's a reason I don't slam the door shut on all those theories of haunting. Too much is unexplainable," Falric said.

"Is this feeling the mist? My clothes are sticking to me, but it's so cold." Alrion tried loosening his shirt.

"That's the mist. It keeps the moisture level very high here. Not good for campfires," Vincent said.

"Good point," Alrion said.

"There's a whole host of reasons why people avoid this place. However, we don't have many options. The mountain path is blocked now, and if we went around the forest, it would take days and days. It's not worth it," Vincent said.

"How long will this take?"

"We will have to camp overnight, but we can make it out tomorrow easily."

"That doesn't sound too bad."

"It shouldn't be. Hang on." Vincent slowed his horse and peered into the distance.

"Do you see something up ahead?" Falric said.

"I think so; I can make out a few shapes. Do you think there are people here?"

"There might be. Why don't you investigate, and we will stay further behind?" Falric said.

Vincent set off again, and Alrion waited before continuing.

I hope it's fellow travellers and not more Blighters, Alrion thought. He had seen enough for one day.

Vincent waved at them to stop, and dismounted. He slapped his horse and sent it back towards Alrion. Then Vincent proceeded alone and on foot into the mist. He walked with care, each step placed as softly as possible. He was not a hunter or a woodsman, but he could be quiet when he needed to be.

It was hard to make out the shapes ahead, but it looked like two people. Two would be manageable if it turned out they were hostile. As he crept closer, he could start to hear voices.

"This mist is terrible, I can't see anything," a man said.

"Well I told you this would happen, you shouldn't complain," an older man said.

"We had no choice."

"Stop grumbling about it then."

"I'll complain as much as I want," the first voice responded, but was quiet after.

They don't sound particularly dangerous, Vincent thought and continued his approach. As he closed in, he was still at a loss as to who they were. The outlines of the shapes improved, and he could see they were on foot without horses, but no details were clear. He had to make a decision, to slow down progress and try to avoid them, or confront them and travel together.

I'll confront them, and decide based on their reaction. I won't be able to determine much of anything without being right next to them.

Their pace was slow, so he increased his speed and called out once he was almost upon them.

"Hello, friends!" Vincent said. They stopped immediately and turned around.

"Is someone there?" one of the men said.

"Yes, hold still and I'll come closer. Damn this mist," Vincent said.

"You can say that again," the voice said. Vincent continued to approach and finally got a good look at the pair. They were two men, one older and one much younger. They wore simple travelling clothes with no jewellery and sturdy boots.

"I'm Vincent, nice to meet you," he said, holding his hand out to the older man first.

"Fitzgerald, nice to meet you."

"Grant, also nice to meet you," the younger man said.

"What brings you to this awful place?" Vincent said.

"We are merchants. We'll sell anything really. But profits aren't as good, so we're looking to see if we can get new lines from further abroad." Fitzgerald gestured into the distance.

"Heading to Altarbright then?"

"You know it, that's the place to be. You heading there also?" Fitzgerald was studying Vincent carefully.

"Yes. We're so close, yet so far." Vincent threw up his hands, referencing the mist.

"Tell me about it. I've had it up to here with this mist and the strange whispers," Grant said.

"Yeah, I'll be happy to be out of here. You two travel safe," Vincent said.

"Hang on, aren't we going the same way? Why don't you join us? At least we could camp together," Fitzgerald said.

"That sounds reasonable. I came ahead to investigate who was here. Since you two seem like stand-up fellows I'll report back to the others."

"How many others?" Fitzgerald spoke quickly, and a panicked look flashed across his face.

"Just two more. My son and father. Don't go anywhere."

"I feel like we've been doing that all day," Grant muttered. Vincent waved and turned to walk back the way he had come.

Something is up with these two, but I can't put my finger on it.

16

COMPANIONS

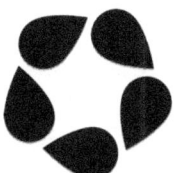

V incent stepped out of the mist and saw Falric and Alrion staring out at him.

"That took a while," Alrion said.

"I was careful, but I spoke to them," he said.

"Who are they?" Falric said.

"They said they are travellers, going to Altarbright to find new goods to trade with."

"It seems plausible, but why come through here?" Falric said

"Exactly. However, like us, they could be trying to save time. There are not a lot of options."

"What's your gut feeling?" Falric said.

"There's something not quite right but I can't place it. I'm not worried about them, though, they don't seem dangerous," Vincent said.

"I trust your assessment. So, what's the plan?"

"They suggested we camp together. It's not a bad idea, and it would raise suspicion if we said no."

"Why do we care if they are suspicious?" Alrion said.

"If they are a danger, it's better we play along and assess. Disappearing on them may cause them to behave differently and come after us," Falric said.

"Isn't that better than us being right with them?" Alrion's stomach started churning with the thought of another intense encounter.

"Keep your friends close, and your enemies closer," Falric said.

I don't like this.

"I agree. With the narrowness of the path, it would be very hard to pass them and impossible to do so without being noticed. If there is something up, I think we can deal with them easily," Vincent said.

"After seeing you with a sword back there, I'm confident of that," Falric said.

An adventure was supposed to be more fun than wading through hordes of feral creatures and camping with strangers who might want to kill you.

"We'll move ahead then. Don't say anything about your true purpose or mission. I said you were my son and father, so play along with that." Vincent looked at Alrion and then at Falric.

"Sure," Alrion said. He could do this. He wouldn't be the one to hold them back.

"I can play along," Falric said. Vincent mounted his horse and pushed ahead. It didn't take them long to catch up to the two figures on the path.

"Ho, Vincent!" Grant called out.

"I'm here. Proper introductions when we stop for the night," Vincent said.

"Sure thing." Grant started walking again, with Fitzgerald just behind. Vincent had to slow his horse to match their pace.

"No more lessons in the forest, not until we are alone again," Falric said to Alrion.

"I understand." It made sense to be cautious with these strangers, even if his father did not consider them dangerous. Progress was slow, and Alrion found the forest even more intimidating now that they were deep inside it.

I wish I could just spur the horse on and rush out of here.

The swaying of the trees and the whispering sounds were almost hypnotic. Alrion strained to hear the whispering properly, to discern if there were actual words, but unlike earlier, he couldn't quite hear.

Did I imagine the whole thing?

Their pace slowed even more, and Alrion looked around wondering why. However, he saw that the path had opened out into a natural clearing.

"This looks like the camp spot," Vincent said.

"It is the only place so far that has been wider than that narrow path," Falric said.

"The layout of this forest certainly is strange. Bring the horses over here." Vincent pointed and then dismounted. They tied up their horses securely to a tree at the edge of the clearing and grabbed their bags.

"I'll introduce you." Vincent walked over to the two other men, who were busy laying out their own things.

"Looks like a good camp spot," he said.

"Aye, I've been on the lookout all day," Fitzgerald said.

"I'm travelling with my family. This is Falric and this is Alrion."

"Nice to meet you both. I'm Fitzgerald and that's Grant."

"Likewise," Falric said. Alrion nodded but didn't speak up.

"I don't know about you all, but trekking through this forest has worked up my appetite," Grant said.

"I think it's safe to say that we are all starving," Vincent said. Grant laughed and reached into his pack for some food.

"What I wouldn't give for a nice warm cup of tea right now." Grant continued munching on some bread.

"Good luck lighting a fire here. The air feels so damp, I think it would actually be impossible," Vincent said. Falric said nothing.

"Yeah. Water, water everywhere but no way to heat it," Grant said.

"Vincent told us that you were merchants," Falric said.

"That's right. We'll sell anything of value. Used to be raw materials for building. We would link up the quarries and builders or deal with carpenters and tanners and so on. Do the deals that the individual craftsmen wouldn't bother with. But times are changing, and there's not as much construction going on. I blame the peace we have had." Fitzgerald spat out something into the tree line and wiped his face with the back of his hand.

"That's an interesting take on it," Vincent said.

"Yeah, he's right, though. There was a lot of rebuilding to be done due to the Blight. Then there were all the people who flocked here when they heard that Avaria was safe and untainted. But those who could afford to move have done so, and those that can't are stuck," Grant said.

"What are you after now?" Vincent said.

"We don't know. Well, we know we are after a solid earner, but we don't know what it will be." Fitzgerald shrugged.

"I have no idea what we will find. But Altarbright seems to be a good trading hub because of the lake, so maybe we will get some goods from outside Avaria?" Grant looked over at his companion for confirmation.

"Maybe, fingers crossed," Fitzgerald said.

"You've never been to Altarbright?" Vincent said. His eyes darted between the two men, watching their faces.

"No, never needed to venture that far. Have you?" The older man seemed to be challenging Vincent.

"A long time ago, I probably wouldn't recognise the place now." Vincent laughed, but it sounded forced to Alrion.

"Yeah, times change. So, what's your business there, if you don't mind me asking?" Fitzgerald said. Vincent paused for a moment and then replied.

"Nothing as serious as your trip. Wanted to show my son some more of the country before he ends up settling down. It's good to broaden your mind some."

"Great idea, travel is a fantastic way of learning more about the world. But I must ask, why did you come to this awful place?" Grant said.

"Why did you?" Vincent said. Grant licked his lips before he responded.

"We couldn't afford the detour, such a long walk otherwise."

"Same deal." Vincent kept his gaze squarely on Grant. The merchant adjusted his position on the ground.

"I see. Do you believe any of the stories about this place?"

"That it's haunted?"

"Yeah. Every person you talk to has a different theory about why it is so creepy," Grant said.

"I don't believe in that stuff. It's just stories," Vincent said.

"You are probably correct. But I still wonder." Fitzgerald looked over at Falric.

"I must agree that it seems very unlikely that anything untoward is happening in the forest. It is just a process that we don't know or understand that is causing these effects," Falric said.

"I'm starved." Vincent cut off the conversation and rummaged through his pack. He passed bread and cheese to Falric and Alrion who devoured it with gusto. Vincent continue to study their new companions while he ate.

He seems quite suspicious of those two. I can see why, there's something not quite right about them. Alrion noticed his father exchanging a grim look with Falric. They both seemed to be in agreement about the strangers.

"I think it's time to turn in," Vincent said. As they started to prepare for sleep, Fitzgerald approached them.

"Look, I've been polite, but I have to ask. What are wizards doing here?" he said. Vincent whirled around quickly and looked at him with caution.

"What are you talking about?"

"I haven't travelled that widely, but I know a wizard when I see one. Those robes are so distinctive. They may be simple and not flashy, but there's nothing else like them. I'm right, even if you don't admit it," he said. Vincent looked conflicted and didn't reply immediately.

How do we deal with this? Alrion thought.

"How would you know what a wizard looks like?" Falric said, a playful tone to his voice.

"We had some visit the town, so I know."

"Which town?" Falric said.

"You wouldn't have heard of it."

"If I'm a wizard, then wouldn't you expect me to have heard of it? If wizards have visited there?" Falric was giving Fitzgerald an icy stare that was at odds with the friendly tone of his voice.

"No, actually. They stayed and didn't return." Fitzgerald stammered and looked down before meeting Falric's gaze again.

"We found these cloaks abandoned in a town we passed through. If you say they are wizard cloaks, then I guess we should be more careful. Thanks for your concern," Vincent said. Fitzgerald looked at him, then over at Falric. He looked like he was evaluating his next move.

"Well glad I could be of help and apologies for any misunderstanding. I think it is time for us to retire, so have a good night and we shall see you in the morning." Fitzgerald turned and walked back to the other end of the clearing, helping Grant get their bedrolls laid out. Vincent turned and approached Falric and Alrion.

"This just gets weirder and weirder. There's something going on. Falric and I will take turns keeping watch tonight. I don't trust them."

"I agree. They are nervous about something, and I did notice them staring at our robes the whole time. They are only distinctive to those who know what to look for. I'm not buying the fact that they had some wizards visit a town he didn't want to name," Falric said.

"What about me?" Alrion said.

"You sleep," Vincent said.

"How can I sleep knowing you're watching those guys to see if they try and pull something?"

"You will. We have a long trip ahead of us, so the more you can rest the better. We'll wake you up if anything starts happening, don't worry about that." Vincent put a hand on Alrion's shoulder.

"At least one of us should get a proper sleep, and as the man learning the most right now it should be you. Your time will come, mark my words," Falric said.

"Sure." Alrion didn't want to make a big deal.

I know I can pull my weight. But they seem really uneasy about this. I'll just have to try and sleep.

They started their preparations for sleep. Falric and Alrion tried to get some rest, while Vincent sat up pretending to read.

～

"Falric, you awake?" Vincent said. Alrion awoke immediately and sat up. He hadn't managed to get into a deep sleep.

"Almost. I'm trying to work out what disturbed my sleep. Be quiet for a moment," he said. Vincent turned back to look at the travellers. They still appeared to be in their beds. Falric had sat bolt upright. His eyes were fixated on the distance.

"This is not good. Wake Alrion and get ready to leave," Falric said.

"I'm already awake. What is it?" Alrion said.

"Trouble. Get ready," Vincent said. Alrion started to stand but sank back down. Something was bugging him. He listened carefully to the sounds of the forest. They were the same as before, the wind and the swaying of the trees. And the strange whispering sound, that was almost inaudible, running beneath the rest of the sounds like an undercurrent.

"Runnnnn AAAAAlrion," the forest whispered and Alrion felt a chill run down his spine. Before he could speak he heard a new sound. Something was rushing in their direction. He looked up and saw a giant flame in the shape of a man hurtling towards them. Vincent grabbed Alrion and hurled him out of the way. They both fell to the ground and heard the flame pass over their heads. A gigantic explosion blasted behind them, and the smell of smoke filled the air.

"I thought you said it was impossible to start a fire in here," Alrion said.

"Looks like I was wrong." Vincent drew his sword.

17

UNDER FIRE

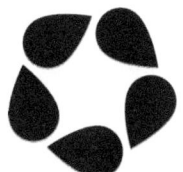

Vincent stepped forward and looked out into the darkness.

"It must be a wizard. Falric are you there?"

"I'm here. It is a wizard, which is surprising," Falric said.

"Aren't all the wizards with you?"

"No, not all wizards. Be careful," Falric said. Vincent gave Alrion a hand up. The young wizard brushed himself off and strained to see what had attacked them. The smoke and mist were hampering visibility. He saw a shape in the distance, walking closer. He couldn't make out who it was.

"It's the wizard," Falric said.

"We don't know what he can do, so just duck and run if you have to," Vincent said. Alrion nodded.

"Don't act rashly, this is extremely dangerous," Falric said. The figure stopped and observed them. Falric held his hands up, and a gust of wind flew out and dispersed the mist and smoke nearby. They finally got a good look at who had attacked them.

He was average height, wearing a full black hooded robe. His face was hidden from view. In his right hand, he held a jet-black staff with a dark crystal orb at the top.

"Who are you?" Falric called out.

"You don't need my name, and I don't need yours. You are well known to me Falric," a voice said. It was somehow amplified and boomed around the clearing.

"What do you want?" Falric said. The man started to speak but stopped himself. Instead, he just laughed. Falric looked at Vincent.

"What's the plan?" Vincent said.

"We should counter-attack from different directions at the same time. He will have difficulty tracking us both," Falric said.

"Just give me the signal." Vincent dropped into a ready stance and started circling around. The hooded wizard stopped laughing and looked at them. He raised his staff and brought it down upon the ground. The earth beneath his staff rose up, a wave of rock and stone lurching from the ground and barrelling towards them.

"Get down!" Falric shouted, and he threw his hands up in response. The rolling wall of earth slowed as it approached them and paused in mid-air.

"Move!" Falric cried out. Vincent dragged Alrion away and Falric dived to the opposite side. Falric managed to hold onto his spell just long enough for them to get clear of the main thrust. The ground suddenly fell everywhere all at once and Alrion felt like he was being buried alive.

After a few moments, Alrion realised he was holding his breath. He breathed in and got air, which surprised him. He struggled up and found that only a light layer of rock and soil had settled over him. His father was more covered, so Alrion dragged him out. Vincent coughed and sat up, looking over at Falric.

"Don't worry, I'm alright." Falric dusted himself off.

"That was insane." Alrion looked around. The clearing was like a war zone.

"Horses are gone," Vincent said, looking out.

"So are our travelling companions. Do you think they were buried?" Alrion said.

"Not a chance," Falric said.

"I think this was a setup. They were waiting for us, then the wizard came. They knew what to look for." Vincent shook his head and retrieved his sword, sheathing it.

"That sounds fair. What can you tell us about that wizard?" Alrion said.

"I don't know who he is. From his dress and manner, you would think he was touched by the Blight. Yet I didn't notice the taint in his Spark."

"Then where did he come from?" Alrion said.

"I'm not sure. But he was clearly after us, and almost succeeded," Falric said.

"Do you think you can find him again? Or be more prepared next time?" Vincent said.

"We'll have to be more cautious. But no, I don't have a way of tracking him. Until we find out more, or manage to capture his staff, we won't have a way of locating him." Falric sighed. "Battle and tracking are not my specialty I'm afraid."

"What did you mean about his Spark?" Alrion said.

"Remember how I mentioned that when you are tainted by the Blight it taints your Spark as well? Other wizards can sense that taint when you use your Spark. It has a strange resonance to it, which you will understand when you notice it. I assumed that due to the attack by the Blighters, the dark dress and dark crystal on his staff that he was tainted. But his magic had none of the telltale signs," Falric said.

"Perhaps you were wrong, and he is just a rogue wizard?" Vincent said.

"Possibly. But it's too coincidental that we were forced out of the tunnel by Blighters and into the forest where he was waiting."

"True, it does seem like we are being tracked," Vincent said.

"How are they doing that?" Alrion said.

"I'm not sure, but I'll think about it. But one thing I know for certain, we need to modify our appearance. No matter how they tracked us to this forest, they were able to confirm our presence by our clothing. We need to be more careful. Perhaps what your grandfather said in his letter is to be taken more literally," Falric said.

"What did he say?" Alrion said.

Finally, he's mentioning something specific about my grandfather.

"In his letter to me, he referred to the Hidden Wizard as being the one to destroy the Blight. I thought he was being metaphorical, or referring to the fact that you had been hidden in your upbringing. But perhaps he also meant it more literally. That you need to be hidden to achieve your mission."

"You could definitely interpret it like that. I just don't know," Alrion said.

"Either way, it's good advice. Is there a way we can disguise ourselves with magic?" Vincent said.

"Not a good way, and it will be difficult to hide that from other wizards. These particular cloaks are also protected from altering. We will just need to do it the old-fashioned way and get some new clothing from the next place we visit."

"Fine. Let's see what we can salvage and get out of this damned forest." Vincent waved his arms in frustration. Alrion understood the feeling. It had been such a frustrating leg of their journey. The slow approach, and the creepy trees and whispers. The additional slow-down of the travellers, the ambush, and the loss of their horses just added to it.

What a terrible day. I'll be glad to put it behind me.

"I can't wait to be out of here," Alrion said.

"Truer words were never spoken," Falric said. They picked through the debris in the clearing, claiming whatever food and supplies they could find. Alrion dug through his pockets, to see if he had left anything. But he found something he wasn't expecting. He removed it from his pocket and looked at it.

It was a book or journal. Small in size, with a blue leather cover, and blank pages inside. He didn't remember it at all.

"What do you have there?" Falric said.

"I'm not sure, I don't remember where I found it, or how it came into my possession."

"I recognise that. You would have taken it from the supply building," Falric said. Alrion thought back and a realisation dawned on him.

The magical artifact! I never even looked at it.

"You're right. The memory is coming back now, why was that room in the dark?"

"Your grandfather believed that magical artifacts were not as simple as they looked. That they could influence who used them and when. So, he bought into the idea completely and instituted a system whereby each new wizard selects his own artifact to take with him. The idea behind the dark room was to increase the chances of the wizard selecting the right artifact, by senses other than sight."

"Really? That's interesting. I do remember this one feeling different to the rest, it was warm to the touch."

"It must have been reacting to your Spark. That's a good sign."

"What is it?"

"That will be revealed in time. It looks like a magical notebook to me." Falric had a wry smile.

"Did you see that?" Vincent pointed at Falric.

"Yes, I believe you would call that a textbook wizard answer," Alrion said.

"Good, you're learning," Vincent said. Alrion couldn't help cracking a smile himself. It was nice to break the tension of what had just happened.

"Well, I think we should get a move on. The sooner we leave this place the better," Falric said.

"Do you think he will come back?" Alrion said.

"The wizard? I doubt it. I feel like this was a show of power, and a test of sorts."

"Some test. I don't want to see the final exam," Vincent muttered.

"I must clarify that we don't do tests like that at the academy," Falric said as they walked.

"I had assumed not, but I'm glad you clarified that." Alrion could still feel the adrenalin pumping through him, although he tried to relax as they walked.

I can't believe I was useless again. I can't seem to do anything right.

He had screwed up back in the mountain path and was rescued in the forest. Rationally he knew that everything was fine and that he had survived. But he just felt like he wasn't useful at all.

I'm going to have to fix that.

It was still quite dark as they set out, being so early in the morning. It made the walk seem longer than it was. The trees continued their relentless rhythmic swaying, and the just-inaudible whispers persisted. Thankfully, though, they didn't seem to address Alrion any longer.

I wonder if that wizard was playing tricks on me, Alrion thought. But a worse thing than that came to mind.

If that's true, then the wizard already knows who I am.

He couldn't explain why that was so chilling, but Alrion got the shivers at the idea. He shoved the thought away and focused again on walking. Hours passed, without any breaks.

"We can't afford to waste any more time in the forest," Vincent explained. Falric was in agreement and Alrion could see why. He told his stomach to be quiet and kept walking. Finally, he saw a change in the mist. For so long it had hung before them, obscuring the path. But now it seemed to be thinning.

"Are we almost out?" Alrion said.

"I think so. Did you notice the mist?" Vincent said.

"Yes, that was it. Although I'm not sure when it changed."

"Not that long ago, it was a fairly quick transition. What do you say Falric?"

"We should be out within minutes if it's like this," Falric said.

"Good." Vincent increased his walking pace. Alrion matched it, keen to see the sun again. It hadn't even been that long, but he had never been in such a strange place before either. Each step granted him additional strength and optimism, and he could see further and further ahead. Finally, he could see a space outside the forest and almost ran towards it.

"This is it," Vincent said as they emerged from the path.

They stepped onto a dusty track, in a deserted area. There were patches of brush and shrubs but no structures or any trees. The vast openness seemed like an incredible contrast after the narrow paths and constricting nature of the forest.

"I feel like I can breathe again," Alrion said.

"It's no wonder people avoid going through that, but we made good time. All things considered," Vincent said.

"Very good time, but too eventful for my liking," Falric said.

"No arguments about that. I'm all for less excitement," Vincent said, and Alrion nodded too.

"How far to the next town? That's where we are going right?" he said.

"It's pretty close, maybe an hour or two? I think we should push through and stop there. It's called Altarbright," Vincent said.

"That's an interesting name, why is it called that?" Alrion said.

"I'll let the good wizard fill you in." Vincent deferred to Falric, who seemed excited at the opportunity. He drew himself up and began his explanation.

"It's actually a very simple name. Before this town became such an important trading hub, it was a sacred place where an ancient people worshipped a goddess in the lake. They created a large altar to worship her, and it was made from a bright gold that was polished daily to maintain its shine. On a still day, you could see the reflection of the altar in the water, and the people believed it was the goddess giving her approval," Falric said.

"Is it still there? The altar?" Alrion said.

"No, it was stolen many years ago. A giant gold altar is just too tempting for thieves. But the name stuck, so we still call it Altarbright."

"That's a shame." Alrion sighed deeply.

A giant gold altar is just the kind of thing I hoped to see.

"Yes, it is. But you can see where it used to stand."

"So, it's a big town?" Alrion said.

"Yes, very big. Avaria has grown from strength to strength. As much as those two back in the forest were hiding something, they were right about what happened when Granthion cleansed the Blight from here. Trade from other countries exploded and Altarbright was the prime spot to conduct trade. The lake is a natural border to some of our neighbours," Falric said.

"Are we crossing the lake?" Alrion perked up again.

"Yes."

"Are we leaving Avaria?" Vincent said.

"No, but we can use the lake as a shortcut." Falric revealed no more. As they walked on Alrion started to see signs of something in the distance. They came upon a crossroads and noticed that many people were streaming in towards the town in the distance, but from other directions.

"I guess nobody comes the way we did," Alrion said.

"For good reason." Vincent laughed. Alrion looked over at the others on the road ahead. There were some people walking, others on horses, and some driving coaches or wagons, multiple horses pulling them along.

"Are they all merchants?" he said.

"Not all but many. Some are just travellers, others are people looking for a better life in a bigger town," Falric said.

"Why would life be better here?"

"A lot of money flows through Altarbright. That means opportunities to make a living, both honestly and not," Vincent said.

I wonder if that thief will be there, Alrion thought, remembering how his ring had been stolen at Carford.

"Wow, this is incredible. I can barely recognise the place," Vincent said. Alrion looked up and was impressed. Huge stone gates rose up before them, with a wall going all the way around the perimeter. Alrion could see lots of large buildings, with a few incredibly tall towers further back.

"Are they wizard towers?"

"No, I believe they are for the officials that overlook the port," Falric said.

"Now this is going to be an adventure," Vincent said, taking in the town.

I couldn't agree more, thought Alrion, excited at the possibilities.

18

REGROUPING

Entering Altarbright reminded Alrion of Carford, only everything was twice as big. The road was twice as wide, the gates twice as tall and twice as many people flowed through. There were a large number of guards milling around, and even guard posts at each end of the gate. People were being let through, but larger vehicles were being stopped for inspections.

"Why are they stopping them?" Alrion said as a nearby wagon was halted.

"They are looking for smuggled goods I suspect." Vincent watched the guard interrogate the travellers and examine the wagon before continuing, "As this is a key entry point into Avaria they are very wary of what comes in and out. This looks much stricter, though."

"Since Avaria has been free of the Blight, officials have been trying to keep it that way," Falric said.

"It can't be that free of the Blight, considering what we ran into yesterday," Alrion said.

"And that's an important lesson," Falric said. Alrion mulled it over as they continued into the town. Unlike the main street that dominated the other places they had visited, Altarbright was a sprawling place with dozens of streets. Even his father was wide-eyed, trying to take in the enormity of it.

"I can see the looks on your faces. You can tell the town is bursting at the seams." Falric chuckled. Once they reached the first crossroad, Vincent stopped.

"The first thing we should do is resupply," he said.

"Agreed," Falric said. "I know a good place."

"Lead the way." Vincent stepped back and gave the wizard a fake bow. Falric nodded graciously and took the lead. He turned left and the other two followed close behind. They walked along another busy street, then turned abruptly into an alley.

"I don't like the look of this," Vincent said.

"You're not supposed to," Falric said. Vincent said no more and put his hand on his sword hilt. Halfway down the alley, they stopped before a door and Falric knocked three times. The door opened, and he stepped through. Vincent ushered Alrion through and entered last.

The interior of the building was quite spacious. They were in a shop of some kind, which was stocked with just about everything and anything. There were racks of clothes, supplies, equipment, and herbs.

"Who runs this place?" Vincent said.

"It's a store run by the wizards. Seeing as how Altarbright is such a hub, there's value in us having a presence here." Falric walked down one of the aisles, running his hand over the goods.

"I see, looks well-stocked."

"We take pride in it. Although I admit it is somewhat easier to do here considering the amount of trade goods that flow through this town." Falric stopped his walk and started to look around in earnest.

"Is there anyone else here?" Alrion said as he wandered.

"No, there's nobody tending the place right now. From time to time wizards get an assignment here, but generally, it is maintained on an as-needed basis by those who use it." Falric picked up a leather-bound book and leafed through it.

"Nobody has been here for a few months." He put the book back down.

"Don't suppose you got horses back here?" Vincent said.

"No, I'm afraid we don't. But we should be fine from here on. I wouldn't want to take them on the boat anyway."

"Fair enough." Vincent started browsing the available clothing. "Is this all normal stuff?"

"Yes, none of it is magical. We need to blend in sometimes," Falric said.

"Now seems like a good time."

"That's the idea."

"Pick yourself something from here," Vincent said to Alrion. The young wizard looked through the rack and selected a green cloak with a hood. It was quite plain, save for a jewelled brooch, and stretched down past his hips when he tried it on.

"The fit looks alright, and you can pull over the hood as required." Vincent checked Alrion's shoulders and pulled the hood over.

"How do I look?" Alrion said.

"Like a young merchant, with something to hide." Falric pushed the hood back, "Now, I think that's appropriate. You next."

Vincent grabbed something similar, in a dark-navy colour. Falric found a plain light-brown cloak that he could wear.

"Isn't that too close to your robe?" Vincent said.

"Not at all. Trust me, an old man like myself is more likely to insulate himself from the cold wind," Falric said. Vincent laughed.

"I'll see what supplies I can rustle up." He walked through the room and disappeared into the back area.

"So, we leave our robes here?" Alrion said.

"Yes, someone will either use them or return them to the academy." Falric returned his robe to one of the racks. Alrion took a closer look and noticed that it was different to his own. It was white inside and had a variety of colours along the trim.

"Is this special?" he asked Falric.

"Yes, only the head wizard wears that one." Falric reached out and straightened up the robe on the rack. His hand trembled slightly.

"Don't you feel odd taking it off?"

"Yes, but wearing it this far was an indulgence. I should have removed it back at the academy."

"I see. It's a new time for us all."

"It sure is." Falric noticed Vincent waiting. "Are we ready?"

"Yes, let's head out." Vincent handed out a leather pack to both Alrion and Falric. "There are a few essentials within to keep us going."

Alrion rummaged through and found some food and some blankets. He closed the pack back up, slung it over his shoulder and left the room.

"Where to next?" he said.

"We need to go to the docks and book passage on a boat," Falric said.

"Sure." Alrion followed along. They returned to the main road from the alley and followed the flow of people towards the docks.

"Do you mind if I wander around and meet you there? It looks like if I just follow this group I can find my way," Alrion said as they walked. Falric looked at Vincent.

"I suppose so. There's not much of interest there for you anyway. If you lose your way, return to the wizard store."

"Yes, good idea. Knock three times and the door will respond to you," Falric said.

"Don't get into any trouble, we've had enough already." Vincent gave Alrion a stern look.

"Promise. I just want an opportunity to explore a bit while we are here."

"You have one hour," Vincent said.

"Done," Alrion said. He diverted to turn right at the next crossroads.

"I wonder what got into him?" Falric said.

Alrion didn't hear his father's response, he was already walking fast in a different direction. He had flirted with the idea of exploring the town, but it had suddenly become an urgent idea once he had spotted her.

He tried to blend into the crowd as he walked, to not let her catch on. He had recognised the woman instantly, even though he hadn't seen her since Carford.

Let's see what you have to say for yourself, Alrion thought as he closed in. She was wearing the same clothes and appeared to be walking casually down the road in no hurry. Not once did she look back, so Alrion felt like he could get closer. As he started to approach her, she darted into a side street.

Alrion quickly ran after her. He couldn't see her once he turned the corner, but there were multiple cross alleys, so he kept running until he could look to see where she went. Once he reached the first set, he slowed and whirled around to look at the other directions. But he felt a presence behind him.

"Hello again," she said. Alrion turned fully to face her.

"That was my line."

"Why? Because you thought you had snuck up on me?" She gave him a dismissive laugh. Alrion's cheeks started reddening.

"I did."

"No, I let you see me and you followed me here." She gestured at the dark street they were in. "If I was up to no good, you would be in real trouble. Consider this a free lesson."

"What about stealing? Doesn't that count as up to no good?"

"No, that's just a habit. And pretty fun. But I'm glad I did it because once I saw what it was, you piqued my interest." She winked at him.

"What do you mean?"

"Well, you were carrying a magic ring. Then looking closer at you, I started to see an interesting picture emerging. An old wizard, a young man presumably also a wizard, and a strange man accompanying them both. Probably a mercenary."

"You think you know a lot."

"I do know a lot, Alrion." She stretched his name out and laughed as she watched his reaction. "Don't act so surprised that I knew your name, I've been paying attention."

"What's your name then?" Alrion struggled to get things back on even terms, but clearly this woman was a step ahead of him.

At least I can learn her name. If she'll even tell the truth.

"Lara."

"Well, Lara, if you have been paying attention then maybe you would have noticed that the strange man accompanying us is my father, and he's also a blacksmith, not a mercenary."

"So cute of you to provide me with all that information, but I don't buy that. I've never seen a blacksmith with such slim arms. They are usually thick as tree trunks." Lara demonstrated with her hands.

"I don't even know why we are arguing about this. What are you after?"

"I'm just after something interesting to do. And following your little group has been just the distraction I was looking for. My you've had some adventures already."

"You've been following us? The whole time?"

I can't believe it. What would make someone do that? And how could we not have noticed?

"Of course! How else did you think I made it here, just as you arrived?" Lara looked to be enjoying Alrion's reaction.

"I still don't get it. Do you want to rob us again? Following us to look for a bigger score?" Alrion said, the frustration showing in his voice.

"I thieve, but I'm not a thief. There's a difference. There's not a lot of value in things, but once you realise they can be taken so effortlessly you get a different perspective. Experiences are worth something, and following you all has been quite the experience already." Lara looked quite satisfied. It just infuriated Alrion more.

"Fine, why don't you hand over my ring then if you don't see the value in it?"

"Oh, but you clearly do, so I'll hold onto it for now. I'm glad we could have this chat, Alrion, but we both need to be places." Lara didn't wait for a response, but spun around and sprinted away.

"Wait!" Alrion called out, but she paid no attention. He saw an old crate against the alley wall and lashed out at it. Without really thinking he shoved the crate with extreme force, hurtling it on a collision course with Lara.

She turned in response to the sound, and once she noticed the crate she bent down, vaulted off the ground and landed on it as it travelled, riding it for a few seconds before jumping off and continuing on her way. She turned and gave Alrion a little wave before she disappeared around the corner.

She's gone.

He didn't try to follow but instead inspected his hands, as if expecting to see something on them.

What just happened there? How did I lash out so quickly? And what if I'd hurt her or someone else?

He had just been given a lesson on the value of control. Nothing serious had come of it, but he had thrown that crate with great speed and little thought. He was a little scared of what he was capable of, even after such little training.

"Maybe because of such little training," Alrion said to himself. Yes, he had to watch himself and judge his reactions. He had the power to harm already, and without a doubt, his power would grow and grow. He walked away, trying to find his way back to the main streets. It wouldn't look good if he couldn't find his father and Falric at the docks.

He took a few wrong turns but found his way back to the main road that he recognised eventually. Following it returned him to where they originally parted ways. From there it was easy enough to let the crowds lead him to the docks. Alrion didn't look at too much as he went, he was trying to solve the puzzle around Lara.

Who is she?

She was always dressed in plain clothes, which were not feminine at all. She was clearly an adept thief, as she had stolen his ring without any trouble at all. He panicked as he felt through his pockets again. But nothing else was missing.

That's a relief. How embarrassing would it be to lose something again, he thought. If what she said was true, she had been following them since that first encounter. He didn't exactly trust her, but there had to be some truth to what she was saying. They were both here, and she knew his name. She was up to something. He started to wonder if she was somehow connected to the mysterious wizard in black who had attacked them.

"Now there's a man deep in thought," Vincent said. Alrion looked up and noticed that he had arrived at the docks. Vincent and Falric were standing by the side of the road, waiting.

"Oh, I'm here already," Alrion said.

"Here already? You almost made us start looking." Vincent glared at Alrion.

"Well, I lost my way, but here I am."

"We've booked passage on a ferry that leaves soon. It will be travelling overnight to our destination," Falric said.

"Where are we going?"

"We'll fill you in somewhere more private," Vincent said.

"Sure."

"Let's get settled in." Falric gestured to a vessel ahead. At the end of the dock was a huge wooden boat, with a large cabin area and massive deck. There were people already stepping onto the boat, and many crowding around up top.

"We're not riding outside, are we?" Alrion said.

"No, we paid for a cabin," Falric said.

"That's a relief, thanks for that."

"It's not for you, it's for me. You'll understand when you get to my age," Falric said. Vincent laughed but Alrion didn't get it. He looked up at the ferry.

"Does it have a name?"

"Sure does, look there on the side." Vincent pointed it out.

"*The Glider.* Sounds promising. I've never been on the water before."

"First trip of many. Let's go," Falric said. Vincent went first and showed their tickets to the deckhand. Falric and Alrion followed. As they boarded, Alrion felt the ferry move gently beneath their feet. The first time the ground underneath him had been so unsteady. It was a strange feeling, as it completely mirrored how he felt. After his encounter with Lara, he felt like he was no longer grounded, and that everything could shift again in an instant.

19

BOATING ACCIDENT

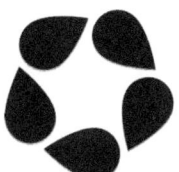

They pushed through the growing crowds and entered the main cabin of the ferry. In front of them was a well-worn stairwell. They walked down the stairs carefully, emerging into a long corridor at the bottom. There were rooms along the corridor, each one marked with a number.

"We are room number four," the wizard said. It was the second door on the right. Vincent entered first and Falric and Alrion followed.

"Wow, this is tiny," Alrion said. The room had a set of two wooden bunk beds against one wall, another tiny wooden bed on the floor, and a small window at the end of the room.

"Space is at a premium, you probably don't want to know how much this room cost us," Vincent said.

"You two can take the bunks, I'll take the floor," Falric said.

"Sure. Top or bottom, Alrion?" Vincent gestured to the bunk beds.

"I'll take the top." Alrion threw his bag up there.

"Why don't you two investigate the ship, I'll mind our things." Falric lay back on his bed and made himself comfortable.

"Don't get too relaxed there," Vincent said with a chuckle and held the door open for Alrion. They left the room, and returned to the stairs, walking all the way back up to the deck.

"Why are we going overnight?" Alrion said.

"They only do two runs a day, one first thing in the morning and one in the early evening. The reason for that is this ferry has a few possible stops, but the end point is a long trip. It's a ten- to twelve-hour trip."

"All on the same lake?"

"Yes, it's a huge one. That's why the ferry takes the long way around, it's a horrendously long trip either way, so they have more stops to service more passengers."

"Makes sense. Where are all these people going?" Alrion pointed at the surging crowds on the deck of the ferry.

"I'd say they are going all the way. To Dendra."

"Dendra?"

"Yes, it's our closest ally country and main trading partner."

"Another country. That's pretty cool."

"Yes, there's a whole world out there. Avaria is just a small part of it."

"Do you think I'll see it all?"

"Definitely. I'm not sure where this trip will take us, but as a wizard, you will travel the world and meet a lot of interesting people."

"Did you travel a lot with grandfather?"

"No, not much at all. I think that it was too dangerous to take me. So, he alternated between staying with me, and leaving me behind. He was also establishing the academy."

"Oh, so you travelled later?"

"Yes, by myself. I roamed a lot after he passed," Vincent said. Alrion didn't know what to say. He was interested in learning more about his father's travels, but noticed that it was an awkward topic. So, he let it go. As he was thinking about what to say next he heard a giant horn sounding.

"What's that?"

"That's the signal. We're off," Vincent said. They pushed through the crowd until they could get closer to the edge of the ferry. Alrion could feel the movement and also see their passage through the water.

"Hang on, what's moving the boat?"

"They have an engine room at the bottom," Vincent said.

"Engine? How does that work?"

"Not sure. It's a closely guarded secret. I suspect there's some magic involved. Probably a wizard set it up, and there are some specially trained people who keep it running."

"Wow."

"It's pretty remarkable. Although the last time I rode it was before you were born, and they had the option for passengers to be backup rowers." Vincent chuckled.

"That wouldn't be fun." Alrion couldn't imagine how much effort would be required to row a boat of this size.

"It was a risk some took, as it greatly reduced the ticket price. But I don't think it is an option anymore. The progress that has been made in the last twenty years or so has been tremendous. It's pretty exciting."

"Sure is. I'll have to find out how this ferry works."

"You'll find out in time, I have no doubt about that," Vincent said. They watched the town of Altarbright slowly fade from view, as they went deeper and deeper into the dark night.

"Not much left to see here, let's head below," Vincent said. Alrion followed, and they descended the stairs to return to their cabin. Falric was lying in his bed, soundly asleep.

"Now there's a reliable security guard," Vincent said.

"I heard that," Falric remarked, keeping his eyes closed.

"At least he noticed us come in," Alrion said, playing along. Falric snorted.

"Hey, Falric, my father said that this ferry runs on magical engines. Do you know how they work?"

"I do indeed."

"You'll have to explain later. But I was thinking, if they're magical and wizards were involved setting them up, then why did you say that the cabin was so expensive? Wouldn't there be a wizard rate?" Alrion said. Falric opened his eyes and sat up.

"You're a quick one. They don't need us anymore. They have their own specialists who maintain the engines, so we don't get preferential treatment. I could have twisted their arm, but we want to go unnoticed, so I just paid."

"Oh, I see."

Another situation where being a wizard doesn't make a difference.

"The world owes us a lot, but they don't sit around being respectful. They move on, so we have to keep earning their trust and respect. Some places are easier than others," Falric said.

"I thought that it was obvious that wizards would be well-respected and listened to. I guess that's not the case."

"No, it is not. Your grandfather earned us a place of favour for sure, but I have not been able to maintain our standing I'm afraid. The world is moving on, and taking our contributions for granted." Falric sighed.

"Maybe I can change that."

"I am hoping so," Falric said with a smile. "How're things up top?"

"Absolutely bursting at the seams, makes this room seem spacious," Vincent said.

"Well, at least we got our money's worth. We are the first stop. It's a little town called Paperton."

"I don't know it." Vincent had a puzzled expression on his face.

At least we're both new to this area, I'm sick of being the only one who doesn't know anything.

"Good. I hope those who are after us don't know it either. We should eat and have an early night. They will be dropping us off at some ungodly hour in the morning." Falric shook his head.

"Sounds like fun," Alrion said. "I take it we won't be able to look at any more spells."

"Not tonight, but soon. We can't have you being a one-trick pony," Falric said. Vincent laughed and grabbed his bag. Alrion did the same and they ate a simple meal.

Alrion clambered up onto the top bunk and lay still listening to the sounds. A lot of murmuring filtered down from the deck above him, but things were fairly quiet down below. He heard a faint hum coming from somewhere and decided it had to be something to do with the engine driving the ferry. The rippling of the water as they pushed through was consistent and calming. Despite his excitement and the earliness of the night, he found sleep was not far away.

Alrion awoke, unsure of the reason. He tried to shake the fog from his head and looked around the room, letting his eyes adjust to the dark. Falric was not in his bed. He clambered down from the bunk and looked for his father. He, too, was gone. Alrion ran across the room but stopped before leaving. He thought he had heard something. He listened carefully, and a terrifying sound echoed through the ferry. Screaming.

Alrion burst through the door and scrambled up the staircase.

Something is going on, and I bet we're involved. I have to see what I can do.

It was no coincidence that he had been left alone in what could be classed as relative safety. But he couldn't sit around waiting for whatever it was to be over, he had to investigate.

He confirmed his suspicions as soon as he reached the deck. The space in front of him was completely bare. He looked over and saw throngs of people around the edge of the boat. But the centre of the main deck was cleared. Only as he looked closer did he notice some bodies on the ground. He searched the crowds and saw Falric and his father at the edge of the group of people. Everyone was focused on a single man, stumbling through the empty space on the deck. He was the one screaming.

Alrion couldn't see what was happening clearly, so carefully made his way over to join his father.

"What's going on?"

"We are under attack. It's a Shade." Vincent's voice was tight and he didn't even look at Alrion.

"A Shade?"

"Yes, it's a rare and terrible creature of the Blight. It is perfectly black and blends in perfectly with darkness. It is practically invisible at night."

"So, it's there somewhere?" Alrion started looking for it.

Great, so we find some invisible death monster while we're on a boat.

"Yes, it's holding that poor man who is screaming," Falric said.

"What do we do?"

"We have to kill it or drive it away. Chances are that it is here for us," Falric said.

"How do we kill it? I won't be able to sleep until I know this thing isn't waiting to sneak up on us," Vincent said.

"Only magic can kill it. Directly or indirectly. Well-made equipment can damage it, but it must be magically enhanced to deliver a killing blow. You have to remove or destroy the heart."

"It's got a heart?" Alrion said.

"It was originally a person. Just one that was twisted by the Blight. Their heart absorbs the essence of the Blight and becomes a black stone. As long as it remains intact, the Shade will reform overnight. No matter what damage you do to the rest of the Shade."

"Sounds fun," Vincent said.

"What do I do?" Alrion asked.

"You stay back and let us handle this. No debate."

"Got it," Alrion said. He knew the tone of his father's voice, the one when he was laying down the law. Vincent didn't use it often, but he would not back down once he did. Alrion could sense the terror in the crowd, and the tension felt by Falric and his father. So, he decided to stay out of the way. For now.

"Is there a way you can make it visible?" Vincent said.

"It's difficult out here in the open. I know of a way that will definitely work, but it's a last resort."

"Alright, keep that in your pocket then. I'll try and bait it, and you do your thing," Vincent said. He drew his sword and stepped out from the crowd. Falric followed closely behind.

"Why does it still have that man?" Vincent asked as they crept forward.

"Not sure, I think they use the screams of the victim to terrify and distract," Falric said.

"Lovely." Vincent crept forward. The screaming man turned towards him. The poor man screamed even louder for help.

"I guess that means we've been spotted," Vincent said. Falric didn't reply. Vincent took care in stepping forward. Alrion edged closer too, trying to get a better look. He noticed that something was poking through the man's stomach.

"I think I can see where it's holding him," Vincent said. Alrion held his tongue, he didn't want them to know how close he was.

"Good, but I'm not sure how much we can do for him," Falric said. Vincent stepped closer again.

"He wants your boy!" the man squealed before screaming in pain once again. Vincent reacted swiftly, swinging his sword towards the man. Whatever was holding him disengaged and let the man fall to the ground.

"Take him away from here," Vincent yelled to a person nearby, who just stared at him in horror.

"Now we can't see it," Vincent said. He swung his sword out and it collided with something and was pushed back.

"It's here. Not sure how I'm going to fight blind!"

"Give me a minute," Falric said. Vincent walked in a circle, running through a sword style that sliced the air in front of him.

It's hanging back, but where, Alrion thought.

"You need to draw it in," Falric said. Vincent stopped moving and closed his eyes. He looked like he was trying another way to discover the Shade.

It's hopeless. There's too much noise here, and I can't see anything. He needs help.

"C'mon Shade, show me your worst!" Vincent called out. He

flinched with what had to be a stabbing pain and reflexively grabbed with his left hand. He was holding onto something.

"To my left, I've got a hold on it!" Vincent yelled. Falric opened his hand and small fingers of flame shot out, arcing through the air. They hit the Shade and started to burn. Vincent waited a moment and then swung his sword at the burning shape. He connected with something, and it pulled away from him sharply.

I can see it now. The fire is illuminating it.

"That worked." Vincent maintained a defensive stance.

"Yes, but it's quite risky. They burn incredibly easily and with great intensity. Not only is it a danger to everyone here, but it doesn't actually damage the Shade at all," Falric said.

Alrion realised the danger of what Falric had said as he watched the Shade transform into the burning silhouette of a man. The flames leaped onto the deck, causing it to catch fire as well.

"This has to end fast." Vincent charged forward.

He has to hurry. The ferry will burn up. What can I do?

Vincent stepped forward and swung at one of the Shade's arms. He connected and hit some resistance, but managed to continue his momentum and slice through.

Vincent tried to reel in his attack and redirect it as the Shade reached for him with its other arm. This time it didn't try and pierce him, but instead smashed him in the same place with what felt like an open palm. Vincent fell down, the wind knocked out of him. He dropped his sword and swore with pain.

The Shade moved forward to attack again.

Now's my chance! Alrion tried not to think too much, and remembered how he had instinctively thrown force at Lara. But it wasn't coming easily. He couldn't waste any more time, his father was struggling to stand up.

Stay away from him! Like that, the spell flowed through him. The Shade was shoved back, and it almost lost its footing. The flames continued to burn as if nothing had happened. The creature cocked its head, staring in Alrion's direction.

"What are you doing?" Vincent yelled at Alrion. He managed to prop himself up, but looked unsteady. Alrion could see the anger in his father's eyes. And also fear.

"Get up, and get back to it. They're adept at fighting magic, so additional attacks will be less effective," Falric said. Vincent bent down and retrieved his sword.

"At least that worked." He pointed at the severed arm, still burning on the deck. "Can you put it out?"

"I have an idea," Falric said. The flames slowly dissipated from the burning limb, and started collecting in the palm of his hand. He compacted them into a ball and hurled it at the Shade. It didn't even try to dodge the attack and was knocked back again. The flames already on it flared up briefly then went back to their prior state.

"Tough bugger," Vincent said.

"You have to go for the heart, or this will drag on forever!" Falric threw another wave of force at the Shade, unsteadying it. But it seemed to be less effective than Alrion's attack.

It's already adapting to our spells. I'll wait in the wings for now.

"Go for the heart? Easier said than done," Vincent muttered. He dashed in again, aiming a slashing strike at the Shade's other arm. But the Shade had anticipated this and jumped back at the same time. As Vincent's strike fell short, the Shade reached out and grabbed the blade, tipping Vincent off-balance.

Stumbling, Vincent managed to pull out a knife from his belt and hurl it at the Shade's chest. The creature was caught by surprise and had no counter. The blade embedded itself in the Shade's chest. Right where its heart should be. The Shade stopped moving and tried to reach the blade with its arm.

I can't believe he did it. But it's not dead yet. It mustn't have pierced through. Maybe I can help it along?

"Falric!" Vincent yelled. Falric responded by throwing a wave of force at the knife, embedding it to the hilt. The Shade stumbled back a few steps. Vincent dropped his sword and ran towards it. It was trying to reach the blade and pull it out.

Vincent reached out with his right hand and pushed forcefully against the tip of the blade handle, tumbling over in the effort. The knife drove in slightly more and the Shade fell backward. It toppled towards the edge of the ferry, boosted by an extra force wave from Falric. The Shade clawed at the ground, trying to stop itself.

"Just die, you monster!" Alrion yelled. Without thinking he unleashed a powerful wave of force. The Shade's tenuous hold failed, and it disappeared over the edge and into the water with a sizzling hiss.

20

UNCHARTED TERRAIN

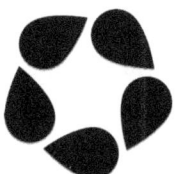

V incent stood up and surveyed the damage. He traced his hand over a giant scorch mark in the deck where the Shade had tried to hang on, and it continued over the edge of the ferry. Flames licked the deck and other areas, flowing through the gaps in the flooring caused by the Shade.

"Do you think it's dead now?" Vincent peered over the edge of the ferry.

"Depends if you destroyed the heart. I don't suppose that was a magic blade?" Falric said.

"I think it might have been. I bought it from Brangtur."

"The city of blacksmiths? There are those there that know the secrets of magical metalworking, so there's a chance. If you bought wisely, that is."

"So, it might be dead?" Alrion said.

"Might be, can't say for sure. We are safe for now. But the ferry has sustained serious damage." Falric walked around, extinguishing flames where he could.

"I can't believe the Shade did so much damage. Some of these areas look like molten metal burned through." Vincent stepped around them.

"The unique makeup of the Shade burns so much hotter, that's why I was hesitant to light it up. Battling creatures of the Blight is not my specialty. But we achieved our aim," Falric said. Alrion joined his father, and examined the wreckage caused by the Shade. He too looked over the edge, trying to see if the Shade was anywhere. Vincent yanked him back from the edge.

"You've done enough for one night. How about you explain what it is you think you were doing?" Vincent's voice was loud and angry.

"I'd also like an explanation before I turf the lot of you into the drink," a male voice said behind them.

"The captain, I presume?" Falric said.

"Yes. Start talking."

"We encountered a Shade, a rather vile and dangerous creature of the Blight. You should be thankful that we dispatched it." Falric adjusted his posture and stood up straighter.

"Oh, I should be thanking you for destroying half of my deck? I can't continue with this kind of damage, not without going ashore and assessing." The captain didn't seem like he was responding to Falric's attempt at authority. Alrion stifled a chuckle.

"You can thank us that you are still alive, and this ferry is not completely and utterly destroyed." Vincent turned his back on the captain and walked off. Alrion turned back to the water, staring out in search for the Shade.

It was here for me, no question. I'm out of my depth, Alrion thought. He looked over at his father, a newfound admiration building. He crossed the deck to talk to him.

"I'm sorry, but I couldn't idly stand by. Don't be too angry."

"I worry about you. And you made yourself known to the Shade. But, you did well. We should include you more in the future, so your involvement can be more planned. And you cannot scare me so badly. Deal?" Vincent held out his hand. Alrion shook it, and his father brought him in close and slapped him on the back.

"We should make ourselves scarce before the captain gets too many ideas," Vincent said.

How did you do that? I've never seen that side of you before," Alrion said.

"I've had some training, a long time ago. But you'll be surprised by the things you are capable of once you have a child of your own," Vincent said with a grim smile on his face.

Alrion headed downstairs to collect their things. The captain had decided to land at the nearest safe place on the shore and assess the boat for repairs during the day. Their group wanted to be ready to leave as soon as possible.

Just what was that? Alrion kept thinking over and over. It was different than the other encounters he had seen. As strange as they were, they made sense. People reduced to animals by the Blight and behaving as such. A wizard gone rogue, attacking them. Not your everyday occurrence, but they made sense in a way. But the Shade was something else entirely. He needed to know more about them.

I'll ask Falric when I get the chance. We might not be so lucky next time.

The ferry travelled much slower, as it diverted course. Alrion struggled up the steps with all the bags, and unceremoniously dumped them on the ground once he reached his father. Vincent gave Alrion a sideways glance, and picked up Falric's bag, handing it over to the wizard. He left his on the ground, but shifted its position with his boot. Alrion looked out over the water.

"I can't tell if we're moving."

"We're definitely moving, but it's a painful crawl. They don't travel this way often; the water is shallower and probably has more dangers," Vincent said.

"Another setback. I fear that we haven't managed to shake our pursuit at all." Falric furrowed his brow.

"Yes, clearly we are still being followed. Although it would have been easy to guess our intentions by following our route. Hopefully, now that we're stranded, we will get a chance to pass by unnoticed." Vincent looked over at Falric.

"Perhaps, that depends on where we end up," Falric said.

"How will we move on?" Alrion said.

"We will find the nearest town, then resupply and hopefully find some horses. I'd hate to have to walk the rest of the way." Falric looked pained just thinking about it.

"I guess we are taking the scenic route then," Alrion said. Vincent laughed.

"You could say that. I'm glad you can have a joke after the night we just had," he said.

"Just being philosophical."

"Good. Some perspective is always useful," Falric said. The sun was beginning to rise, and they caught their first glimpses of the shoreline. Ahead they could see a place to land. A section covered by small stones, which gently sloped up to grassy terrain.

"Could be worse," Vincent said. They watched in silence as the ferry closed the gap, and the crew steered it onto the shore. Vincent looked over at the side of the ferry and pointed out the damage.

"Now that's worse than I realised. That Shade sure tore the ferry up."

"I hope we've seen the last of that creature," Falric said.

"You need to explain Shades more, in case we come across them again," Alrion said.

"Of course. I will brief you on our way to the nearest town. To be honest I didn't expect to come across one on this journey, they are quite rare." Falric shook his head slowly and sighed. "There's been a lot of things I didn't expect, or was prepared for. But don't worry, I won't hold anything back."

"Thanks. That's all I can ask for."

"Be careful what you wish for," Vincent said. Alrion didn't reply. The crew steadied the ferry and adjusted the landing gear so that the passengers could walk down to the shore. Alrion stayed close to his father, and they inched along amongst the throng of people pushing and shoving to get off.

As they stepped onto dry land, the groups of people started to thin out. Some hung close to the boat, hovering around the captain and asking questions. Others started hiking off immediately. Vincent took the lead and walked with confidence, leading them through the throngs and further inland.

"This is a stroke of luck." Vincent pointed to a dirt track ahead.

It's barely there, and doesn't look heavily used, Alrion thought. He looked at his father and was about to speak, when Vincent interrupted.

"Look, I know it doesn't seem like much, but right now all we need is a route back to civilisation. And this is our ticket." Vincent looked behind them. "Others have figured this out too, let's get a move on." Without waiting for a response Vincent pressed ahead. Falric sighed and started to walk again. He appeared to be having a little difficulty. Alrion kept pace with Falric, not wanting the older wizard to strain unnecessarily.

"I appreciate you staying with me, lad. My joints aren't what they used to be. You wanted to hear about Shades didn't you?"

"Yes. Ideally before we encounter another one." Alrion laughed, trying to make a joke out of it. But there was an awkward tension hanging in the air.

Falric doesn't know when we will have another attack.

"As you were saying, now is a good time to begin. Shades are strange creatures, only really spotted in more recent times. I think the first reported and verified occurrence was around thirty years ago."

"What are they? I mean really."

"Shades are people, or at least were. As I mentioned before their bodies are different. They are stronger, more resilient, and retain more of their normal form. If you think of Blighters as being stage one of contamination, then Shades are stage two."

"More like stage ten," Vincent muttered.

"Well in terms of development and challenge, yes, it is a big step up. But I don't think there are any other stages between Blighters and Shades."

"Can Blighters become Shades?"

"No, but that was a logical conclusion to make. The answer is in something else. There are those called Tainted Ones, which we need to discuss."

"Tainted Ones?"

I've never heard of those either.

"Yes. Imagine a Blighter, except that they retain their mental faculties and can pass themselves off as a normal person. In most ways actually, they are still a person."

"They look and act like a person? What's different?"

"They have been tainted by the Blight but did not convert to the animalistic form that you have seen in the Blighters. In rare cases they can still infect others. But they have all the intelligence and cunning of a man, perhaps even more so."

"They still just sound like a normal person. Or at least a bad one."

"More or less. But there's one more thing that is crucial to understand. They are also connected to the Blight," Falric said. Alrion stopped walking instantly. Something about the statement seemed important.

"Connected to the Blight? What do you mean by that?"

"We believe that all creatures that are tainted by the Blight share a common communication method. It might be a shared mind or shared thoughts, but they can somehow communicate through their shared link to the Blight." Falric seemed to be distracted and looked up. Vincent was joining them. He motioned to Alrion to continue with his question.

"So, they can coordinate?" Alrion said.

"Exactly. And that's where Tainted Ones come into their own. As they have access to a normal mind, they can control and manipulate Blighters. The number and success do vary depending on the Tainted Ones doing the controlling," Falric said. Alrion let the idea work its way through. He spoke up again after he had time to process it.

"You think one of these Tainted Ones sent those Blighters after us in the mountain."

"Exactly."

"And those travellers we met in the forest might have been Tainted?"

"I think it is quite likely. They aren't common here in Avaria, but there's nothing stopping them from coming here."

"But that wizard wasn't a Tainted One?"

"No, I don't think so." Falric leaned against a nearby tree and waited. Alrion let the ideas sink in and settle.

I'm still missing something.

"What's this got to do with Shades?" he said.

"I wanted to take the opportunity to be as forthcoming as possible, now that we need to be completely vigilant for creatures of the Blight." Falric adjusted his position and let out a tired sigh. "But the connection is this: Tainted Ones can also become Shades. I don't know the exact process. It could be they are sought out and transformed by other Shades, or it could be they take on too much of the Blight. But we know of at least one Shade that used to be a Tainted One."

"Do the Shades remain intelligent?"

"Yes, very much so. But their bodies are changed significantly. They not only look perfectly black, they are transformed. Their body changes from flesh to something else. Strong like stone, but still soft. As I mentioned before their hearts crystallise and can regenerate their new body. It makes them incredibly difficult to kill."

"Do they communicate too?"

"They must do, but I haven't heard of any speaking with a person. Our theory is that they are so connected with the Blight that they can only communicate with other creatures of the Blight. Namely Tainted Ones and Blighters." Falric looked to Vincent, as if to invite him to comment. But Vincent remained silent.

I think I'm starting to understand this. But I wish I had been introduced to this sooner. It would have been much less of a shock than just encountering that Shade. I'll just confirm I have it right.

"If I'm understanding this correctly, then Blighters and Tainted Ones are two sides of the same stage of Blight taint. But the Shades are the next level."

"Exactly. Once set upon something, Shades are relentless. I hope we managed to kill the one that attacked us last night. But if we did not, at least we have severely damaged it and slowed it down."

"I hope it's gone for good. I don't want to face that thing again," Vincent said.

"I need to accept the fact that it's probably still after me but will be delayed. And that someone put it onto our path," Alrion said.

"I believe so. It could be the travellers we met, it could be the wizard that attacked us. It could even be someone else we have not yet encountered." Falric had an apologetic look on his face.

"But you don't know. That doesn't make me feel better," Alrion said.

"It's the truth. We know enough to take steps in our defence," Falric said.

"He's right, Son. We have to keep adjusting what we are doing and keep an eye out. The more we change our pattern, the more we can stay one step ahead."

"We're shipwrecked and on foot."

They clearly have the upper hand.

"But we are alive," Falric said.

"What do they want with me? I can't do anything yet?" Alrion's frustration was starting to come through.

I've done everything asked of me. I've played along. But disaster after disaster keeps happening. And there's no guarantee that I can even do anything remarkable.

"They must be fearful of what you may do, or what you might learn. It's a good sign that we are on the right path. I wish it were less dangerous, but at least we are following the right path." Falric gave Alrion a warm smile.

"I guess so," Alrion said.

That Shade terrified me. It was so different and alien. And looked relentless. Something about its inability to communicate made it even more terrifying. Like there was a force of evil on my trail. I'm not ready for this.

Alrion decided to not let himself dwell on it. He started to walk again and his father nodded, pushing ahead once more. Alrion took a greater look at the terrain they were walking through. It was lightly wooded, with a clear path to follow. As they had progressed, the path had improved.

"Strange area. Why is it deserted but also has a good path?" Alrion said.

"I would say people come down to the lake from a town nearby, but don't necessarily inhabit this area," Vincent said.

"That sounds reasonable," Alrion said. "Is Avaria a big country? In the grand scheme of things?"

"Avaria? No, it is quite a small place. But it rose in power and popularity after the cleansing of the Blight," Falric said.

"Did what my grandfather do prevent the Blight from existing here?"

"No, there's actually no protection here at all. It was all one event, a single cleanse. However, as a consequence of that, any Blighters or exposed Tainted Ones were dealt with swiftly and harshly. They stick out more, and people are more inclined to be proactive in removing them. So, it's a safer place overall."

"How bad is the Blight elsewhere?"

If what I've experienced is a safe place, I hate to think what the rest of the world are going through.

"There are some places where there are more people affected by the Blight than those not. Some even think that's because the origin of the Blight is nearby. But it varies. I must admit I haven't travelled a lot lately, so I'm not sure. Vincent, you haven't travelled in years, have you?"

"I haven't been outside Avaria since before Alrion was born."

"Yes, so we are as curious as you. But don't worry, we won't need to leave Avaria to complete your tasks. The Pool of Knowledge is hidden within its borders." Falric winked.

"Good. Are we close?" Alrion asked.

"Closer. I apologise but I want to keep our final destination under wraps a little longer. We've had a dark trail nipping at our heels all along, I won't feel safe sharing details like that until we can figure out how they are tracking us." Falric looked weary.

"As much as it frustrates me, I concur," Vincent said.

"As long as we're getting closer," Alrion said.

"Well, we're getting closer to something. I'd say that's a town ahead," Falric said. Alrion could see houses in the distance, puffs of smoke rising from their chimneys.

"That's a relief, I had wondered how long we were going to be wandering," Vincent said.

"You were wondering? I would have relished twice a walk at your age." Falric scoffed at Vincent.

"Next, you'll be telling us how in your day you had to drag yourself out of the womb and fix yourself a meal," Vincent said. Alrion laughed.

"No respect," Falric muttered, but the grin on his face was unmistakable.

21

THE BRIGHT CARAVAN

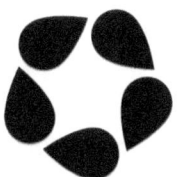

There was no sign proclaiming the name of the town, or any formal entrance. They just ended up within the town. Alrion looked around as they walked, spotting a tanner, blacksmith, and a healer.

"Falric, do local healers use magic?"

"Some do, although many do not."

"Is healing magic hard?"

"It can be, but the basics are not too bad. And incredibly useful. Are you interested in learning some?" Falric's eyes lit up.

"Yes, at least that's something I can work on outside of being attacked."

"Good point. If our trip continues the way it has been, we are going to rack up some injuries. I'll teach you a spell soon."

"Thanks." Alrion hadn't even considered the possibility before now, but seeing the healer's house, with its mystic symbols scrawled all over the walls had inspired him.

"I'm going to find out some information." Vincent pointed out a boy who was wandering through the town and intercepted him.

"Excuse me, can you please tell me where we are?"

"You don't know? This is Bowlern." The boy seemed less than impressed at Vincent's lack of knowledge.

"Bowlern? Don't know it. Our ferry landed nearby so we weren't planning on visiting."

"Wow, that's exciting. Nothing much happens here, it's pretty boring mostly."

"Is there a general store or somewhere we can buy things?"

"Yeah, but there's not much there." The boy looked down for a moment, but then perked up. "Actually, you're much better off checking out the caravan."

"The caravan?"

"The Bright Caravan is in town. They have heaps of cool things, and since they travel around a lot they can probably help you more." The boy's eyes were alight with excitement.

"Thanks, kid," Vincent said.

"You're welcome, I hope it helps." The boy ran off.

"I've got a good feeling about this," Falric said.

"A caravan?" Vincent said.

"We can find out what route they use, get some supplies, and ask them about the area more. It could be very useful."

"I don't think I've seen one before," Alrion said.

"You'll know it when you see it," Vincent said.

They continued walking through the town, Alrion keeping his eyes open. He had heard of caravans mentioned but never witnessed one. He wondered how it would help.

As they neared what looked like the edge of town, he saw a row of brightly coloured wagons arranged in a semi-circle. There were streams of people, and lots of horses either wandering or tied up. Everyone appeared to be moving constantly, and the noise of conversations, banging, and general business filled the air.

"Wow," Alrion said. They were right, he did know it when he saw it. The people looked like a different sort, but he couldn't quite pinpoint why. But they were so strange when compared to the other townsfolk they had seen on their trip.

"This could be good," Alrion said.

"I hope so, we could use a break," Vincent said.

They made their way through the campsite, heading for the Bright Caravan. A lead wagon with 'Bright Caravan' painted on it occupied the entire space, the letters a garish yellow on a light blue background.

"Let's talk to their leader." Falric directed them to a man with a large decorative hat sitting near the lead wagon. He was surrounded by other people who were asking him questions.

"I'd say that's our man," Vincent said.

"He certainly stands out," Alrion said. As they approached the man the small crowd around him spread out and turned to face them.

"How may we help you fine folks? My name is Farver and the Bright Caravan is at your service." Farver tipped his hat, then replaced it on his head with a flourish. His voice had richness to it and energy that seemed out of place.

He looks a lot older than he sounds, Alrion thought.

"Farver, nice to meet you. I'm Falric, and this is Vincent and Alrion." Falric gestured to his companions. The movement looked positively spartan in comparison to what Farver had just done. "We just arrived here, and are looking to move on to Paperton. I was wondering if we could buy some supplies from you, or get some advice on the best way to go."

"Ah, Paperton. We don't trade there anymore, we're too big now and access is tricky. But we pass close by on our way. It's actually quite easy, there's a main road that will take you most of the way there."

"That's great. Do you have any horses you could part with?" Vincent said.

"No, I'm afraid we don't. But we can help you with some supplies."

"That'll do. Where do I go?"

"The rear wagon holds all our supplies." Farver looked Vincent up and down. "Are you good with that sword?"

"Good enough to be still walking and talking."

"We really can't spare the horses, but maybe you could travel with us until we are close to Paperton. It's slow going, but it would beat travelling on foot. You don't have any faster options."

"And in return?"

"In return, you help us out if we run into any difficulties. Saves you walking, and you can help yourself to supplies and food. I'll feel more comfortable, and maybe you won't even be needed."

"That's a pretty good offer." Vincent looked over at Falric.

"Are you expecting difficulties?" Falric said.

"No, it's a safe run and we are big enough to deter most would-be bandits. But I've heard some rumours flying around and thought it would make sense to travel together," Farver said.

"Sure, just give us a moment to discuss," Vincent said.

"By all means, but we will be packing up and leaving soon so we can make it to a good campsite this evening. If we don't see you, we will assume you are staying here."

"We'll let you know either way. I'll be back soon." Vincent walked away with Falric and Alrion close behind.

"What's wrong? Don't you trust this guy?" Alrion said.

"He's probably alright, but you never know. I'm more concerned for them, though."

"You think we will make them a target?" Falric said.

"Exactly. We have been attacked at just about every step since we left the academy. If it happens again while we are with them, there might be casualties. That would be on us."

"It's a concern for sure. But surely by being with them, we could be more invisible? The three of us walking alone will stick out. By going with the caravan, we might blend in and destroy the trail," Falric said.

"True. It's a risk either way." Vincent looked quite conflicted. He didn't seem particularly happy about either option.

I know that look. I've seen it before when he's been in the workshop and trying to choose between two awful choices.

"I'll leave it up to you to decide," Falric said.

Exactly what my father wouldn't want.

Alrion could see Vincent running through the scenarios in his mind. After a minute of deliberation, the blacksmith spoke up.

"Let's do it. The benefit outweighs the risks, and if they run into any trouble unrelated to us, we can sort that too."

"And if trouble does come looking for us, we can divert them away," Falric said.

"Agreed. Let's head back and let him know. Are you fine with this Alrion?"

They asked my opinion. Wow.

"It's what I would have chosen. We have the opportunity to help them and it may help us too." Alrion beamed at the sense of being included, finally.

"Great." Vincent started back towards the caravan. As before, the crowd around Farver parted when they were close.

"I see you approaching again, am I right that you're on-board?" Farver said.

"Yes, we're in. Thanks for the opportunity," Vincent said. Farver made a quick hand signal and a young boy ran off towards the rear of the caravan.

"He will let them know you are joining us. Head down and ask for anything you need urgently. There'll be another opportunity later today when we stop to make camp."

"How long until we make it to Paperton?" Alrion said.

"I expect we will part ways around midday tomorrow. It shouldn't take you more than a few hours to complete your journey from that point."

"Thanks again, we will see you later," Falric said.

"My pleasure. Donna will sort you out," Farver said. The three of them stepped away and watched him swamped by people once more.

"Busy guy," Alrion said.

"Yes, but very clever. He sized us up and determined we were not a risk, and could be useful to him. But he also offered a mutually beneficial proposition. He's a smooth operator." Vincent sounded quite impressed but wore a frown.

"Isn't that good?" Alrion was confused.

"Oh yes, it's good. It means that he has been doing this a while and knows how to work with people. He's quite alert, so let's assume that there will be trouble and have our guard up. I don't take him to be the type to worry unnecessarily."

And there it is. Trouble ahead.

"I agree," Falric said. They continued over to the rear wagon in the caravan and saw a tall, thin woman with short brown hair and glasses on. She was on the move constantly, packing things away, and rearranging storage in the wagon.

"You must be Donna?" Falric said.

"That's me. You must be the new folks. Anything, in particular, you need before we head off?"

"Something to snack on?" Alrion said. He couldn't ignore his stomach any longer.

"Not much here, it's all been packed away. I can find you something, though. Anything else?"

"No, I think we're fine. We may need some bedding later," Vincent said.

"We will handle that later tonight. Take this." Donna shoved a parcel at Alrion, then returned to rearranging things.

"Thanks, see you later," Alrion said.

"Bye," Donna said without turning around. She started muttering to herself and increased the pace at which she was working.

"What did you score?" Falric said.

"I think these are biscuits?" Alrion opened the packet and inspected the hard, round objects.

"You enjoy those. I have some stale bread for later," Vincent said with a chuckle.

"Sure, I'll take my chances with their food," Alrion said.

"Suit yourself," Vincent said. "Let's make ourselves useful."

"Sure." Together father and son helped pack up the caravan. Donna was quick to give them jobs once she saw them helping. Falric sat off to the side, supervising and chiming in with clever quips when he saw an opportunity.

"Bend with your knees!" Falric cried.

"He's enjoying himself too much," Vincent said. Alrion flashed him back a smile.

"Well you two, thanks for your help. You did more than my so-called helpers." Donna sighed.

"Since we're coming along, we thought it was worth giving you a hand," Vincent said.

"It made a difference. And now you can help me in another way. The three of you can ride in our wagon, and my helpers can walk alongside. That'll teach them to let guests outwork them."

"It's a tough job, but someone has to do it. You name it, we're your men," Falric said.

"Typical that he's all hands on deck when it comes to sitting around," Vincent said.

"Of course. Efficient use of resources. I have years of experience sitting down. I've been training all my life for this." Falric grinned at Donna.

"I'm all about efficiency. Now off you go, before you hold us up." Donna pointed to the rear of the wagon and the three of them headed over. They found a small space at the end, where they could sit on crates and barrels and enjoy the fresh air.

"This was a good idea." Vincent leaned back and looked relaxed for the first time in a long time.

"Agreed. If we can't get horses, then traveling with the caravan will do nicely. This trip has been a lot more eventful than I had expected. The sooner we reach Paperton the better," Falric said.

"Is that the last place we will be going?"

"No, but our way will be simpler once we get there."

"Still cryptic," Vincent said.

"I don't want to disappoint." Falric waved his hand in a mystical way. Alrion laughed. The conversation died down and he watched the countryside as they went.

The progress of the caravan was very slow, it was easy enough for the lazy workers to walk alongside the wagons. But they travelled consistently and without breaks.

"We are making good time. All things considered," Falric said. Vincent nodded.

"Looks like we won't be stopping for lunch." He pointed at the men walking alongside and saw that they were eating as they walked.

"I guess it would be too much effort to stop and restart this big a group," Alrion said.

"Exactly. And if they are wary of trouble, the more time they are in motion the better. There's probably some food here, let's check," Vincent said. He rummaged through the boxes and brought out some more biscuits, only these were plainer and more bread-like.

"These should do the job." Vincent handed them out but didn't start eating. Alrion bit into one and was surprised by the flavour. They were crispy, salted, and felt substantial.

"Pretty good," Alrion said. Vincent took a bite and seemed satisfied.

"Don't eat too many. You'll get too thirsty."

"Got it."

"This is nice and peaceful. Let's hope the rest of the journey is as uneventful," Falric said, and Vincent and Alrion murmured agreement.

The afternoon progressed steadily. Alrion could tell that they seemed to be climbing slowly, the ground rising in elevation.

"We're going up," he said.

"That's probably why they aren't going to Paperton. It's down by the water, and hard to access with this number of wagons," Falric said. Alrion was about to respond when he noticed the wagon jolt. It rapidly slowed, then stopped.

"Must be trouble, let me investigate." Vincent jumped out immediately and ran towards the front of the caravan.

"Let us also exit, I have a bad feeling," Falric said.

22

DIVIDED

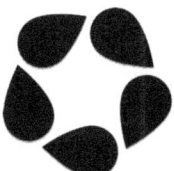

Alrion looked ahead and could see the whole caravan had stopped and there was a huddle of people next to the front wagon. He watched his father step into the huddle and converse with them.

"Definitely looks like something is happening," Alrion said.

"Let me see," Falric said. He closed his eyes and concentrated. His eyes opened, and he started walking away.

"I need to warn them."

"What is it?"

"Blighters," Falric whispered and Alrion took off after him. As they neared the huddle it opened as if welcoming them in.

"We've had a sighting," Vincent said.

"Blighters," Falric said.

"So, let's take that as confirmed. Do we know where they are coming from?"

"Not sure, we may even be surrounded."

"I have an idea. But you're not going to like it."

"No, if it's what I think it is." Falric shook his head furiously.

"I'm going to move forward, see if I can lure them away. The caravan is a sitting duck, and will be hard to defend."

"By yourself? That is suicide," Farver said. The people surrounding him murmured their agreement.

"It's a calculated risk. Not all will follow, but it will split them up and I can probably track where they are coming from. If there's a Tainted One directing them I can take him out and scatter the rest." Vincent sounded resolute.

"Then I can defend the caravan from any stragglers," Falric commented.

"Is this really a good idea?" Alrion said.

My father can handle himself, but this is something else. It doesn't feel right.

"It's the best we have. There's no time. If we get separated I will move on to Brangtur. That should confuse them. I will wait for you there," Vincent said.

"Sure. But we will be seeing you soon," Falric said.

"Take care of the old man." Vincent gave Alrion an affectionate pat on the shoulder.

"Dad, are you sure about this?"

"Don't worry about me, I can handle myself. Got a horse I can use?"

"Yes, take mine. She's black with a white stripe up around the front wagon. With luck, you will bring her back," Farver said.

"Done." Vincent ran towards the horse and jumped up into the saddle. After steadying himself he rode off along the road.

"Be safe," Alrion said, mostly to himself.

I know I'll see you again. But it doesn't feel like it will be soon.

Falric drew Farver aside.

"I am no tactician, but make sure you evenly spread your people out. The more we spread out the Blighters, the better. They will get more confused and be easier targets. Give me a horse and I will ride up and down the length of the caravan, taking them down as I can."

"Who are you?" Farver said.

"I'm a wizard. Battle is not my forte, but I can be useful. Very useful."

"Whatever you need. This caravan isn't just our livelihoods, it is also our home. Take Master Falric here to our fastest horse," Farver said.

"I'm coming too," Alrion said.

"Good, I need your help. Help me spot targets, and pay attention. It's going to get chaotic."

"Absolutely." Alrion felt the nerves come back, and his stomach churning. But inside the maelstrom was a tiny piece of calm.

This is what you should be doing. Just trust it.

"Incoming!" a voice yelled from the rear of the caravan. Falric was in the middle of mounting up when he stopped.

"Actually, you take the reins, so I can concentrate on the fight."

"No problem." Alrion mounted up and leaned forward, giving Falric room to sit behind him.

"Go!" Falric said. Alrion kicked the horse into action and headed towards the commotion. As they thundered along the caravan, he saw a pack of Blighters converging on the rear wagon.

"Ride past them in an arc," Falric said. Alrion spurred the horse on, heading directly at them and when close, steering the horse away. As they rode alongside the Blighters, a stream of fire flew out from Falric's hands and consumed them. Alrion continued the arc and turned the horse around.

"Good. Let's go back and look for more," Falric said. Alrion could see that the Blighters had either been killed outright or were being finished off by caravan folk. They returned to the main wagons and saw several Blighters splitting up and going after individual people.

"Slow down, I need more finesse here," Falric said. Alrion did as instructed, keeping a safe distance but riding closer to the Blighters. Falric pointed at one and a thin spear of fire shot out and pierced a Blighter through the eye. He dropped to the ground instantly.

"Wow, that's precise," Alrion said.

"Yes, but it takes a lot of concentration. Let's get the rest."

"On my way." Alrion picked up the pace and headed to the next Blighters. This time he slowed between two of them, and Falric let loose two more spears of fire. They continued in this fashion until they had reached the head of the caravan.

"There's a few here," Alrion commented.

"You aren't joking," Falric said. There must have been fifty Blighters streaming towards the caravan, a lone figure in the distance behind them.

"Who is that?"

"It's not the wizard; I'd say it is a Tainted One directing this lot. I want you to ride through the pack, so we can go after him," Falric said.

"I hope you know what you're doing." Alrion spurred the horse on.

"I'm going to have some fun with this," Falric said. Alrion wondered what he was talking about but soon saw. A giant bird comprised of flame hovered above them, swooped over their heads, and rushed ahead. The flame bird attacked the group of Blighters head on, the intense heat incinerating all it touched and blazing a path through them.

Alrion rode hot on its trail, making the most of the impact. As they rode through Falric fanned flames on either side, torching those that were still alive but confused by the attack.

One of them stumbled towards the horse, despite the burning flames. Alrion had no time to think. He summoned his power, channelling it into a forceful push knocking the Blighter far away. It didn't get up again.

"Good instincts. Leave the rest of the stragglers and let's go for the leader," Falric said. Alrion's face lit up with the thrill of battle and his successful contribution and urged the horse on, towards the lone man standing at the back.

The man was just standing there, motionless.

"Something's not right," Alrion said.

"Slow down and approach at a walk," Falric said. Alrion dropped his speed and the horse trotted towards the man, who remained motionless. Alrion could sense that Falric was up to something. He kept his eyes on the man and saw a cage built of fire assemble itself around the enemy.

"That should hold him, let's go have a chat," Falric said. Alrion looked back to see how the caravan was faring.

"Don't worry about them, they can finish up."

"Why did he let us capture him without a fight?" Alrion said.

"I'm not completely sure. However, I suspect it has to do with their communication link. I can imagine it would be disruptive having large numbers of Blighters in pain and dying all at once."

"Interesting." Alrion tucked that thought away for later. He dismounted and helped Falric down. Up close, the Tainted One looked normal. He had short dark hair, green eyes, and was looking down at the ground.

"Who sent you?" Falric said. The man looked up, not really seeing them. It was as if he was gazing past them.

"Who sent you?"

"The reclaimer."

"The reclaimer? Who is that?"

"He is the one that reclaims the world for us. For those touched by the Blight. He gives us a future."

"Does he have a name?"

"He is the reclaimer." The man had a fanatical look to his features.

"Is he a wizard?" Alrion said. The question seemed to jolt the man out of his trance-like state.

"What's it to you?"

"You attacked us. Why?" Alrion said.

"It's all part of his plan."

"Tell me more of this plan," Falric said.

"That's not part of the plan." The man reached into his boot and retrieved a small vial of liquid, downing it in one gulp.

"You have triumphed here, but you will not win," the man said, then collapsed to the ground. Falric released the fire cage and walked up to inspect him.

"He's dead. It must have been poison."

"That's crazy," Alrion said.

"Perhaps, perhaps not. However, there is a serious plot here that we cannot ignore. I am continually surprised by their ability to track us."

"What about my father? The fight is done now."

"Yes, the immediate danger is over, but I doubt he will return. He has good instincts, I think he will try and lure them away from us." Falric seemed quite clear on that.

There's something too neat about all this.

"You planned this? All along?"

"No, but we considered it if we were attacked again. He convinced me that it was a good idea. Don't worry about him, he can take care of himself. You and I also have an important job to do."

"I know."

"Let us return, and talk to Farver. He will want an update." Falric walked back to the horse. The two of them rode back to the caravan, Alrion trying not to look at the damage and devastation.

"Is that it?" Farver said as they approached.

"Yes, their leader is dead. Our friend is out looking for any others," Falric said.

"What were they after? I have not heard of such attacks."

"I'm not sure, but perhaps they were after us," Falric said. Farver's attitude changed completely. He regarded Falric with caution.

"Really?"

"It's our best theory. I am a wizard after all. We appreciate your help and hospitality, but we cannot endanger you any further."

I can see the relief on Farver's face.

"I appreciate your honesty and your gesture. Given what has happened, I think I would be forced to ask you to leave otherwise."

"No problem here. We will gather a few things and be on our way."

"Please take the horse as a token of friendship. It will speed you on your way."

"And if trouble follows us, it will be further from you."

"Indeed, it serves us both." Farver smiled.

"Thank you, and good luck," Falric said. Farver bowed.

"I'll fetch some supplies." Alrion darted off to the rear wagon.

"That was quite a fight," Donna said.

"It was quite intense. Is everyone alright?"

"I think so, apart from a few scares and some damage, I think we came out unscathed. Thanks to your help."

"Thanks. If you don't mind, I will grab a few things before we leave."

"You're leaving?" Donna gave him a sidelong glance.

"We are travelling with a wizard. We may be drawing their attention." Alrion braced himself for the response, but Donna seemed unfazed.

"Oh, I see. Well, take what you need and good luck."

"Thanks, Donna. Safe travels." Alrion quickly grabbed some blankets and food and stuffed them into his bag and ran off.

The sooner we leave the better. This is way too awkward. And I don't feel comfortable that we've put these people in danger.

"All set?" Falric said.

"Yes."

"Off we go."

"Sure." Alrion looked back and reflected on the situation.

The Bright Caravan is not as bright now, but it will endure. He nudged the horse forward and they galloped away.

Their progress on the horse was much faster than the caravan was travelling. Despite some initial discomfort they settled into the ride. Alrion was running through their last encounter with the Blighters over and over in his mind. He spoke at last.

"Falric, I have a question about magic."

"Go ahead."

"How come you seem to use a lot of fire magic? Is that on purpose, or is that just a coincidence?" Alrion ducked to avoid a low hanging tree branch and steered the horse towards the middle of the path.

"Good question. The simple answer is that everyone has different affinities with the various elements. A talent if you will. It just so happens that I have a talent with fire. It comes more naturally, so I end up using it more. That reinforces my comfort and ability with fire. It is generally a self-supporting cycle."

"Everyone has their own specialty?"

"More or less. Everyone will have an element that they lean towards, that is easier and generally more powerful for them." Falric leaned to the side, and a thin column of fire burst from his hand. It incinerated another branch that was looming from the other side of the path. The branch crumbled into ash, and started to fill the air. That reminded Alrion of something.

"Do you think the wizard that attacked us is fire-based as well?" he said.

"You really have been thinking about this. I'm not sure; I don't know enough to say. Maybe, but maybe not."

"I guess we will find out. I just thought it might be a way to narrow down who it is. Is there a way to test for an affinity?"

"We generally don't, it just comes out as part of the training. It is worth recognising and remembering. Knowledge about yourself is just as important as knowledge about magic and others."

"Makes sense to me." Alrion nodded along.

I wonder what I have? Maybe it is fire because I created such a big flame in that initial test.

"If you're wondering about your own affinity, then we shall have to wait and find out. Although if you're anything like your grandfather, it won't be so readily apparent."

"What do you mean?"

"He used all elements interchangeably without any sign of preference. Either he had no preference, or he masked it well."

"Interesting." The more he found out about his grandfather, the more amazing he seemed to be.

No pressure there.

"Yes, it made him a more rounded wizard. A very talented and dangerous man when he wanted to be."

"I guess I'll see how I go. Is all magic associated with an element?"

"Most, but there's no hard and fast rule on it." Falric leaned out again, unleashing a wave of force to push away some rubble that Alrion hadn't spotted. The horse startled a bit, but recovered quickly.

He's more aware than me and I'm steering us. Not a good look.

"How about healing magic?" Alrion said.

"Water."

"I can see how that would work."

"Yes, we will get to that tonight. Once we reach the campsite that the caravan was aiming for," Falric said. Alrion was satisfied with that response and kept riding.

After all that's happening, a healing spell would be nice. A chance to repair and not just destroy.

23

A NEW SKILL

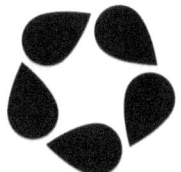

The terrain was sparse now, with grass, shrubs, and only the occasional tree. They were slowly ascending as they went, climbing what seemed like a small hill.

"We must be close now," Alrion said.

"Yes, not far to go. At the top of this hill should be a nice flat site. It's the most popular campsite in this area. Well, it used to be, a long time ago," Falric said. Alrion kept his eyes on the horizon, trying to spot their destination.

The countryside rolled on, and he lapsed back into just enjoying the ride and keeping his eyes on the dirt road. Finally, they crested a particularly steep section and emerged onto what had to be the campsite. To the side of the road was a large dirt area, with a big pit dug in the middle.

"That's where they light their fire," Falric said. Alrion rode on past it, observing the ground.

"Just stop somewhere at the end over there." Falric pointed. Alrion looked where Falric had suggested and picked a grass covered spot. He jumped down and held the horse steady while Falric dismounted. Then he led the horse to a nearby tree and tied it up.

"This will do nicely. It will be dark soon, and this is a good place to rest." Falric eased himself down onto the ground, sitting on his robe.

"What about the caravan?" Alrion said.

"They will have to make do I'm afraid, they won't make it here in time. It's for the best, though, if anything comes for us they won't be involved."

"True. I hope my father is alright."

I wonder where he is now. Maybe he's close we weren't delayed that long.

"He is, don't you worry. After we complete our task, we will go to Brangtur and meet up with him. The journey will do you good."

"Is it far?"

"Yes, quite a distance, and he's got a good head start on us. But that just means we have some time to advance your training."

"Speaking of which?"

"Yes, after dinner we shall go over a healing spell."

"Great." Alrion laid out their food and they ate in silence. Alrion was thinking about the battle they had just survived, and his small victory.

I'm not quite pulling my weight yet, but I'm contributing. It feels good. It feels different to being a blacksmith. It's less forced and the potential is huge.

Falric had done an amazing job with the Blighters and he wasn't even considered a battle-hardened wizard. There was a lot of room for Alrion to improve there. He could already tell there would be many battles in his future. It was hard for him to stop going over how he had screwed up in the tunnel beneath the Thundering Mountain.

Just get over it and focus on the path ahead. You can't go back and do better.

"We were going to discuss the healing spell," Falric said. "A very useful spell, with near infinite uses. It is water-based, which will help in your understanding of it. However, there is one thing that I must state at the beginning."

"Yes?" Alrion was fully alert.

"It is largely ineffective on yourself."

"I can't heal myself?" Alrion's heart sank.

But I was going to keep myself alive with this!

"Not effectively, no."

"Why not?"

"How should I explain this? The Spark is a special energy created by your body. You cannot use it to rebuild your own body. Does that make sense?" Falric was giving Alrion that same 'I'm sorry we just don't know but you'll learn to accept it' look that he had done a few times now.

"Sort of but what's the reason?"

"Your grandfather would have a good philosophical response to that, but I can't give you the technical explanation, I just understand it as fact. It's one of the basic laws of magic."

"That seems like quite a flaw," Alrion said, the disappointment clear in his voice.

"You could look at it that way or you could think about it this way. It works more effectively on other people. So, it is best used to support companions who are assisting you." Falric pointed to himself and smiled.

"I'll be able to heal you?"

"Not just me, anybody. But think of two wizards healing each other, sounds more useful now, doesn't it?"

"Yes, I suppose."

"Remember to think about what utility it can provide, and what that means for you. I think it's clear that you should not travel alone. And the healing spell is a good incentive for others to travel with you."

"That's a good way to think about it."

I did want another way of contributing, so it still does that.

"Of course. So, should we continue?" Falric said.

"Yes."

"Good. Another thing to mention, which you may have already guessed from the restrictions I explained, is that this spell absolutely requires the Spark to function. It cannot work otherwise."

"That makes sense, from what you said."

"It does, and will make more sense once you have tried it. The best explanation for the spell is like this. You know how with the push spell, you visualised the force it took to move an object?" Falric mimicked a push motion.

"Yes."

"This spell also includes a visualisation, but an entirely different one. Hand me that spoon." Falric pointed at a spoon that Alrion had used to eat some soup with. Falric wiped the spoon on his cloak and showed it to Alrion.

"Now it's not exactly polished, but what can you see?"

"I can see myself in the reflection. It's a bit warped though."

"No surprises there. Now I add a bit of water, what can you see now?" Falric said. Alrion stared intently at the water.

"Move the spoon around, and see what happens to the water," Falric said. Alrion did as instructed, slowly moving the spoon, and observing the water.

"Well depending on the position of the water, I can see myself."

"Great. I would have preferred to discuss this in another location, like say the Great Mirror Lake but I think you can understand it. But the key to this visualisation is your reflection in the water."

"Sure." Alrion wasn't quite sure where Falric was going with this. But his explanation of the push spell had been quite effective.

"You have some scepticism, which is good. Allow me to explain further. What I need you to do here is picture yourself reflected in the water. The way you are now, without injury. And what the spell does, is use the water as a medium in which to return your body to the state it is in now," Falric said. Alrion took a minute to absorb the information.

"That's crazy."

"Maybe a little, but your body is more water than anything else. Does it still sound so crazy?"

"Yes," Alrion said emphatically. Falric laughed.

"I can't argue the point; it's a little out there but you'll come around to my line of thinking. Anyway, the water component of this spell is both a medium and a visualisation aid, but the Spark is what makes the spell work. So, take any thoughts of crazy and get rid of them."

"I'm sorry, I'll try and focus more."

"Good. Don't worry, everyone goes through this. However, this is not an easy spell, and you wanted to learn. It's a vital lesson, for my health as well as yours."

"Yeah, I can see why it might be useful being able to heal you," Alrion said.

"Yes, like I said its uses are infinite. Now, let's try something." Falric sidled closer to Alrion.

"Take a good look at my hand," Falric said. After he had Alrion's attention, he continued.

"Make a mental picture of how my hand looks. All the lines, the spots, the roughness in parts. Is it firm in your mind? Good. Because now I'm going to do this." Falric took a knife and cut across his palm. A red line instantly appeared, and blood began to ooze out immediately.

"What!" Alrion called out.

"That really stings. Please heal my hand if you don't mind."

"How do I do it?" Alrion started to panic.

This is too intense.

"Find your Spark. Instead of letting the fire of it take over, think about the cool clarity of the water. Imagine a sheet of water hovering over my hand, and its reflection showing my healed hand and guiding my hand back to that state." Falric was quite calm in his explanation, even though the blood continued to flow. Alrion closed his eyes and listened to Falric's words.

He had trouble reaching his Spark, but his frustration quickly jumped up and helped him locate it. He wrestled with it, trying not to channel it the same way as he had before. He knew instinctively that an explosive burst could be quite catastrophic.

"Careful, my hand is starting to heat up."

"Sorry." Alrion continued his concentration. He used Falric's words to construct a visualisation, to see a circular sheet of water reflecting a healed hand, and a stream of mist flowing down to repair the hand, guiding it into the new state. In his mind, the hand was slowly repairing itself. He could see the cut closing, the skin knitting together to repair the slice. Once he was finished, he could see in his mind a perfectly formed hand, untouched.

Alrion opened his eyes and looked for real. Falric's hand looked different but there was a mess of blood on it.

"What happened?" Alrion said.

"Don't worry, it just wasn't as picture-perfect as your visualisation. But it's fine," Falric said. He took some water and slowly poured it over his hand. The blood washed away, and the hand looked completely healed.

"Wow! I did it! I don't believe it."

It's a miracle. I healed his hand. That's not possible.

"You sure did, you have good instincts. Looks and feels fine."

"But why did it look so bloody?"

"Well just because you healed me, doesn't mean that it wasn't a bit of a process. With time and skill, you can make it a cleaner fix. But it was nothing a bit of water couldn't clear away."

"I get it. But, wow, I can't believe I healed you." Alrion grabbed Falric's hand and examined it up close.

"Yes, I am also a little surprised." Falric took his hand back.

"Really? You cut yourself unsure if I could heal you?"

"Of course, it's the best way to learn. Besides, if it really bugged me I could stick a bandage on. It's minor enough."

"Ha-ha alright," Alrion said. He was beaming from the success of the spell.

"You have done well, and this is actually an important milestone. However, before we move on, let's quickly reflect on this spell. It is powered by Spark, but requires a precise visualisation."

"You need the proper knowledge to do it."

"Exactly, you're catching on. If I had just told you to heal my hand, who knows what would have happened," Falric said. He laughed, a mixture of mirth and horror at the thought.

"That could be messy. But all is well."

"Indeed. The reason why this is an important milestone is that you have successfully used visualisation to focus your Spark in a different and unusual way. This means that with practice and preparation, your ability to cast many and varied spells can be expanded."

"Great! I'm sorry for being sceptical. Twice now you have taught me new spells, in a very effective way."

"Don't worry, it's completely normal. And we are skipping through this process rather quickly."

"Now I can learn more spells." Alrion felt like he had caught the bug. He needed more spells to cast.

"You can even learn some by yourself. Let me fetch something." Falric rummaged through his bags and removed an old book with a navy-blue cover, but without a title.

"Here, take this." Falric handed the book to Alrion. Alrion felt the weight of it and the age.

"What is this?"

"That is my spellbook. There is a wealth of knowledge contained within that tome. All kinds of wonderful spells, with notes about how to cast them, and which pillar of magic is key."

"This is incredible." Alrion leafed through it. "Hang on; there are so many blank pages."

"Yes, well you see it is a magic spellbook. You infuse the spellbook with the new spells, and it understands what they are. And it will only show you those that are within your means."

"Have you cast every spell in here?"

"Yes, I built that spellbook myself. Your grandfather had his own, with pages even I could not read," Falric said, chuckling to himself.

"Thanks. Can you really give this to me? Isn't it too much?" Alrion started to hand it back. Falric refused to take it.

"Not really, all the knowledge is up here now." Falric tapped his head, "and it's good for you to discover some things on your own."

"I really appreciate it; I will take good care of it."

"Good, that is all I ask."

"One other question, about the healing spell."

"Sure, what is it?"

"Can it heal anything?"

"Just about. There are a few odd cases, but it is quite versatile."

"What about the Blight?" Alrion said. Falric smiled.

"I was wondering if you were going to ask about that. No, the Blight is a different thing altogether. I don't know the spell your grandfather used, but it was not a healing spell. Not at all."

"Oh, OK. I was just curious."

Did you really think it was going to be that easy?

"It was a good question, and many have pondered why. Why is the Blight not treatable as a wound or illness? Food for thought. However, let's not get too bogged down in those things. I think we have had a pretty big day, and I'm keen to turn in."

"I'm a bit tired," Alrion said, not realising it until Falric brought it up.

"That's also due to the healing. It is quite Spark intensive, so keep that in mind."

"Will do."

There's a lot of things I need to keep in mind.

"Now help me clear up here," Falric said. Alrion helped him put everything away and they readied themselves for sleep.

"It's a clear night. So lovely to sleep under the stars," Falric said.

"I agree. I used to do this often, back in Hamley." Alrion sighed. "I was supposed to go the day you arrived but never did. And I never spoke to my friends about leaving."

"They will understand. It's a different life you need to live now, and your quest is more urgent than we initially thought. Cherish the quiet life you had there, and perhaps one day you'll achieve it once again."

"Are you speaking from experience?"

"This is more excitement than I've ever had. I was destined to live as an administrator. When I was a young boy, I was growing up in Paperton. Bound to be a scholar, until your grandfather found me. And yet I ended up behind a desk anyway!"

"I guess we never know what's in store for us." Alrion looked at the stars. They appeared different tonight. A little brighter.

"We never do and it's a privilege for us to have this quest. We have the chance to make a difference in the lives of many people. However, enough philosophy, this old wizard is tired. Goodnight, Alrion."

"Goodnight," Alrion said but he could already hear Falric snoring.

How did he fall asleep so fast? Alrion wondered. It had to be something about being old. Alrion couldn't sleep easily, despite his tiredness. He thought about the fight they recently were in, the Blighters and the Tainted One. Then about his father.

I hope you are alright. Why couldn't you meet us at Paperton? Alrion thought. Surely, a diversion wouldn't require such a long journey. Well, he would get to the bottom of it but first they had to get to Paperton and wherever the next destination was. As he fell asleep, Alrion imagined what it would be like to be a fully trained wizard, fearless and with spells at his fingertips.

24

FIRE AND EARTH

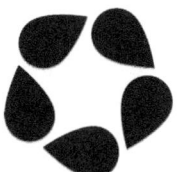

Alrion woke, a feeling of dread filling him. Something was not right. He sat up swiftly and turned his head, looking for Falric. He wasn't there, and it looked like he had just upped and left.

"Not good," Alrion said to himself. He rose and tried to shake the sleepiness from his head. He sensed something happening in the distance, so took off at a run.

He heard sounds, which helped him pinpoint what was happening. He couldn't describe what they were exactly, but it sounded like the earth was cracking. Alrion reached the road, but the sound was coming from further away. He kept running, trying to track the noise, and figure out what was going on.

I hope it's not more Blighters. This wasn't supposed to happen, Alrion thought. He increased his speed and searched the horizon for anything of note. He started to notice disturbances in the terrain. Land turned over, soil everywhere. Scorch marks on trees and the grass.

This is some kind of battle. Maybe it's the wizard?

He pushed on, the urgency of the situation raised in his mind. If there was a fight, he had to help somehow. He couldn't do much, but he could do something. The noises got louder and louder. It wasn't just that he was closing in, but the fight was escalating. He pushed through a small bunch of trees, sure that whatever he was after was on the other side.

As Alrion emerged from between the trees he stopped dead still. The ground was torn up, big mounds of earth missing. Large rock formations littered the space, and a few small fires burned. But what took Alrion's breath away was the view of the two wizards locked in battle. Falric, and the wizard in black.

A ring of flame surrounded Falric. He was shooting a wave of fire from his hand at the black wizard, but the black wizard had protection from a wall of earth and was hurling lances of stone at Falric. Alrion realised that what he was sensing was the magic being wielded by these wizards. It was their Spark, raging in conflict. He looked between the two, unsure of how to help. Now that he was here, he didn't know whether to go to Falric's aid or try and attack the enemy wizard.

I'll try a push attack. Maybe I can destabilise the wizard and give Falric an opening.

He was just preparing when he saw Falric's face. Falric had spotted him, and a sudden look of anger surged across it. Alrion was surprised and shocked. Falric shook his head, then turned his attention back to the black wizard.

What does that mean? What should I do? Alrion thought. The black wizard caught his attention. All his stone lances had been melted and turned away by Falric's fire. He was trying a new approach.

The ground started to crack and split apart, and Falric lost his footing temporarily as the dirt beneath him rose up in a jagged chunk. However, he wasn't just being raised, a whole section of the cliff was being pushed towards the edge. In concert, a rolling wave of earth was coming in to block any possible escape.

Falric could sense what was happening, and started to react. However, he stopped all of a sudden. His gaze met Alrion, and he closed his eyes. Falric and the mound of earth he was standing on toppled over the cliff. The wave of earth crashed over the top. And then all of a sudden, the seismic activity ceased, and the black-garbed wizard walked over to inspect his handiwork.

I'm next, Alrion thought, and he ducked back behind the trees he had just emerged from. He continued to peer through to see what the wizard was doing. He seemed to be watching carefully for any signs of Falric. After he was satisfied, the black wizard looked over at where Alrion was hiding. Alrion froze with fear, unable to act.

I can't fight that, he thought. The black wizard's gaze remained fixed on Alrion's location for a moment, then continued. The wizard relaxed and started walking away, back toward the road. Alrion ducked down and crept away in the opposite direction, trying to stay hidden. Once he had reached the last piece of cover, he stayed in the brush waiting.

After he thought it was safe, he emerged to inspect the scene of the battle. There were huge tracts of earth missing or displaced, some appearing molten and still glowing. He avoided those and carefully stepped over to the edge. Below were the lake and the shore, but there was a huge mess of earth and rocks now on the ground. A colossal chunk of the cliff was missing and dispersed down below.

Falric is down there somewhere. But there's no way he survived.

But he couldn't abandon his friend and mentor. So, he found a way to clamber down the broken cliff, the destruction forging a path for him. He picked up some cuts and bruises on the way, but he arrived at the bottom on unsteady feet. The extent of the damage was even worse up close. He couldn't believe how much rubble was here.

Better get started.

He wasn't sure where to look, so started moving larger stones that looked like they could roll. It was slow progress and felt reassuring but when he stepped back to survey his progress, it looked like he had achieved nothing.

"Falric!" he called out. His desperation had increased, and time was against him. There was little chance that the wizard would come back. He listened closely for any signs of a response. Nothing.

I've got to do something, Alrion thought. His frustration was rising. He couldn't help Falric in his time of need. He felt useless.

"Damn it!" Alrion cried out, kicking out at rocks. He latched onto the feelings of doubt, frustration, and helplessness and tried to use them. He felt his Spark and amplified it. Then he pictured in his mind, all the earth and the rocks and the dirt flying away and revealing Falric. He focused all his might and once he had reached his limit let it all out in an explosive push.

It was cathartic and freeing. And destructive. He couldn't see anything due to all the dust in the air. He closed his eyes and waited for it all to settle. His senses were heightened by his tension and the magic he had just unleashed, and he could feel the dust falling to the ground. His breathing slowed, and panic took over.

What if the wizard sensed the magic and returned looking for Falric? Alrion thought. He felt a pit in his stomach, knowing that he would be powerless in that situation. As visibility returned to the area, he surveyed what he had done. Damaged and scattered rocks covered the whole area. But all he had done was remove a layer or two of rubble. There were still plenty of rocks covering the ground.

How could there be so much? Alrion wondered as he walked around. He prodded rocks here and there, hoping that he would find a giant nook with Falric lying safely within, but he found nothing.

"No!" Alrion called out, softer this time. Despair was rising within him as he realised that Falric was gone. Even if he had survived the fall and the rockslide, he was too weak to free himself and Alrion had been unable to excavate the rocks either. He could do nothing more. Alrion slammed his arm against a nearby pile of rocks, briefly enjoying the release but not relishing the pain. He looked around once more and felt only one thing: alone.

Alrion walked along the shore, looking for a way to return to their camp without having to climb up the rocks. He was also secretly hoping that he would spot something on his way but once he passed the impact site, nothing else suggested that anyone was there. With each step away, his heart felt heavier as he walked away from his mentor. He remembered his fear of the black wizard returning, but in that moment, he didn't care.

How can I be the chosen one, when I can't even help one person? There's no way I can reach the Pool of Knowledge by myself.

He kept walking, unsure of what to do next but knowing he should at least collect their things. He arrived back at the camp, expecting to see it ransacked and destroyed but it was exactly as he had left it. Alrion carefully examined Falric's belongings, trying to find any clues as to how things had happened. His bag was undisturbed, and his bed had been slept in.

It just looks like he awoke and went straight to confront the black wizard.

He rifled through Falric's things, looking for anything that might be of use. There was a notebook and some clothes, but nothing of note.

He already gave me the spellbook, Alrion thought. That would have been the most valuable thing. Alrion packed up Falric's things and left the bag on the ground. Then he did the same for his own belongings. Soon he was staring at an empty campsite, with two bags and a horse tied up. He mounted the horse with both the bags and started to ride away.

He took the long path around, returning to the shore where Falric had fallen. He dismounted and walked on foot to the middle of the destruction. He dug out a few rocks and placed Falric's bag into the nook.

"Farewell my friend, you deserved better. I am sorry I couldn't be more help. I feel responsible for the whole thing. You were only here to protect me, but you shouldn't have lost your life." Alrion choked back the tears. "I'm not worth it, no matter what that trial said. I can't go on, I can't complete our quest. But I'll return your spellbook to the academy so that your knowledge will not be lost." Despite his best efforts, a tear dripped onto the bag, and he quickly covered it with more stones.

This is not right. Why did this happen? Alrion thought as he walked away. He mounted the horse and turned away, wanting to put the whole thing behind him as fast as possible. He took his time returning to the road, not wishing to injure the horse, then kicked the horse into a gallop.

Let's go home, he thought. It would mean dealing with the issue of his father having gone ahead, but he would understand.

I'll send a letter when I get to a proper town.

It would still be an adventure getting home, but he just had to retrace his steps. With care, he could do it; it would just take time. He barely even took in the scenery, instead focusing on what he would need to return. He almost didn't notice the lone figure standing on the road ahead. When he did he stopped abruptly, almost falling off the horse. He couldn't see who it was, the shape of the person concealed by a cloak.

Alrion's first thought was that the black wizard had indeed found him but after the initial shock, he saw that it wasn't the case. The figure was too short and didn't have the same aura of dread and despair. No, this was someone else. But it was too coincidental that they were just standing there, looking at him. Waiting.

I guess I don't really have a choice. That's the way home, and that person is in the way. I'll have to go and see who they are.

He nudged the horse forward, and slowly approached the mysterious figure.

At least since I'm mounted I can make a hasty escape if required. He knew that trouble was up, one way or another.

25

THE RETURN

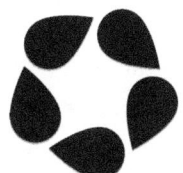

"Hello there, stranger," a female voice said. At first, Alrion didn't recognise it but knew it was familiar. He squinted at the figure, trying to discern more detail about who it was.

"Don't tell me you forgot about me already?" the voice continued, tinged with disappointment.

"Show your face," Alrion said. The figure drew back her hood.

"Lara, wasn't it? I don't really have the patience for your games today." Alrion glared at her. She seemed a little startled by the depth of his anger.

Of all the times to show up!

"Not even to get your ring back?" Her voice lost some of its playfulness.

"Sorry, too late. Don't care."

"That's a big change of heart. Where are your friends?" Lara looked around, concern starting to show on her face.

"One is dead, the other has gone ahead." Alrion was too weary to sugarcoat his response. He sagged down in the saddle a little.

"I didn't expect that ..." Lara said.

"Neither did I."

"So, where are you heading now?"

"Home. If you feel like following me again, I can guarantee that it will be a boring trip, so you shouldn't bother." Alrion nudged the horse forward. It took a few tentative steps.

"You don't have the look of someone who completed his quest." Lara challenged him with her eyes. He stopped the horse again.

"My quest? What would you know anyway?"

"I've been watching and following. I know your group was up to something. Something important. But it looks like you are giving up." She jabbed an accusing finger at him.

"Not that it's any of your business, but you're right. But I don't care for your judgement. You are just a petty thief." Alrion nudged his horse forward again.

I can't deal with this right now. I just have to get away.

"I am neither of those things." Lara tossed something at Alrion hard. He caught it against his chest and looked closely. It was the pouch containing his ring, the one given to him by his father.

"This doesn't change anything. Just leave me alone." Alrion pocketed the ring and directed the horse to the side to navigate around her. Lara stepped in front of the horse.

"That was a sign of good faith. Just talk to me about this." She paused to watch his reaction, and then continued, "You may think of me as a nobody, but I've followed your trail since Carford and I've seen some crazy things on the way. The more I think about it, the more I realise that something important is happening and I want to get involved. So just talk to me."

Alrion looked and listened. The edge from her voice was completely gone. It was flat and direct.

Maybe she is telling the truth? He thought. He wanted to just storm off, but there was something oddly sincere about what she had said. He searched her face for a reason to ride away. He didn't see one, and let out a deep sigh.

"There's a campsite not far from here. Let's go there."

"Are you going to make me walk?"

"Fine." Alrion shuffled forward on the horse and gave her a spot to jump on. She clambered up with ease and held onto him.

"Don't fall off." Alrion turned the horse around, riding back to the campsite. He didn't really want to return, but it was the only sensible place to go and it wasn't far. Lara didn't even try to say anything, which was fine by him. It would be hard enough talking to her as it was, so any break in the conversation was good.

When they arrived back at the campsite, Alrion immediately looked over at where he had spent the night. He could see the impression where Falric had slept. He held back a tear, it was still all so raw. He mechanically dismounted and pulled out a blanket from his pack, and laid it out on the ground. Lara sat down, and he sat next to her.

"So, what are we talking about?"

"What happened here?" Lara said. She sat quietly, waiting for him.

"We stayed here overnight. I awoke early, noticing something was wrong. I found my friend Falric battling an evil wizard." Alrion looked at Lara, but she remained silent, waiting for him to continue.

"I was frozen, unsure of what to do. Falric noticed me and waved me away, so I hid. Within minutes it was over, and he was buried under the rubble of the collapsed hillside."

"I'm so sorry. He looked like a genuinely nice person. Is that wizard still around?"

"No, I think he has left now."

"Is that the same one that has been following you the whole time?"

"How do you know about that?" Alrion couldn't hide the suspicion in his voice.

"Like I said, I've been following along, and you have left a massive trail behind you. So much destruction."

"It's not my fault, and that's why we split up. To try and confuse them and stop the pursuit." Alrion threw up his hands in frustration. This talk wasn't helping.

"What are they after?"

"I don't know. Either me, or what I am after."

"Which is?" Lara leaned in closer.

"I don't know if I can trust you."

"Why not?" She leaned in closer again, staring into his eyes. There was an intensity there that surprised him.

"Like you said, you have been here all along. You could be part of their plan, and giving me the ring is a ruse to gain my trust!" Alrion let loose. Lara flinched a little, but maintained her gaze.

"Don't hold back there. Look, I don't know what else I can do to convince you, but let me say this. You're alone, and you're abandoning your quest, whatever it is. Do you really think it's acceptable to do that and make your friend's sacrifice meaningless?"

"What do you mean my friend's sacrifice?"

"From what you said it is clear that Falric ended the fight before you could intervene. He did that to protect you from the other wizard."

"It does seem like that," Alrion said, looking down at the ground. He felt worse.

Why is she doing this?

"I've been drifting for a long time. Floating from town to town, taking what I needed to survive, doing odd jobs. Not classy stuff. I didn't know what I was seeking all that time. More running than seeking to be honest. But now I know. It's a purpose. I've been adrift with no purpose." Lara looked resolute. Like she had finally decided.

"And now?" Alrion was curious to hear what she had to say.

"And now I've seen that you are on an important mission and you need my help. I want to help."

"Why do I need your help?"

"No offense, but you're greener than the grass. You've no experience of the world, and despite what you have been doing on this trip you're still new. I have many useful skills, I've been just about everywhere, and I can spot danger coming. I've got great instincts," Lara said. He didn't respond immediately.

"What do you get out of it?"

"I get to do something meaningful. I am tired of wandering aimlessly."

Maybe this is a real offer. Can I really say no to that, and turn my back on everything?

"Where do we go from here? If I agree that is."

"You tell me what we're doing, and we turn around and we hit the trail again. You set the rules of engagement." Lara stood. Alrion joined her.

"I'm tired, and I've been through hell this last day. You're right, in that I was giving up. I feel helpless and alone and like a failure. What's to stop us failing at the next trial anyway?" he said.

"I tailed you here, without being spotted by your pursuers, across several forms of transport and without any of you spotting me except when I baited you. Don't underestimate what I can do," Lara said.

Alrion considered her words and paced around the campground. He was unsure. Her help seemed too convenient and unexplainable but since he was about to abandon his task anyway, what did he have to lose? If they failed together, that was her fate for joining him.

If I try again and fail, it's no worse than abandoning. It's better, because at least I tried. I can't turn my back on Falric, and everything he believed in.

"I'll tell you a bit more. And if you still want to come, I'll take your help. There will be some rules."

"Of course."

"I'll explain later, as required but I guess this is key. As you originally guessed, my friend Falric was a wizard. In fact, he was head of the Wizard Academy. He was also the successor to the wizard Granthion, who cleansed Avaria of the Blight." Alrion watched her reaction, and was secretly pleased that her eyes widened.

"I've heard of Granthion, that's amazing."

"It was an incredible feat. Here's where it gets crazier. I am Granthion's grandson, and Falric was convinced that I have the ability to cleanse the world of the Blight."

"What?" Lara practically shouted. Alrion let out a tiny laugh.

"Yes, that's right. I know it sounds ridiculous."

"For a wizard like Falric to believe it, it must be true." Lara recovered from the shock and looked even more intense than before.

Just who is she?

"And that's why we were on this journey. There is a place not far from here, called the Pool of Knowledge."

"I've heard of it." Lara didn't sound like she was bluffing.

"What?"

"I have an interest in hidden things and places, especially incredibly valuable ones. Don't look so surprised." Lara seemed annoyed.

"I guess in your line of work, it wouldn't be too strange. Anyway, my task is to visit the Pool of Knowledge and see if I can learn the spell required to cleanse the Blight."

"We have to get there!" Lara started heading for the horse.

"We? You're still up for this? Knowing that there's an evil wizard and potentially every creature afflicted with the Blight out to get us?" Alrion watched Lara stop and turn around to face him.

"Of course. I have a stake in this. Not only do I believe in fate, and that I found you for a reason, but also, I have a personal connection. The Blight took my brother. It tore our family apart, and I would not want that to happen to anyone else. If I can help, if I can make the difference to remove the Blight from the world, I will do it. A hundred times over." The fire in her eyes was unmistakable, and undeniable.

"I'm sorry to hear about that. Until recently I never had to deal with the Blight."

"It's fine, but don't you ever try and abandon this quest again. If you do I will hunt you down." Lara let slip a tiny smile.

"Deal. However, don't steal anything else from me, or I'll hunt you down myself. And while I may not be as tricky as you, I'm learning a lot of tricks of my own."

I don't understand this. But it seems right somehow.

"Deal. So, what's the plan?"

"We need to get to Paperton. That's my next lead, as far as I know there will be people there who can direct me further."

"Paperton is not far. In fact, it is the only place of note around here. I'm sorry to say this, but that wizard after you is probably headed there."

"Then I guess we need to hurry along. But there's one thing I need to do before we leave here."

"What's that?" Lara had been returning to the horse but turned back again.

"I need a new spell, something with a bit more firepower."

"Such as?"

"Fire. I was being pretty literal." Alrion chuckled.

"Oh, right. How do you learn those?"

"I have a book, given to me by Falric. Fire was his specialty, so it seems fitting to learn the basics next. I want to have something else up my sleeve before my next encounter. I've seen firsthand how useful it is in dealing with the creatures of the Blight."

"Can I see?" Lara said.

"Sure, this is it." Alrion pulled out the spellbook. As he leafed through it, he gave Lara occasional sidelong glances.

"Look, I promised I wouldn't steal anything else from you. Not that I would try anyway, all the pages are blank."

"Ha, to you maybe. To a wizard, they are full of instructions, diagrams, and other useful information. Falric said that the spellbook was somehow protected magically."

"That's good to know."

"You know not all magic requires a wizard, but that's a talk for another day. This looks promising, basic fire conjuring." Alrion went quiet and studied the pages carefully, leafing back and forth in the same section. Lara watched him with curiosity.

"I've never seen magic up close."

"It won't be that spectacular. Let me concentrate." Alrion closed his eyes and ran through the spell in his head. It was simple really, there was a visualisation aspect, but it seemed easy. His Spark could easily start a fire, he had even done it before any training as part of his initial test.

He rotated his hand so that his palm faced up, then concentrated on his Spark. He channelled his frustration and anger at his power-lessness, drawing upon his Spark and expanding it. Then he channelled it into his hand, imagining a flame appearing above his hand, extending upwards. He could feel the heat and hear the whoosh as it flared up.

"Wow!" Lara called out and jumped backward. Alrion opened his eyes and saw a flame dancing above his hand. It was alternating between being small and contained, and rising like a giant pillar.

"It's harder than it looks," he said apologetically, and focused on it more. He took the huge surge of Spark within him and put it in a box, then visualised it to be the lamp that he had originally used when Falric came to test him. The flame started to take shape and looked like it was contained within a lamp.

"It's actually working," Alrion said, some surprised joy sneaking into his voice.

"It sure is!" Lara was transfixed by the dancing flame, her eyes following its motion.

"I think I'll quit while I'm ahead," Alrion said, as he felt his focus dropping a little. He mentally extinguished the flame and it puffed out in an instant. He examined his hand carefully, expecting to see some signs of the fire.

"Hand survived?" Lara said.

"Yes, it looks fine. Just a little warm." Alrion turned it over and felt it with his other hand. "I feel better."

"Better because you learned another spell?"

"Partly. Better because I released some of my frustration into the fire."

"Sounds good to me. And you avoided burning down this entire area."

"Yeah, that's also a plus." Alrion managed a small chuckle.

"Are we good to go?" Lara looked quite impatient.

"Yes. We really should leave. How long to Paperton?"

"Riding we should be there today, provided there are no more adventures." Lara climbed up onto the horse, leaving a space at the front for Alrion.

"I can't promise anything, but I think there's been enough excitement for today." Alrion checked to make sure everything he needed was packed and looked over the campsite one more time.

"It feels better leaving this time. More hopeful, less depressing." Alrion untied the horse.

"Good. You can do this."

"Thanks. I appreciate the help, I know I've been cautious and not trusting, but sorry in advance I will continue to be. Just realise that it's not because I'm ungrateful." Alrion clambered onto the horse, and steadied himself. He grasped the reins. Before he could direct the horse, he felt Lara holding onto him. It felt completely natural.

"Don't worry, I understand. You'll see, your trust today is well-founded."

"I take it we follow the road?"

"Yes, I'll show you the path when we need to divert to Paperton."

"Let's go then." Alrion wheeled the horse around and started their journey. The wounds were still raw, but he left some of the pain behind him.

26

THE PAPER GATEKEEPERS

The ride went smoothly, and they progressed swiftly along the main road. Alrion explained more to Lara as they went, including some basic information and filling in some of the gaps.

"You've come a long way. I probably haven't given you enough credit," she said.

"Not really."

"I apologise, but now's the time to prove it. We are almost there." Lara pointed into the distance. Alrion could see Paperton now, nestled down in a valley next to the lake. It was a sprawling collection of stone buildings with tiled roofs.

"Doesn't look very organised," he said.

"That is the town of scholars. It looks perfectly appropriate. Like stacks of paper left haphazardly around the place." Lara laughed.

"When you put it that way it does seem about right. You've been here before?"

"A while ago, but only as a visitor. I can direct you to their main hall, from what you said we should start there."

"Sounds good to me. Here we go." Alrion began the descent. As they traversed the winding path down to Paperton Alrion understood why the caravan did not take the route anymore. At times the path was relatively narrow, and the turns were tight. It would take the caravan a very long time to navigate that path, with no guarantee that they would be able to complete the journey.

"What can you tell me about them? The scholars?" he said.

"Not much, but they are sticklers for rules and regulations. They have laws and by-laws and statutes and all other kinds of things that must be followed. They do not believe in just figuring it out. You may have some difficulty getting their help."

"Thanks for the tip. I'd rather know before going in there, so I can try and start on the right foot." Alrion pulled the reins harshly, avoiding a nasty tumble. Lara didn't say anything, but did grip his shoulder so hard he felt her nails dig in.

Almost killing myself by falling off a horse wouldn't be the best introduction

"They sure do love their paperwork there." Lara picked up the conversation without much of a pause, "But you definitely need their help, from what Falric mentioned to you only they will know how to get to the Pool of Knowledge."

"Imagine that. What we need is kept safe by paper-pushers and not guards."

"A refreshing change."

"Definitely." Alrion could see more of the town now. It had a quaint quality to it, like it was a small village that had grown organically. It didn't have the harshness of some of the larger towns he had seen.

"Keep along here, there is a large hall at the end of this road," Lara said as they entered the town. Alrion couldn't see what she was referring to, due to the winding of the road but he followed the route, taking in the odd architecture as he went. Unlike other places, there weren't many people on the street.

"Where is everyone?"

"Not sure, maybe there's something on?"

"I hope we're not too late," Alrion said. If the black wizard knew about Paperton he could already be here.

Just focus on the task here. You can worry about him later.

A few turns later and Alrion finally spotted what Lara had been talking about. A giant stone hall sat above the rest of the town at the end of the road. It had a large black and white clock mounted at the top, and multiple stone columns framing the entrance.

"That must be it."

"That's it. It's the heart of their town, and also the brains." Lara laughed. Alrion smiled.

That was a terrible joke.

"Into the scholar's den," he muttered as they pushed forward. He noticed several horses tied up out the front, so he slowed and dismounted. After Lara bounded off, he tied up their horse and started to ascend the steps to the front door. He could hear the sound of talking from inside.

"Try and keep quiet so we can figure out what is going on," Lara said.

"Sure." Alrion slowed his walk and looked for people who might challenge him but there was nobody around. He reached the main doors, which were closed. With care, he pushed against one door.

It's not locked!

He continued to open the door and slipped inside, holding it for Lara to join him.

Alrion found himself inside a massive hall. The main floor was full of people, with a stage and a lectern at the end housing several others. He looked up and could see gallery after gallery of people in attendance as well.

"The whole town must be here," Alrion whispered.

"Must be. Let's keep it quiet," Lara said and Alrion nodded. He moved closer and lurked behind the back row of people.

"That concludes item eighty-seven of the agenda. Seal the room for the last agenda item," a strong male voice called out from the front. Two imposing men stepped forward towards the doors and stopped.

"Who are you?" the first man said.

What do I say? They'll probably realise I'm a stranger. I better just be straight with them.

"I'm Alrion, a visitor."

"This is a private meeting, get out." The man reached out to assist them leaving.

"I'm sorry but I really must see your leader. It's an urgent matter." Alrion stood his ground. Lara stood with him.

"You may file a meeting request tomorrow, and it will be processed in due course. But you must leave now." The man sighed wearily and pointed to the door.

"He's a wizard, very important business. Can't we file the paperwork later?" Lara said.

"Wizards have no special permissions, they must also follow the same rules and regulations as the rest of us," the second man said.

"You don't understand, this is an emergency. Now is the time to raise this, and I think with everyone here the perfect chance to brief everybody at once," Alrion said.

"No. Please leave before we are forced to escort you out. With force." The first man took a step forward.

"Why are we delayed in securing the room?" the man at the front called out.

"Out of my way," Alrion said, his frustration building. He threw his hand out in front of him, mentally attaching a push to it. Not a normal push but a spear-like column that forged ahead. It parted the mob, clearing a path ahead of him.

Each displaced scholar gasped and turned with surprise. Alrion capitalised on their confusion and walked along the newly made path, using the distraction to progress. Lara followed closely behind, smirking at any of the scholars that looked over at her.

The scholars stood back in silence, surprised by the intrusion. Alrion walked all the way up to the front. His burst of frustration had made him act tough, but it was running thin now. He had realised what he had just done, and was alternating between feeling embarrassed and trying to stoke the fires of frustration and urgency and stay on the offensive. He looked up at the speaker standing at the lectern. The man was old and wrinkled, with a long grey beard. He regarded Alrion with disdain.

"Are you the leader?"

"No, you impudent whelp, I am the Speaker. What gives you the right to barge in here?"

"My name is Alrion and I have a very urgent need. I don't have the luxury of waiting for the paperwork to be completed. I must speak with your leader about the Pool of Knowledge." Alrion was surprised that his voice sounded more confident than he felt.

"You are wasting our time with such fairy tales," the Speaker said.

"No fairy tale at all. I was brought here by the wizard Falric who not only confirmed that it exists but also that Paperton was the place to gain access." Alrion had fudged the facts a little, but he needed to confirm that the scholars could actually help him.

"Falric. Yes, we know him. Perhaps he can clear up this confusion?" The Speaker looked behind Alrion. Lara smiled back at him.

"Unfortunately, he was killed this morning by an evil wizard. One who is on his way here. That's why I am in your hall without my mentor, and also why this matter is so urgent," Alrion said. A gasp went up among those on the stage.

"A major loss, if that is true. However, how are we to know that you are who you say you are, and Falric is indeed lost to us? How do we know you are not the one that killed him?" the Speaker said. Alrion paused for a moment. He had to rein in his annoyance and think of a solution.

"Show them the spellbook," Lara whispered to him. Alrion nodded and rummaged through his bag.

"Look at this, it is Falric's spellbook!" Alrion said. He handed it to the Speaker.

"Looks legitimate, but the pages are all blank."

"It is protected by magic, but surely a scholar such as yourself can read some of the pages."

"I can indeed, I was testing you. I can see his mark on the book. It would be hard to come into possession of this without him desiring it. But are you even a wizard?"

"Yes. I am a wizard." Alrion decided to demonstrate, and at the same time do a little tribute to Falric. He closed his eyes and focused again on his Spark, fanning the flames, and increasing the intensity. He channelled it into a flame and tried this time to give the flame some shape. More than the simple flare he had done earlier.

"What?" the Speaker called out.

"I like what you did there," Lara said, enjoying the reaction. Alrion opened his eyes to see how his spell had turned out. Shock and surprise were on the Speaker's face. The whole group on the stage were on their feet, backing away. It was even better than Alrion had hoped.

A flame extended from his upturned palm, but it didn't just go straight up. It bent and split into many smaller and connected flames, depicting the outline of a book with the letter 'F' in the middle of the cover. It filled the air above the stage, the heat threatening to set the stage alight.

"That's quite enough," the Speaker said, and Alrion let the flame dissipate.

"Are you satisfied?" Alrion said.

"While your demonstration was acceptable, we need to confer before we come to you with a decision."

"How long will this take?"

"As long as it needs to take," the Speaker said. Alrion felt Lara leaning in close.

"Great that you got this far, I don't think you can push your luck much further. Be gracious," she whispered.

"That's all I can ask. I shall wait for your response. But please do be mindful of the urgency here. A deadly wizard is after the Pool of Knowledge, and we need to be ready for that."

"Don't worry; there are those who have been prepared for such things. Please wait in the guest rooms until you have an answer. We will return the spellbook to you at the same time," the Speaker said.

"Thank you." Alrion turned to leave. He tried to ignore all the strange looks and keep his composure as he walked through the crowd.

I can't believe I did that, he thought. Nevertheless, he pushed the thought away. He couldn't afford to undermine himself with doubt. There would be plenty of time for that later if he so wished.

A short man pushed through all the people and stopped in front of Alrion.

"Alrion, my name is Caleb. I have been tasked with directing you to your accommodation."

"Caleb? Thanks. This is Lara."

"Nice to meet you, Caleb. Are you a scholar too?" Lara said.

"Of course, but a junior one. That was quite a display back there."

"It had to be. I hope this process doesn't take too long," Alrion said.

"I think they like you, they never agree to convene on such short notice."

"Wow, I'd hate to see what happens if they don't like you." Alrion laughed.

"It's always according to the letter of our law, but if you really ticked off the wrong person you could be waiting months for the most basic decision to be taken." Caleb had a serious look on his face.

He's not joking around.

"Sounds pretty awful," Lara said.

"It probably sounds worse than it is. I don't think they would force outsiders to wait for months. That's saved for internal squabbles. Let's just get ourselves out of the hall," Caleb said.

Within a few minutes, they were outside, even with the commotion and the curious scholars trying to stop them with questions.

"Now we can breathe. What an exciting time!" Caleb said.

"You think this is exciting? It gets better, or worse depending on your perspective," Alrion said.

"Surely better, a little excitement could never hurt. Paperton is quiet, with good reason. It was explicitly designed to be so. It's conducive to research and learning."

"Makes sense to me. Do you get a chance to travel?"

"Yes, but only once you are formally admitted into the Fellowship."

"I hope you get there soon. I too lived a fairly sheltered life, but since I set foot outside my home it's been quite an adventure." Alrion was already starting to feel a kinship with this Caleb. They had a lot in common.

"Much appreciated, I look forward to the opportunity. Here we are." Caleb stopped in front of a small house. It was a simple structure, painted all in white with a bright blue door. Caleb unlocked the door and walked inside. Alrion and Lara followed.

The house was tiny but functional. Alrion saw a sitting room with a couch and two chairs, a basic kitchen and larder, and a bedroom.

"I hope we won't need to stay that long." Alrion put his bag down, and Lara did the same.

"Hopefully not, but the place is kitted out for longer stays just in case," Caleb said.

"How long do you think I'll have to wait?"

"A few hours at the earliest, it's quite a strange request."

"Can you tell me anything about the Pool of Knowledge?"

"Not much, it's a well-kept secret. The less that people know, the better. We wouldn't even acknowledge its existence for most visitors."

"Sure, but can you tell me anything?"

"Just generally available information. Access is restricted, nobody gets to go there. Which is why it is incredible they are even deliberating about your request. I don't know exactly why it is so restricted, but I get the impression that it is about protecting the pool from the wrong people." Caleb looked uncomfortable talking about it.

"That's pretty vague. Why not just tell us something interesting, even if it is just a rumour?" Lara said.

"Fine, that's a fair point. And maybe you'll get to see it anyway. They say it is an actual pool, and the knowledge of the world is contained there. You can see why they would want to protect that. Knowledge is power after all," Caleb said.

"That's exactly why I need to be there. Also, why the black wizard wants access too. Knowledge is a key pillar of magic. In most cases, you can't cast the spell if you don't know it is possible." Alrion saw Caleb nodding along.

I don't think I'm telling him anything he doesn't already know.

"Very interesting. I'm sorry I can't be of more help, but I don't know enough. I will suggest though that you rest. We don't know how long they will be deliberating. They will send for you when there is a decision," Caleb said.

"Thanks for your help. Will they be sending you?"

"Not sure, but likely."

"Then I hope I see you soon," Alrion said.

"Me too." Caleb waved and left the tiny house.

"He's right, you know," Lara said, after the door closed.

"About what?"

"Resting. It has been a long day, and you don't know how long the wait will be. But when they say yes, you need to be ready."

"I agree in theory, but resting now will be hard. I'll try." Alrion headed off for the bedroom. He knew he couldn't sleep immediately, so he decided to try and mentally rehearse some of his spells. He didn't have his spellbook or the time to try and learn something new, but he knew that he would need as much magic as he could muster for whatever lay ahead.

27

THE ABANDONED GATE

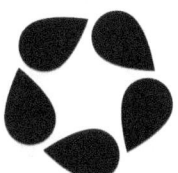

Alrion awoke to the sound of a bell and sat upright. He hadn't even remembered falling asleep. He dashed out of the bedroom.

"Talk about a rude awakening," Lara said. She was lying on the couch, and let out a little yawn. Alrion could see it was still dark outside. He walked straight to the front door and opened it. Caleb was standing outside, holding a torch and a handheld brass bell.

"Alrion, the hall has completed their deliberation. You have been summoned to receive their judgement."

"Thank you, I will come immediately," Alrion said. Lara jumped up and joined him.

"Any indication of what the decision is?" Alrion asked.

"I am acting in the official capacity of the Notifier. I cannot engage in discourse."

"Fine." Alrion didn't really expect an answer but was desperate to find out. He had no idea how long he had slept, and he felt like he was already behind. They walked swiftly back to the hall. Caleb opened the main doors and held them open. After Alrion and Lara walked through, he closed the doors behind them and stood guard.

Alrion heard the doors locking behind him.

"They mean business," Lara said.

"They sure do, I just hope it's good for us," Alrion said, his doubt growing. The hall was empty save for the men collected on the stage. Alrion walked through the echoing empty hall with as much courage as he could gather, but he felt like with each step the giant space was mocking his approach. Such a huge and old structure seemed to impose itself unfairly upon him. The Speaker was standing at the lectern. As Alrion approached he spoke up.

"Alrion, the student of Falric, stop right there and await your judgement!" Alrion stopped, confusion and fear foremost in his thoughts. He waited for the Speaker to continue.

"We have deliberated over your case, your history, and your actions before us. We must say that we are concerned by your brash behaviour and the ignorance you have shown in your plea," he said before pausing.

I don't like where this is heading.

"We have balanced that against the great need you have explained to us, and the passing of the great wizard Falric, one of our own. Would that he was here today, we would feel a lot more comfortable," the Speaker said, again pausing.

"They're not comfortable, do you think this means they're considering it?" Alrion whispered to Lara.

"Sounds like it to me, but you never know with these types," she said.

"As we are just the initial gatekeepers, we have decided to allow your request. Your merit will be judged by others more worthy. Approach, so that you may be admitted." The Speaker beckoned for Alrion to come closer. The young wizard took a moment to process what was said.

"Go, don't let them second-guess themselves," Lara hissed at him. Alrion stepped forward and continued walking towards the stage. It sounded like they had grudgingly agreed to his request, but there was another barrier to get past. Whatever the circumstances it didn't matter, it was progress. Alrion ascended the stairs onto the stage and approached the Speaker.

"These are strange times Alrion, and we must act in kind. At the rear of the stage is a doorway, which will lead you to a secret passage. That passage will take you to the Ancient Gates. There you will be tested, by the wisest and strongest among us. If they consider you worthy, they will grant you access."

"Thank you, for your help. Is this the only way to access the Pool?"

"Yes, there is no other way. Therefore, this other wizard you mentioned has not come, or we would know about it. We will prevent him if he is as you have described."

"Be careful, he is incredibly powerful. What test awaits me further in?"

"We cannot comment on that. It is for you to discover." A smile crept over the Speaker's face, but disappeared quickly.

That's something Falric would say.

"Can I have my spellbook back?"

"Yes, but not until you return. You may take nothing with you, save the clothes on your back. And she must wait here." The Speaker pointed at Lara.

"No problem, I can't help you in there anyway. Take care, Alrion." Lara gave him a reassuring smile, and he couldn't help smiling back.

"I guess I should go then. Who knows how much time I have?" Alrion nodded at the Speaker, then turned to walk across the stage. The group of scholars stood and stepped to the side, the path between their chairs leading to a darkened area. Alrion walked through as confidently as possible, trying not to think of all the eyes watching and scrutinising his every step. As he passed them, he could see more detail in the distance. It was a simple wooden door, reinforced with steel bars and a steel handle. He reached out and grabbed the handle, pulling the door open.

A cold breeze reached him, and he could feel moisture in the air. Ahead was a dark tunnel, hewn out of the rock. There were lit torches at intervals along the tunnel.

"Here I go." Alrion stepped inside and let the door close behind him. The sound of the door locking had finality to it. As if the way back was now sealed. He could only go forward. Alrion walked down the hallway, wondering what test awaited him. It sounded like there were some special elders that he needed to confront next.

As if the scholars I just dealt with weren't enough of a pain, he thought. However, if any of the stories Caleb had told him was true, then it made sense. All the knowledge in the world would be a huge gift for any person, as well as an incredible responsibility. One that needs guarding and using sparingly.

I don't think I'm worthy, not yet. But it's my quest, and I must continue.

The secret behind his grandfather's spell would be here, and the knowledge needed to make it work for good. Maybe he could teach others instead, maybe he would just be a conduit for that knowledge. But he wouldn't know what lay ahead until he completed this task.

Alrion progressed down the path and started to see what was at the end. It widened out into a larger room, cut out of the rock. Torches circled the room and highlighted a giant circular stone door. On either side of the door were two stone thrones, roughly cut with sharp angles on a raised platform. But the thrones were empty. A set of stone steps led up to the platform.

There's nobody here, Alrion thought as he stepped into the room. He had expected somebody to confront him, and the presence of the two thrones suggested it would be two people but there was no sign of a living soul. He noticed carvings on the door, so he approached to investigate.

One way or another, I need to get this door open, he thought but he had a bad feeling in the pit of his stomach. Something was not right. The door was not supposed to be abandoned. Especially since they knew he was coming.

"Just focus on the task," Alrion whispered. He ascended the stone steps carefully, focusing on reaching the top. As he climbed the last stair, he walked over to the thrones and looked at them. One had three wavy lines carved into the right armrest. The other had a star carved into the left armrest.

I wonder what they are for? Do they mean something?

The thrones were otherwise unmarked. He stepped forward and took in the big circular door. There were pictures carved into it that depicted people, and books, and a pool.

It must be related to the story of this place. Or part of a riddle, Alrion thought. He noticed some writing carved into the base of the door and bent down to examine it.

The provider of all things gives access to those who are worthy.

"This is a riddle," Alrion said quietly. He examined the pictures up close, trying to discern their meaning. He pressed carefully over different shapes and symbols on the door, to see if anything happened. The stone door remained silent and unresponsive.

I don't think there's a secret handle, it must be something else, Alrion thought. At the very centre of the door, he saw that the stone looked slightly different. He ran his hand over it and noticed something. The surface and colour of the stone changed slightly when he touched it. However, within a second, it had reverted back.

"This section responds to touch, that has to be significant," Alrion said as he stepped back and regarded the whole door. No other areas looked the same.

The area that responds to touch must be the place for my answer. But what is the answer and how do I represent it?

He decided to tackle the riddle first. It referenced a test of worth, and the prize at the other end was access to the Pool of Knowledge. By Alrion's reckoning, it had to be a test of knowledge or application of knowledge. A student who was worthy would be granted access to more knowledge. He decided to look again at the pictures on the door.

The first depicted a man lying in a house with the sunlight streaming in. The second showed him working and planting crops. The third depicted him returning home with the sun setting and stars visible. The stars made him think of the carving in the throne, so he went back and had another look at it.

"Stars provide light at night and so does the sun during the day," Alrion said aloud. He looked at the other throne.

"I don't know what these wavy lines mean, they could be the sun's rays but maybe that is already covered? What else could it be?" Alrion said under his breath as he walked back to the stone door and examined the pictures once more.

The man is growing crops under the sun, the heat from the sun helping them to grow. Maybe that's it?

He tried drawing the wavy lines with his hand on the stone centre. Nothing happened. Alrion thought over the riddle some more. It had to be something else. The constant in all the images were the man and the sun.

Well if you think about it, the sun seems to be giving him something in every picture. In the first, it wakes him up. In the second, it helps him to grow food. And in the last one it helps him return home to rest, the stars taking over, Alrion thought, pointing at the sun in each picture. That was the common element and tied in with the riddle.

"Worth a try," Alrion said and reached out. He placed his hand onto the centre of the door and traced a circle shape. He heard a clank and stepped back. The massive circular door moved forward, then started to roll to the right exposing another corridor behind. Before Alrion could see what lay beyond, he was assaulted by a strange smell.

What is that?

He stepped forward and looked around. Something was there on the ground, but he couldn't quite make it out. He focused and drew forth his Spark, igniting a small flame above his upturned palm. With the additional light, he could see what it was. Two bodies.

These must be the guardians, Alrion thought. They were wearing dark-blue robes and looked quite old. After examining them, he could see what the cause of death was. Thick stone rods pierced them. Alrion stumbled back as the realisation dawned upon him.

The black wizard must have done this. He used a lot of earth magic against Falric. That means he's already here and has been for a while.

Alrion wasn't prepared for this, even though he thought he was.

The Pool of Knowledge was there beyond the darkness, but the black wizard was probably also there. The one who had killed Falric.

Alrion turned back, considering a retreat. It was tantalising and seductive, but it didn't solve his problem, and he ran the risk that the Pool would be destroyed. He didn't take that wizard for the sharing type.

"You can do this," Alrion told himself as he carefully stepped around the dead bodies. However, as much as he tried, he didn't really believe it. Not yet.

28

THE SPARK IGNITES

Alrion walked steadily down the pitch-black tunnel, his tiny flame only lighting the area in front of him. His mind played tricks on him, projecting dread shapes from the blackness. However, he forged on, determined to reach his goal. The sound of his steps was small and insignificant as they echoed around the tunnel. He could smell something else as he got further and further from the slain gatekeepers. He couldn't quite place it, but it was like damp.

I'm looking for a pool, that would make sense, he thought, happy to have something other than the menacing dark to focus on. He started to see something in the distance and tried to make it out as he walked.

It was a light-blue glow coming from up ahead. An unnatural glow that suggested it was magical. Feeling bolder, Alrion upped the pace. Perhaps there was a chance he could access the Pool safely. The tunnel narrowed, then started widening rapidly. He was about to reach his destination.

The tunnel ended in another cavernous room. In the centre of the room, he saw what looked like a naturally created stone formation. The blue glow was from the liquid within. It seemed to swirl around slowly, without any reason for it but another detail grabbed Alrion's complete attention.

A man stood in front of the Pool, with his head bowed and his back to Alrion.

"So, you're here at last," the man said. Alrion stopped. He knew it was the black wizard, and that things would finally come to a head. There was no avoiding it. So many thoughts ran through his head.

What do I say?

"You were waiting for me?" Alrion stepped closer trying to get a better look.

"Yes. I knew that you would show yourself eventually. And I wanted to thank you." The wizard turned around, keeping his face hidden.

"Thank me? For what?"

"If it wasn't for you, I would never have known that this place existed," the wizard said. Alrion was confused.

How have I helped him?

"Reveal yourself then." Alrion could see the wizard thinking it over.

"I suppose it is only fair, for you to see who killed your mentor and will be killing you next." The wizard pushed back the black hood and showed his face. He had a cruel smile which looked scary with the blue light from the pool dancing over it.

"Branthor!" Alrion called out in disbelief. It didn't make sense. Falric's right-hand man, and most trusted wizard. It did explain how the black wizard had been tracking them and knew their destination.

"Why? How could you do this?"

"There are many reasons, but it comes down to the fact that I am sick of being treated like a second-class citizen. Just because I am not of your bloodline." Branthor spoke the words with real venom, his mouth curled into a sneer.

"What do you mean?"

"This here, this Pool is a revelation. The knowledge of the world, and in particular the knowledge of Granthion. All of it is available to me now. I can set things right, do what must be done."

"I don't understand. Why is this so important to you?"

What happened to him?

"Your grandfather performed the cleansing ritual twenty years ago. Nobody knew it was even possible; he kept that nugget to himself. He didn't share any of his knowledge. But his process was imperfect." Branthor stepped forward and showed his forearm. "See this mark?"

"What of it?" Alrion noticed the curved black line.

"Those who are tainted by the Blight are all marked in a similar way."

"You're tainted?"

This doesn't make sense. Falric said that he wasn't, that he would have sensed the change to his Spark.

"Yes, and no. I was in fact. But your grandfather's spell cleansed me, or so it would seem. I can use my Spark without fear of corruption and my mind is my own. But, it's not that simple." Branthor said. He started approaching Alrion, very slowly.

"My connection to the Blight remains. I can feel the others and if I concentrate, I can communicate with them. I am straddling worlds, the light, and the dark. I cannot lose myself to the darkness, but I cannot escape it. I am cursed because of the spell used by your grandfather!" Branthor's voice was rising in anger and intensity with every word.

"What do you intend to do? Aside from killing everyone in your way?"

"I'm going to take the knowledge from here, and I'm going to create a new breed of man. Tied to, but free from the Blight. And we will rule this world like no other has before."

"That's crazy. You want to make others like yourself?" Alrion instinctively took a step back.

I don't like where this conversation is going. He's out of his mind.

"Of course. The Blight has strength to it. The kinship and shared communication creates a powerful force. United in purpose. Foot soldiers, commanders, and specialists all working in perfect unity. We can take this curse and turn it to our advantage. Until now, I had no hope. I could not unlock the secrets of the Blight, of how to alter or reverse the process. But now, I have all I need." Branthor clenched his hand into a fist.

"Why kill me then?"

"Because I won't let the knowledge leave this place. Once you are dealt with, I will destroy the Pool and kill all who have access. The secrets that were once denied to me will be denied to all but those I choose. It's time for me to be in the inner circle, not left to suffer in ignorance."

"This isn't the only way, we can work together to cure you."

"It is far too late for that. I will not waste the knowledge here on such a petty plan. No, I will do far more. I will place my stamp on the world!" Branthor waved his hand and a wall of stone rose behind Alrion, blocking the tunnel behind him. Blocking his only way out.

There goes my chance at escaping. And he can't be reasoned with.

"As my way of saying thanks, I will let you die in honour. Fight me, and perish in battle," Branthor said.

"You killed Falric. You killed or injured countless others. You would kill me and start up your crazy quest for revenge on my family and the world. I will not let that happen!" Alrion said. His anger, and hurt, and loss fanned the flames of his Spark. He could feel the heat rising through him. Building and gathering. He poured more of himself into it, feeding the flames, adding fuel to the fire. Then something happened.

His Spark blew up, surging, and building with a life of its own. As if it were feeding and sustaining itself.

"Impressive, you have managed to ignite your Spark. But it won't be enough little wizard." Branthor raised a spear of earth from the ground and flung it at Alrion. Purely on instinct, he unleashed a force spell to deflect the spear. Even with all his strength behind it, he only just managed to move it far enough so that it thudded right next to him.

"Nice start, but you can't keep this up." Branthor started raising chunks of earth from the ground, moulding them into giant stones.

He's not going to let up. He's going to keep going until I'm dead.

Alrion combined the fire and push spells, sending out a rolling wave of fire at Branthor. It twirled and writhed as it flew, as if it had a life of its own. Branthor countered by dropping some of the stones down and forming them into a quick wall to shield himself.

At least he can be hurt, he's defending himself, Alrion thought. He had no idea how to fight a wizard, so that was reassuring that Branthor deemed his attacks dangerous enough to defend against. But it's all he had. While Branthor was distracted, Alrion picked up the stone spear next to him and readied it. He ran a few steps to the side and aimed it around Branthor's wall.

As he threw it, he put all his power into a force spell behind it. The column of stone flew through the air, spiralling as it went. Branthor noticed it, closed his eyes, and held out a hand. The stone spear slowed, then disintegrated.

"Earth is my strong suit. You can't hurt me with it," Branthor said, chuckling.

"If you're so good with it, why did you attack us with fire back in the Whispering Forest?" Alrion said.

Maybe I can buy myself some time to come up with a better attack. He's quite confident.

"Hah, that was just fun and games. The fire did its job of confusing Falric, and I didn't intend to kill you then. I just wanted to keep you running. Worked perfectly." Branthor changed his stance and put his hand on the ground.

A wave of rock rose up from the ground, undulating towards Alrion. He ran to the side as fast as he could, trying to get away. The rock wave was so fast and wide that he wasn't going to make it. Alrion closed his eyes and tried to push himself aside with magic. It didn't work well, but he got enough of a result to narrowly escape.

"You have good reactions. You are definitely talented. Such a shame. Perhaps I should rethink my approach. Do you wish to join me?" Branthor said. Alrion paused, catching his breath. He wanted Branthor to think that he was giving the option real consideration.

"No, I'm not going to betray everyone like you did. I want to improve the world, not make it suffer."

"Very well, I had to ask. It would have been nice to have a talented protégé like yourself. Oh well, there are plenty more where you came from. A whole academy in fact." Branthor focused again, causing rocks from the ceiling to start falling down above Alrion.

Not good, Alrion thought as he tried to avoid the falling debris. But try as he might, he got nicked and slammed by smaller rocks.

"I can do this all day. What's your next move?" Branthor said. He was clearly enjoying himself. Alrion was so busy scrambling to avoid being crushed and buried, he couldn't think of what to do next.

All or nothing.

Alrion weaved through the falling stones, changing his direction to head straight at Branthor.

I just need one good hit.

He noticed the rocks thinning out, as he got closer to Branthor.

"Rushing to your death? I appreciate the sentiment," Branthor said, mocking Alrion. As the young wizard closed in he accumulated as much heat and power in his hand as possible, pouring in everything he had.

One shot, he thought. Suddenly he released it all. An explosion of flame erupted from his hand, giving Branthor almost no time to react. But the wizard had expected it, and a rock formation rose to block the flame. The shield of earth didn't stay still, it continued moving forward. Alrion's flame melted through half of it but enough remained of the moving earthen barrier that he was smashed back into the rubble. Alrion lay still, the wind knocked out of him.

"It's been fun, Alrion, but you are no match for me. Perhaps one day, but not today."

"It's not over," Alrion said, coughing. Everything hurt, but he hadn't given up.

"It is now." Branthor closed his fist. The rock around Alrion solidified into spikes and plunged into him. He felt a sharp pain, then blackness.

29

ONE STRIKE

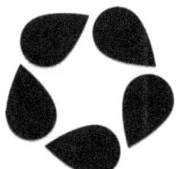

Alrion regained consciousness and tried to move. When he couldn't, he remembered what had happened.

"I'm surprised that you're still alive, but keep doing that and you'll end it faster," Branthor said. He was standing over Alrion, a wicked smile on his face.

"What now?" Alrion said, struggling to get the words out.

"I guess I have a decision to make. I can kill you immediately, let you bleed out, or I can hope you last long enough to infect you with the Blight."

"What?"

"Yes, you heard me right. I can call a creature here to turn you. It's not ideal, but it would make you easier to control and I could always restore you later once I have the capability. Decisions, decisions." Branthor turned and started pacing.

"Where are you going?"

"To drink from the Pool. Now that you and Falric are out of the picture, it is safe to do so. I wasn't able to get much information from those so-called guardians. I'm not entirely sure how it works." Branthor continued to the Pool at a leisurely pace.

This is an opportunity.

Maybe there was a way he could free himself while Branthor was occupied. He started to probe his restraints to determine how he was held and what damage had been done.

"Can you believe it is actually a pool? These stories are never so literal, it is refreshing," Branthor said. "Still with me? Don't worry, I can see that you are." Alrion decided not to respond and save his energy.

He discovered at least two stone spikes that had pierced through him and were restricting his movement. There were likely more. He felt weak and knew that he was in serious trouble. Branthor may not have killed him outright, but he had badly wounded him.

"What do you think the protocol is here? Do I just stick my head inside? Is there a special cup to use?" Branthor said as he inspected the Pool closely. He didn't wait for Alrion to respond.

"You're being awfully quiet back there, I had best drink immediately. Perhaps my newfound knowledge will give me some great ideas about what to do with you."

"You could heal me," Alrion said, his voice a little stronger than he expected.

"Don't be silly, why would I do that? If I turned you, the Blight would save you. Besides, healing just isn't my strong point. Never really saw the point." Branthor turned back and bent over the Pool.

"No point in delaying further, I hope it tastes good." He knelt down and cupped his hands, filling them with water from the Pool. He drank the water swiftly, wiping his face afterwards. While he was distracted, Alrion tried weakening the spikes so that he could detach them from the ground and hopefully remove them. He could get to one with his hands, but the others would require magic which would potentially tip off Branthor.

"Doesn't taste like anything, so that's a good sign. I'm probably not poisoned. Did they tell you how long it takes to work?" Branthor said, walking back to Alrion.

"I know nothing."

"Truer words than you realise. I've come to a decision."

"What's that?" Alrion gently probed with a force spell, feeling where the stone spikes had impaled him. He didn't realise he could morph a push spell this way. He wasn't sure how much Branthor could detect, but if he was careful and used minimal Spark perhaps he could get by unnoticed.

"You shouldn't be wasted; you would be a good addition to the cause. It's not ideal, but I think you should be infected. All you need to do is stay alive long enough for the process to happen."

"I'd rather die."

"Empty words. You can't do anything. And I doubt you have the strength of Will to do so anyway."

"How long do I have?" Alrion said.

I need to buy some time, keep him occupied.

"Not long, probably an hour or so. It looks like I was tidy with my attack, I don't think I hit any vital organs. You should be happy."

"Happy that you've pinned me down and want to infect me with the Blight?"

"Exactly. It's a privilege, you just don't know it yet. Now then, how do I access this new knowledge?" Branthor said.

"Maybe you are not worthy." Alrion coughed, pain wracking his chest.

"If anybody here is not worthy, it is you. You are a simple fledgling, just following orders. It's a miracle you made it this far. If I had wanted to destroy you earlier, I had ample opportunity. Yes, you are not worthy. But in time, you will prove useful." Branthor continued pacing around the room.

Alrion felt himself weakening by the second. Even if Branthor was right and his wounds were not immediately fatal, in his weakened state he would not be able to resist when they infected him, and all would be for nothing. He couldn't let Branthor win. He had to find a way.

Suddenly, he had an idea. One last roll of the dice. One gamble for it all. He smiled and forced a laugh, the pain in his chest worth it.

"What are you laughing about?" Branthor looked at Alrion with suspicion and started to walk back.

"You don't even know how to activate the knowledge you have acquired. It's actually hilarious. It doesn't matter if I die here today, you will not succeed. You have failed all by yourself," Alrion said.

"You ignorant little ant. How dare you act all high and mighty? You're on the brink of death, and I could kill you at any time. Time is what I have, time is what you lack. Even if it takes me years to obtain the knowledge I require, that is fine. You will be powerless to stop me. In fact, you will be helping me very soon." Branthor's flare of anger simmered down into malice, a wicked smile mocking Alrion.

Alrion tried to respond but instead coughed harshly.

Maybe it's too late, he thought. Regardless, it was now or never. He forced out a harsh whisper that was inaudible.

"What was that? Having trouble talking back? Let me hear your clever retort," Branthor said. He approached Alrion and leaned closer.

"C'mon, let's hear it." Branthor pointed to his ear. Alrion grabbed his entire Spark as if he was wielding an iron fist. He wrenched it all out and threw it in a single surge. Everything he had, in one attack but focused on the stone spears and spikes impaling him. He forced every single one out of his body, and into Branthor's chest.

The speed and force of the attack surprised Branthor, and he was so close he couldn't react in time. Alrion almost passed out from the pain, but he had the presence of mind to clutch at his own chest, trying to stem the blood flow.

Branthor stumbled backward, a stunned look on his face.

"How?" he said, muttering the word just loud enough for Alrion to hear.

"I got lucky." Alrion reached for his Spark, and found a small pocket available. His head was spinning, and the pain was threatening to make him faint, but he focused just enough to start a healing spell.

"You fool, that will never work. You can't heal yourself," Branthor said.

"I don't need it to work, I just need it to hold me together a little longer," Alrion said. He didn't have much Spark left but used what he could. He remembered Falric's lecture about the healing spell. About how it relied on the Spark, so it wasn't effective on your own body but he didn't care.

Alrion focused his Will on making it work better, on his own body responding to the treatment. He drew on whatever power he had within to somehow hold himself together. He refused to die here, or wait for infection by the Blight. He would complete his mission, and live to fight on.

"You'll never make it out of here," Branthor said as he fell to the ground.

"That's my line," Alrion said. Branthor was breathing with difficulty.

"I can survive this, just you wait."

"Not going to, I'm going to leave while I can." Alrion dragged himself up to a seated position. He felt over his chest and found that the wounds had sealed up somewhat.

At least my guts won't be falling out, he thought. He steeled himself and forced himself up into a crouch. A sharp pain went right through him, but he managed to stay in the position. He leaned against some nearby fallen rocks and lifted himself to a semi-upright stance.

"Don't think that you've won," Branthor said.

"Save your energy," Alrion said, and started to head towards the Pool of Knowledge. Its glow was calling him. But he took his time. Each foot placed in front of the other, methodically and with care. Any loss of concentration would cause him to fall over, and he wasn't sure if he could get up again. When he hadn't heard any more taunting from Branthor, he paused and looked over.

Branthor was quiet, his eyes were closed but his chest still moved up and down, although in a slow and laboured way.

He's not my problem, Alrion thought and continued on. Gradually he continued, at a crawling pace.

"Almost there, hold it together," he told himself. One more step.

Then one more. Then he arrived. The Pool glowed, its mystical blue water looking every bit as magical as he assumed it was.

I just need a sip, at least for now. Let's not overdo things.

He bent down slowly, making sure he was stable. He reached out with his right hand and steadied himself with his left. As he touched the water, his strength failed him, and he toppled into the Pool headfirst.

30

BAPTISM

Alrion awoke with a gasp. His body was cold, too cold. Everything hurt, and he struggled to move. He realised that he was immersed in the Pool of Knowledge.

I could have drowned.

He had fallen in a lucky way, with his body leaning against the contours of the bottom of the pool and his head out of the water. He managed to shuffle backward so that he was sitting more upright in the water.

I hope I haven't ruined it, he thought. He forced his right arm to move and cupped some water within it, after a few attempts. He managed to gulp the water down and did it a second time for good measure.

Since I'm here, I'd better make this work.

The fluids seemed to revive him a little, so he decided to make the best of it and get moving. In one big movement, he stood up and tumbled out of the Pool. He landed on the ground with a *thud* and regretted it instantly.

At least I won't drown.

With some care, he got back onto his feet and started walking away.

How long was I out? He wondered. The room he was in looked the same, there were no signs of the passage of time. Branthor was still there, but Alrion couldn't see if he was still breathing.

"Not your problem, just keep moving," Alrion told himself. He turned to face the exit. The blockage that Branthor had created had been damaged during the fight but was still mostly intact. Alrion paused and looked around. He selected an area that looked promising and staggered over. There were multiple holes and large cracks all concentrated in this one place.

Don't fail me now, he thought, searching for his Spark. He could sense some there, but grabbing at it was like water slipping through his fingers. With enough persistence, he did manage to gather some Spark and placed his hand on the middle of the weakest area. He unleashed his entire Spark into an explosion of force, rocking the stone wall.

Sections of the wall collapsed, and large cracks formed throughout the rest. The impact was much greater than he expected.

I better not get buried alive in here with Branthor, he thought, watching the wall crack, and contort. The motion finally died down, and he eased himself through a large hole.

"That wasn't so bad," he said and started walking away. A loud crash startled him, and he turned back. The rest of the wall collapsed in waves, showering where he had been standing in rubble. Alrion gulped hard and decided not to think too much about it. He looked ahead.

The tunnel was pitch black, but Alrion was unable to cast any magic. He found the tunnel wall and used it to guide him along. The intense darkness and his slow progress made him lose all sense of time. He knew he had to hurry, in case the reinforcements that Branthor had requested arrived but he also knew that if he rushed, he would fall, and his luck wouldn't extend enough to let him get up again.

After a long, painful slog, he reached the door. It had sealed behind him. He felt a mixture of relief and annoyance.

Well, maybe it opens the same way on this side, Alrion thought. He felt his way along the stone door until he noticed the change in texture in the centre. He was careful not to move too far over, in case he stumbled over the bodies of the guardians. He drew a circle with his hand and stepped back. Nothing happened.

"Work, damn you!" Alrion cried out, and smashed the door with his palm. A loud *thunk* rang out and the door started to move. Alrion staggered back to avoid it and leaned on the tunnel wall. A crack of light, then a flood washed over his eyes. The dimly lit entrance hall was a bright beacon of hope. Once his eye adjusted, he stepped out cautiously and leaned on one of the stone thrones. He edged around it and let himself sink into it. He was too quick to do so and felt the pain as his body hit the stone, but it was a relief to sit down.

Maybe I shouldn't have done this, I won't want to get up, Alrion thought but then he pictured a horde of Blighters or worse streaming down the tunnel and he stood up again. He had to keep moving.

He felt somewhat renewed by the better-lit entrance and the fact that he was close to civilisation again. He just had to struggle on. Step after agonising step. He was so deathly tired.

I could just sink down over there, close my eyes and rest.

The cold stone looked so inviting but he knew if he did so he would never wake. And while there was some comfort in that in his weary state, he didn't want it. So, he pushed on, ignoring the cries of his body.

He finally reached the wooden door that led to the main hall and he rejoiced. He pulled the door open with such force that he almost lost balance and fell through the doorway, but he caught himself and only fell to one knee. He looked up, expecting an audience, but the room was empty. The Speaker and the council had all left.

Great, Alrion thought. His trek was not over. He picked himself up and continued walking. Across the stage, down the steps, and through the hall. His lonely trek felt like the entire length of his journey up until this point but all he could do was move forward, so he did. One step at a time. He reached the giant doors at the end of the hall, which were also deserted. Alrion sighed, and pushed on them, gaining access to the outside.

It was still dark out, and the streets were still. He remembered the way back to his lodging and praised the fact that it was close. He considered calling out but didn't think he had the voice to do it. He kept walking, pausing to lean on buildings and fences as required.

"Just keep going, you made it this far," he told himself. "You can't waste the knowledge that you have gained." Alrion spotted the small house and felt a wave of relief. It wasn't far now. His body started to fail on him, sensing that his destination was nearby.

"Hold on," he whispered. The last dozen steps were almost impossible. He took them one at a time, resting between each one. When he finally reached the door, he reached out to knock and fell against it with a crash.

Alrion sat upright. He had blacked out, and not really dreamed.

How long has it been? He thought. He looked around and noticed that he was in a bed. Lara and Caleb were sitting next to him and looked up with concern.

"What happened?"

"You collapsed outside, I brought you in, and Caleb came looking for you a bit later. You're barely alive, so don't push your luck," Lara said.

"You must search the Pool; the black wizard is there."

"We already did. There's nobody else there in the areas we can access, apart from the bodies of the two guardians," Caleb said, his features downcast.

"Is he alive? That seems impossible."

"There was also a fairly significant cave-in. It will take a long time to properly excavate," Caleb said. Alrion slumped back down in the bed, his body reminding him of his many injuries.

"What happened in there?" Lara said.

"The wizard was waiting for me. Turns out, I knew him. It was Branthor, the new head of the Wizard Academy."

"Why would such a distinguished wizard act like that?" Lara looked shocked.

"Apparently, he was infected by the Blight many years ago, and was cleansed by my grandfather's spell. However, the effect wasn't complete. He was still connected to the Blight. Once he realised that the Pool of Knowledge existed and contained the knowledge of my grandfather, he wanted it for himself. He has crazy plans to make more like him." Alrion still couldn't believe what he was saying.

"That's insane," Lara said.

"Did he drink from the Pool?" Caleb said.

"Yes, he did."

"If there's a chance he is alive as you suspect, that is not good. The Pool does not discriminate and provides the same benefit to all who drink from it." Caleb looked quite concerned.

"What do you mean? And I thought you didn't know much about it?"

Something's not adding up here.

"I'm afraid I wasn't entirely honest with you. Yes, I am a junior scholar but that is because I am training to become a guardian of the Pool. The two you discovered were my mentors. They were great men, and powerful in their own right." Caleb sighed again, and his shoulders slumped.

"What? Why didn't you tell me more?" Alrion tempered his anger out of concern for Caleb.

"It was part of a test. They sent me in to report my evaluation of you as part of the decision. It wouldn't be a fair test if you thought I had valuable information."

I went in there blind!

"I'm not particularly happy about this, but can you at least answer some questions now?"

"Of course."

"How does the Pool work? What does it do? I can't seem to tell any difference, and neither could Branthor."

"The Pool of Knowledge is not just a source of knowledge. It works both ways. By drinking the waters, you drink from its knowledge. However, you also contribute your knowledge. Did Branthor drink before you did?"

"Yes, he did."

"That's good; you may ascertain key knowledge that he had." Caleb stroked his chin, deep in thought.

"That could be useful. How does it work, though?"

"There are safeguards in place. Can you imagine the enormity of that reservoir? All the knowledge compiled from years of scholars and other learned people?" Caleb's eyes were alight with excitement. "Your mind must take in and absorb all that information."

"So, when do I get it?"

"You have it already, but there's a catch. You are not in control of the delivery of the knowledge. It will be fed to you as you need it, as your mind processes it as necessary."

"It's some sort of subconscious control?"

"Essentially. The most common mechanism is through dreams, but sometimes people can access knowledge they never knew they had as if it were their own. It's a strange and inconsistent process."

"Sounds like it. At least, though, I got everything. So, from what you mentioned, I now have all of my grandfather's knowledge." Alrion watched Caleb's response carefully.

"Yes. All that he knew, amongst many other things, are now within your mind. But that's the problem; you can't pick out the things you want on demand."

"I just have to trust my mind to process it?"

This could be a problem.

"Yes. Few are selected to partake and feedback knowledge to the Pool. Branthor killed the only two here that had drunk from the Pool. Precious little is written down about the exact ways of best accessing the information. I will be their successor, in time. There is more preparation for me to do."

"You aren't ready yet?" Alrion sank back down into the bed. He had succeeded, but there were so many more problems to resolve.

"No, I need to expand my knowledge and also practice techniques to more easily access what I require. Had you more time, we could have better prepared you. But now it is done."

"It is, and that is reassuring. How many other people have this knowledge?"

"I will have to consult the records, but outsiders have not accessed the Pool for many years. It is possible that only you and Branthor have it right now."

"I guess we will find out soon enough. My head is killing me, is that normal?"

"Yes, although I am surprised you have noticed based on the other injuries you sustained." Caleb grinned at Alrion.

"I definitely got lucky." Alrion cracked a smile too.

"You sure did. Speaking of which, you should rest some more," Lara said. "It will take a long time to recover, and from what Caleb said I think it will take even longer since you are also incorporating the knowledge from the Pool."

"I think you're right. Thank you both, I really needed your help I would not have survived otherwise."

"That's what we are here for." Lara picked up his pillow and fluffed it. Alrion laughed and even Caleb chuckled.

"Take care," Caleb said and left the room. Lara winked and then left also. But Alrion noticed her looking back at him before he collapsed back into sleep.

Lara left the small building and walked along the main road of Paperton. She took a thin path hemmed in by trees and bushes and ended up down near the lake, in a secluded spot free from passers-by. She looked around for the man she was supposed to meet, but could not see him.

"How is he?" a male voice said from behind her. Lara spun quickly to confront him. It was a man dressed in a nondescript brown robe and he had his face hidden by the hood.

"He's alive, but barely. He had an encounter with another wizard, called Branthor. It's a miracle he survived."

"Did he access the Pool?" The man's voice was insistent and had hints of desperation.

"Yes." Lara watched the man's reaction. He seemed to relax a little.

"Good. Stay with him, keep him safe."

"He won't need my protection soon."

Hopefully I can get this guy off my back. Then I don't have to hide anything from Alrion anymore.

"Wrong. He has gained knowledge and is increasing his power. But he is naive, and needs someone to watch his back while he learns more of the world." The man stopped talking and waited patiently. For her answer.

"Why do you need me?"

"Because you are the best person to accompany him and allow him to grow. Have you changed your mind?" Lara paused before replying. "No."

"Good. Remember that I know who you really are. Until next time." The mysterious man disappeared in front of Lara's eyes. She looked at where he had been, but couldn't see a trace.

"Wish I could do that," she whispered and left to return to Alrion's side.

31

IN DREAMS

Alrion dreamed. At first, it was just so many flashing images, he couldn't make sense of them. There was a vague awareness in his mind that this was to be expected, and not to worry, so he didn't pay them much attention.

The swirling images slowed down and he became immersed within them. He could see an old man standing in front of him. The man sat at a wooden desk and wrote in a book. It looked similar to Falric's spellbook but much older and more ornate. Alrion walked up and looked over the man's shoulder. The man was writing a new entry.

Cleansing the Blight

Alrion found that particular entry very interesting. He continued to hover, watching the man write.

This must be my grandfather, Alrion thought but he didn't look at the man, instead, he focused on the spellbook. He could see the words as the man wrote them on the page, but as they were being written they turned invisible.

Why? Alrion wondered, but he also knew why at the same time.

The spell was beyond him, so he couldn't read it. Much like with Falric's spellbook. Knowing that he couldn't understand it, he walked around to get a better look at the man. Alrion had expected an old man, but he looked to be middle-aged.

"If this is my grandfather, why is he so young?" Alrion thought but the more he looked, the more he knew it was his grandfather. The wizard known as Granthion. The family resemblance was there, he could see his father within the man's face.

Granthion continued writing for what seemed like a long time. Then he finished and closed the book. He stood up and looked directly at Alrion.

"This is for you," he said and passed the spellbook over. Alrion was shocked, but he accepted the book.

"Please tell me how it works," Alrion said.

"You already know, you have the knowledge."

"But how do I access it?" Alrion needed answers.

"You must be worthy of the spell, then you will know it."

"That's fine, but I need help. I have nobody to guide me," Alrion said. Granthion looked thoughtful, then took a few steps, staring into the distance.

"Very well." He waved his arm. A door with a silver shimmering outline appeared in front of them. Granthion gestured at it. Alrion stepped forward and opened the door. Within he could see the Pool of Knowledge.

"I've already done this." Alrion looked back at Granthion. The wizard pointed at the doorway again. Alrion turned, trying to see what was important about the image but it had changed.

Instead, he saw another room carved into the rock. Spread throughout the room were four old men. They were bald and wearing strange robes and long yellow scarves. Emblazoned on the scarves was a symbol Alrion didn't recognise. It looked like a mountain and a sun with additional markings.

The four men were seated on the ground and concentrating. In the middle of them was another doorway glowing white, but Alrion could not see inside it.

"What is this?" he asked, turning back to Granthion, but the wizard was gone. Alrion quickly looked over at the doorway again, but it was disappearing and the scenery around him was fading away. Everything turned white and Alrion started falling.

He awoke with a jerk, pain rocking his body.

Back to reality.

"You OK there?" Lara said.

"Yes, I think so." Alrion checked his body. Everything was as before.

Definitely a dream.

"You look like you saw a ghost."

"Maybe I did." Alrion chuckled. He had to make the best of the situation.

"That's going to require an explanation."

"I'm also interested if you don't mind." Caleb stepped into the room.

"You were also here?" Alrion said.

"I was checking in on you. You've been out for a while. Although I must admit, I wanted to observe the process since I haven't seen anyone react to the Pool of Knowledge. It's an educational experience."

"I definitely agree with you there." Alrion collected his thoughts. "I had a strange dream, with all these images swirling around. I think it was a way of incorporating the knowledge, because I couldn't read any of it. But then it got really strange."

"How so?" Caleb asked.

"I saw my grandfather writing out a spell, only I couldn't read it. When I questioned him about it, instead of explaining he showed me some visions. One of the Pool of Knowledge, and one of something else."

"Clearly your grandfather has passed on and isn't visiting you in your dreams," Lara said.

"That sounds more plausible," Alrion said.

"It could be a way to help you focus. You are seeking something to do with him correct?" Caleb said.

"Yes, I am."

"It would make sense if your mind was using him to call attention to whatever it showed you next," Caleb said.

"If you saw a vision of the Pool of Knowledge, and then something else. Well, to me that sounds to me like you just got a vision of our next destination. What did it look like?" Lara said.

"It didn't make any sense. A few old men, wearing strange clothes and some sort of doorway between them." Alrion struggled to recall all the details. Like a dream, some of it was fading.

"It will probably make more sense in time. Does it always work like this?" Lara said to Caleb.

"As far as I know. It's a protection mechanism, and designed to allow gradual integration of knowledge."

"Well, it's a start. Hang on a minute, you said our next destination?" Alrion looked at Lara.

"Yes, have you forgotten already? I signed up for this, not just the first step. But the whole thing. Besides, you need my help. You almost died without me at your side." Lara smiled. Alrion laughed.

She's right.

"If having you around can prevent this terrible pain I'm experiencing, I'm all for it."

"Great. You tagging along too, Caleb?" Lara said. Alrion wasn't sure if she was serious or not.

"Unfortunately, no. I am not the adventuring type, and I need to prepare to take over the role of guardian of the Pool. There is much I must learn. But perhaps I can be of use to you again in the future, once I am more acquainted with how it works." Caleb bowed.

"We mustn't forget that you have a place here and an important duty." Alrion held out his hand and Caleb shook it firmly. Alrion grimaced and almost managed to disguise the pain.

"Thanks for understanding. This is goodbye, for now, I will be shutting myself away for a while to complete my accelerated training. I have to do it in complete seclusion and secrecy. All the best for your recovery, I hope we meet again soon." Caleb bowed again.

"Thanks for your help, I hope everything goes well. I'm sure I'll need your help in the future if all I have to go on is these cryptic images." Alrion waved goodbye and watched Caleb leave.

"He's a particularly good man, I doubt any of the other scholars would have taken such an interest in you. He cares," Lara said.

"I think you're right. I hope he does well, and finds a way to protect himself and the Pool. I think basing their main defence around secrecy didn't quite hit the mark." Alrion thought back to how easily Branthor had infiltrated the Pool.

"But this place has been hidden for many years. It took a surprising betrayal to unveil it."

"It did," Alrion said.

What happened to Branthor? I wonder.

"You have to be at peace with what happened. You could do nothing more, or nothing less. He may be alive, or he may be dead. We don't know."

"And that's what's killing me. If he's alive with the knowledge of the Pool, then it is only a matter of time before he puts his plan into action. And it will probably involve coming after me and everyone with me." Alrion's hand hurt, and he looked down. He had clenched it into a fist. With an effort he forced it to relax.

"Then you had better sort yourself out, so next time he doesn't actually kill you, or those with you. Just in case." Lara winked at him.

"Sometimes I wonder how I ended up here, and with you no less. I never really thanked you. You convinced me not to give up, you helped me navigate the hall of scholars, and you've been watching my back while I have been helpless. I can't thank you enough, but I will try and make our adventures memorable enough to help pay you back," Alrion said.

"Don't get all mushy on me. I did what needed to be done, and I take satisfaction that you gave that Branthor a real surprise. You sort out the Blight and we will be even."

"Quite a tall order, don't you think? We won't be even until then?"

"Nope. You're stuck with me until then," Lara said, laughing.

"So be it, I guess I'll just have to make the most of it." Alrion tried to stifle another laugh but failed. His ribs complained.

"You may as well. Also, Caleb brought back Falric's spellbook. I put it with the rest of your things. They are all in the corner there." Lara pointed to a bulging pack in the room.

"Thanks."

"You should take a look when you can, just to make sure it is all there. Maybe something else will trigger that jumble of knowledge you have up there. I'm going to go stretch my legs, back soon," Lara said.

"Sure, take care," Alrion said.

Strange girl, he thought after she had left. However, she had done a lot for him already, so she had earned his trust. The impossible goal before him seemed that little bit more achievable. He sat up straighter, testing his body. Once he was moving a little, the pain wasn't as bad.

I should at least do something, he thought and decided to look through his things. What Lara had said made sense, and since he was resting up for a while, anything that kept his mind ticking over was useful.

Alrion struggled to swing his legs off the bed so that he was seated on the edge. Then he shuffled himself over, not trusting his legs with his weight just yet. With the right amount of leaning and good luck, he managed to grasp the leather pack with his left hand and drag it over onto the bed. The contents started to spill out, but he was happy with the result. He tucked himself back into bed and started to leaf through them.

He noticed the spellbook first and flipped through it. There were a few extra pages that he didn't remember from before, so that was useful. It made him think back to something Branthor had said.

I ignited my Spark. Falric never mentioned that. I wonder if it's like a tap that I have turned on now, he thought. Even through his pain and discomfort, he could feel it there, weak but accessible. It wasn't like when he first started, having to work it up. It flowed freely, and he could more easily access it. He was tempted to try it but restrained himself.

I'll ask another wizard when I can.

Alrion returned to the spellbook but it couldn't hold his interest. He looked through his other things. It was all there. His ring, which he had retrieved from Lara. Some clothes and equipment, but his food was gone.

It probably wasn't fit for consumption now, he thought with a chuckle. Finally, he found the notebook that he had taken from the academy.

"This old thing. Falric never explained what it was for," Alrion said. He opened the book to the first page. However, this time it wasn't blank. There were words on the page.

Well done, you have completed the first trial all by yourself. However, don't rest too long, there is much more to do. Whatever happens, you must remember this: you are never alone.

Alrion stared in disbelief on the page. Something was strange about the message. The tone of the speaker seemed familiar. When he examined the page closely, it wasn't written in ink. It was as if the message was etched into the page itself. Like it had always been there.

Who are you? Alrion thought, feeling the letters with his fingers. Another mystery to solve. He put the notebook aside and closed his eyes.

Rest faster. You have to keep moving.

"Am I interrupting something?" Lara said. Alrion opened his eyes. He hadn't meant to fall asleep again, but he felt better for it.

"No, I'll fill you in later. But I've made a decision." Alrion sat up, with slightly less pain this time.

"What's that?"

"As soon as I am fit, we will set out for Brangtur."

"What's there?" Lara gave him a curious look.

"My father. And with any luck by the time we get there, I'll know where my next trial is."

"Trial?"

"Yes, it's clear that there's no easy solution for this. I'll have to earn my chance to cleanse the Blight but I'm going to do it. Nothing will stand in my way." Alrion was surprised at the words coming out of his mouth. But the more he probed his feelings, the truer they were.

"With my help, that's a given," Lara said, and walked over to sit beside him. And for the first time, Alrion truly believed it was possible.

THE STORY CONTINUES

VAULT OF SILENCE

BOOK TWO OF THE HIDDEN WIZARD

A fledgling wizard mastering his power.

A fallen monk.

A secret trial hidden in a desert temple.

Alrion barely survived. His success came at a terrible cost. Driven to improve his skill and prove his worth as a wizard he pushes on.

His dreams show him a vision of his next goal, the Vault of Silence. It is a secret trial guarded by an order of monks and designed to test a person's will. To get there, he must find a guide and negotiate his way through sprawling cities and a vast desert.

But the creatures of the Blight are organising. They have a leader and have infiltrated the general population. To reach the Vault of Silence Alrion will need to make new allies, learn new spells and face an old foe. Can he rise again to the challenge? Or will he be crushed by overwhelming odds?

ABOUT THE AUTHOR

Vaughan W. Smith is a fiction writer from Sydney, Australia, who explores big life questions through story. His favourite genres are Fantasy, Mystery, Science Fiction and Thrillers.

www.vaughanwsmith.com

www.ingramcontent.com/pod-product-compliance
Lightning Source LLC
Chambersburg PA
CBHW020415110726
47899CB00006B/1994